NO REASON
TO STAY

AK White

Corinne,
Here's to great books, vibrant
conversations, and a fabulous new
friendship. Write on, sister!
Regards,

Produced by:

FriesenPress
Suite 300 – 852 Fort Street
Victoria, BC, Canada V8W 1H8

www.friesenpress.com

Distributed to the trade by The Ingram Book Company

Dedicated with love to SCW

The wise crow knows

I am a child of the fall.

Copper and brass, gusty wind blows.

Vivid, cloudless skies watch shivering,

naked trees stand tall.

Hope, sweet and eager, does rise

From rust-soaked vistas to shining eyes.

Here to forever my beating heart goes;

Something the old crow already knows.

CHAPTER 1

...he still held the heart of stone...

My life certainly is not like it used to be. I grimace at such an obviously absurd notion; as if life now could ever be the same as it had been. Pulling a cotton blanket up around my shoulders, I snuggle in for extra warmth and rest my head against the fabric of the sofa cushion. Life is mysterious; in constant change and endless flux it is a continuum of unfolding. And even in my darkest, most troubled moments I am fully aware that I would not desire it to be any other way.

I could blame Philip Glass for my momentary lapse into philosophical pondering. After all, it is his music floating from the speakers that has evoked my feelings of reflective contemplation. The sweet, pure notes from the second movement of his violin concerto gather and build, then tumble, cascading down into each other only to rebuild as voluptuous strings join voices and rise again.

My heart swells with yearning, the music awakening a dizzy flood of melancholy. Even as I breathe a breath of wanting, I know that I have already had more than most. The movement, ending with a single violin voice, ebbs gently outward; slowly, softly, fading to nought.

I think of days gone by, days when I could leap and bound around the living room, dancing myself silly, until, with no oxygen left in my lungs, I would collapse in a heap on the couch panting for air, a smile on my face and exhilaration in my body.

Our moggy, Tetley, would crouch down low, ready to run at a moment's notice until I, the wild dancing beast, had once again subsided into normalcy. Only then would he neatly tuck his little paws inward and let out a soft, barely audible cat sigh. No, my life is not like that anymore.

I can feel the music running through my body, nerve endings alive and hopeful, but the will to make my body move has gone. The cancer has taken too much from me for that.

The view from my window seat faces south; it is a wide, expansive vista out over the vegetable garden and lawn that gently slopes to the forest. The tall evergreens are set back far enough to allow ample sun exposure on the south side of the cabin. Nicely situated on ten hectares the structure is completely isolated from the neighbours.

Years ago, this isolation caused me constant anxiety. What-ifs came in a steady stream the first year that I lived on the farm; my head filled with thoughts of things that could go terribly wrong for a single woman living on her own. Then, as time passed, this solitary lifestyle gradually ceased being a concern for me.

Life has tossed me many worries along the way and I feel as I have grown older that I can negotiate most of what life has to offer without becoming overly anxious. This is one of the upsides of aging: living life isn't any easier; it just feels like it is. And, of course, I have also learned that being alone is different from being lonely. I've experienced both and though I have yet to develop a taste for loneliness, I have become quite accustomed to being alone.

From the couch I can see a Bald Eagle circling low over the tree tops. Fascinated, I watch him spiraling closer and closer; his wingspan is unbelievably wide and his eyes are a piercing gold colour. Rarely have I seen an eagle this close to the house. Then, with ghostly silence, he melts upward into the dark sky of November. I dab a tear from my eyes; my achingly beautiful, wildly free visitor has left me all alone.

My husband had been an avid wildlife photographer. Well-read on many bird and mammal habits and habitats, he had always been an endless source of information. With his camera, he had captured thousands of remarkable images over the years. A sighting like today's would have brought him tremendous joy; a joy that we would have shared and treasured had fate not devised another plan for us.

I flip the blanket back with a sigh and gingerly get to my feet. Charlie is disturbed from his nap and he glares at me, giving me the feline finger by flipping the end of his tail.

"Ahh, Charlie," I say, unconcerned that I am having a full blown conversation with the cat, "don't get your knickers in a twist. I'm just going to make some tea then I'll be back." He continues to glare at me with his golden-green eyes, then, with a huffy sigh and a grunt, lowers his head on top of his pristinely white paws. I have never regretted adopting him from Heidi as an infant stray over eleven years ago.

★ ★ ★

My Iyengar class instructor, Heidi Hefler, is a good friend and she mentions she has rescued six tiny kittens from a dumpster in the alley behind the yoga studio where she teaches. She is trying to find good homes for all the kittens and implores me to come by to have a look.

Despite the fact that we love cats, my husband and I decided against getting another cat after Tetley died. We plan to start traveling more often and we hate to leave cats at the cattery, so it is with a great deal of protest and reluctance I agree to have a look at the kittens.

"I am not going to take one, but I'll come by to have a look," I say with conviction.

"Sure," she responds, smiling. "Come after work tomorrow if you want."

"Okay. I should be there about five if we don't run late."

Running late is a common occurrence at the medical clinic I manage, but as luck would have it I finish just minutes past five. I grab my purse and light cotton sweater and head for Heidi's house. She lives three blocks off the main street through town and only six blocks from the clinic.

The sun is shining and the golden afternoon rays filter through the leaves of the trees lining the street, creating a dappled oasis as a fresh May breeze lifts the scent of flowers into the air. I hum the melody of a Chopin nocturne that I have running through my head as I walk, enjoying the way the fabric of my hemp skirt laps at my legs in rhythm to my strides. My flat-heeled sandals slap the pavement as I stride down the street revelling in the feeling of movement after a long day behind a desk.

I love days like these when spring pushes back at winter and wins. Not being one who enjoys winter sports much, I tend to wait impatiently for the first signs of spring after a long five months of winter. Of course, my painting and yoga classes help me to get through those long, dark, snow-bound days.

As I near Heidi's house, I can see her kneeling in the garden, weeding and planting in her flower beds.

"Hello," I call, waving as I approach.

"Hey, how are you?" she queries, smiling as she rocks back on her heels in a position only a yoga instructor could achieve and wipes a dusty hand across her forehead. "I'm just finishing up here. Go on in and introduce yourself to the kittens. They're in the living room. I'll bring us some refreshments in a few minutes."

"Sure, take your time. I'm in no rush," I reply.

She returns to her digging as I walk up the meandering stone path to the front door of the heritage house. I slip my sandals off and leave them on the porch before I quietly enter the house. I can hear the plaintive meows of the kittens and pause just long enough to appreciate the stained glass windows, elaborate crown mouldings, and original wood floors.

Tentatively I push open the ornate French doors leading to the living room. The kittens, some sleeping, some playing with each other, are corralled in a large cardboard box with the flaps cut off and a fleece blanket lining the bottom. I approach quietly, watching in amazement as they clamber on top of each other willy nilly. I laugh in delight at their antics.

"They're pretty amazing alright," a deep and accented male voice drawls from the corner of the room.

Startled, I turn and say in a rush, "I'm sorry, I didn't know anybody was in here." My breath hitches and heat crawls up my face. Sitting in a comfortably reclined position near the window, a man holding a small hardback book regards me with interest. My thoughts are jumbled as I struggle to make polite, socially acceptable conversation but all I can do is stare.

At the age of thirty-eight I have encountered many handsome men in my day and have never had difficulty keeping my wits about me. Take Joe in yoga class, for instance. He is fit, muscular, attractive, great teeth and yet never once has he stopped my breath. The man with the Australian accent, however is another story. Long athletic looking legs clad in jeans stretch out to the floor, bare feet crossed lazily at the ankle. He holds an air of self confidence and arrogance about him.

I try again, "Uh, hello..." I stumble on my words. *Was it hot in here?* I brush the back of my hand across my temple. "I'm here to see the kittens. Heidi said to come in and have a look. I didn't mean to disturb you." There, now I sound a bit high pitched, but at least normal.

"No probs. You're not disturbing me. I was just baby-sitting the munchkins until Heidi is done in the garden." He lays the book down and with easy languor, rises to his feet. He is well over six feet tall and at five feet seven inches I feel like a pipsqueak next to him.

"I just love this little one," he says reaching into the cardboard box, "because it's the runt. See how tiny this one is?" Lifting an orange and white tabby from the litter he cuddles it close to his chest.

The kitten is so adorable that for a moment I am distracted from the man beside me. Reaching out my hands I say, "Here, may I hold him please?"

"How do you know it's a boy?" he queries as he hands the kitten to me. Our fingertips brush together as I take the kitten from him. Startled, I draw my hands abruptly away and drop my gaze.

The kitten looks up at me with still smokey-blue eyes and lets out a demanding meow as he tries to climb up my shirt with needle sharp claws.

"I'm just guessing," I finally respond to his question. "He seems like a boy to me. Yikes, he may be small but he's sure determined." I laugh as I try to disentangle myself from the kitten. I glance at the man as I kiss the top of the kitten's head.

"I'm Alexandra, by the way. My friends call me Alexi."

"I'm Gabriel and my friends call me Gabe." His dark eyes are intense, interested. Heat shoots through my cheeks again.

"Are you thinking to adopt one of them?" I ask, nodding towards the box of kittens.

"I'd love to, but I'm only staying here with Heidi for a few more weeks, then I'm heading north to Alaska, I think." Smiling to reveal strong teeth and a small dimple in his right cheek, he bends forward and from the box scoops up another orange tabby in one hand and a tuxedo in the other.

"Do you travel a lot for your job?" I ask hesitantly, gently swaying from side to side as I tickle the kitten's belly.

"No, not for work. I've been on a traveling adventure for a few years now. I've been all through my homeland, most of southeast Asia, some of continental Europe, and now I'm giving Canada and the United States a go."

"Wow, that is quite an adventure," I say struggling for enthusiasm. Being a home body myself, it sounds more like purgatory to me. To each his own, as they say. He certainly looks the nomadic type with his frayed jeans, shoulder length, wavy brown hair and bare feet.

"It must be nice to have a job that allows such freedom," I comment. I put the runt back in the box and pick up another kitten. This one, mostly white with a splattering of black, is half asleep and snuggles into the palm of my hand trustingly.

"I've been lucky, really," Gabe replies. "Do you remember about three years ago there was a fantasy movie trilogy that was filmed in Australia and released world wide?" I nod. I had not seen the movies but recall they had been extremely popular.

"Well, I was the art director for those films and made a huge whack of money. I was fortunate enough to have sound financial advice and continued to do very well in the markets. So now, I can do what I want and don't really have to worry about working again." He seems a bit sheepish as he explains.

"Heck, I don't see the light at the end of the tunnel for another twenty-five years! I'm lucky, though, because I really like my job at the clinic." He looks at me in surprise, as if he had never heard of anyone enjoying their job.

"I wonder what happened to Heidi?" I ponder as I put the sleeping kitten back in the box. "She offered me a cold drink and I'm parched."

"I'll get us something to drink. Come through to the kitchen." He leads the way from the living room, down the hall to the old-fashioned kitchen at the back of the house.

It had been beautifully restored with a Belfast sink, a huge island with a stove top built-in and a row of barstools lined up on one side of the island.

"Make yourself at home," he says and pulls out a stool for me. "Now let's see what she has to offer. Hmm, there's orange juice, homemade iced tea, or beer. What do you feel like having?" A lock of hair falls across his forehead as he leans forward to peer into the fridge and he casually shoves his hand through the wavy mass.

Good grief, does the man have any idea how impossibly attractive he is? I think to myself. There is definitely an attitude of arrogance about him, but there is also a casual awareness of himself in each of his actions. Pulling my thoughts together I decide on the iced tea and voice my choice. He serves it in a tall, slender glass and pulls a beer from the fridge for himself and pours the deep brown liquid into a heavy glass beer mug.

"I see you're drinking an oatmeal stout from the local brewery," I say, clinking my glass to the edge of his. "Cheers," we say in unison.

"My husband would approve," I say, nodding to the beer in his hand. "He loves micro-brewery beer."

"Your husband?" He queries, raising a dark eyebrow.

★ ★ ★

A sharp whistling breaks my reverie and I realize the water has come to a boil on the hot plate. I add two fragrant Earl Gray tea bags and carefully pour the water into the white teapot.

It's the teapot that I found at a yard sale years ago. Beautiful, classic white, made in England, and just perfect for tea-for-two. I had been so pleased when I found my priceless treasure. Now, some twenty years later, it has a chip on the lid and tannin stains on the spout that defy cleaning. And of course now it steeps tea-for-one.

The kitchen, rustic but neat and clean, has a wood-burning cook stove with mint green enamelled doors and a bread warmer above the cooking surface. When I had first looked at the cabin some five years ago, I had been delighted by the stove because it was just like the one my mom had in her kitchen when I was a child.

The small cabin had also reminded me of my childhood and I had become emotionally attached to the property immediately. Within a few days of viewing the farm I made an offer that was accepted by the sellers. I listed my own house in town and was fortunate to have a buyer within a few weeks.

My prognosis was not good; all the specialists agreed that more than twelve months was not possible. Yet here I am, beating the odds one year at a time. The change of lifestyle, selling the house, quitting work, and moving fifteen kilometres out of town to the farm had been a godsend.

Having felt firsthand the hardship of living off the land as a child, I was never, as an adult, tempted to return to that difficult way of living. My husband, Mark, however, had been raised in Manchester, and had a completely romantic notion of what living off-grid and off the land involved. For many years of our married life we had discussed the possibility of us living remotely in such a manner. I had always managed to get my way. We had been one hundred percent grid-dependent and neither of us could grow vegetables of any kind.

It had not taken me long after my diagnosis to realize that what I wanted more than anything was to search out the lifestyle that had for so long appealed to Mark. I would make peace with my cancer, subdue my fears, set my course, and try to live Mark's dream for both of us.

The tea, brewed dark and sweetened with a smidgeon of organic cane sugar, tastes wonderful and I wander back to the window seat and nestle in beside Charlie. Stretching out his paw, he pulls my hand towards him, indicating that he wants me to scratch him behind his ears. He's a smart cat and has trained me well. Kitten gets his ears scratched.

It is cold and gloomy out today with low cloud and a brisk wind. Late November can really go either way; it can be beautiful blue skies with pale sun or it can be downright miserable. I had been going for short walks up to the mailbox every day, but today not only do I feel tired out, but the weather is too inclement for my taste.

I know that I need to send a couple of e-mails and finalize a few more loose ends pertaining to my estate but I don't feel like doing that either. Instead, I stroke Charlie's soft fur and gaze into his golden-green eyes. This little fella has been with me through the glory days, through the days of endless struggle, and all the days in between. And now, with my health declining rapidly, I have to formulate a plan for his care after my death. I am desperate to get a response to my letter soon.

My younger sister, Jillie Everest, has agreed to handle all my affairs after my passing which, considering the ups and downs we've had over the years, is really very gracious of her. My older brother, Michael Wainwright, lives in Germany with his wife, and their sons attend university there. Because of the distance he has not been able to offer much help as I gradually decline. My siblings have not been in accord with my decision not to seek traditional medical attention for my cancer.

My decision to abandon Western medicine was not easy and many times I have panicked wondering if I have made a huge mistake by not following the typical cancer protocol. In my most sane and stable moments, I am completely happy with the path I chose for myself as I face my illness. Coming from a medical background at the clinic made the decision even harder, but in the end, I did what I wanted. No radiation, no chemotherapy, no drugs.

Despite the fact that Jillie does not support my decision, she continues to work tirelessly to help me in every way that she can. Of course she would take care of Charlie once I've passed if she could, but she is terribly allergic to cats and can only come to my house if she's loaded up on antihistamines.

Jillie's daughter, Amanda, moved to Montreal for university and after she graduated as a Naturopathic Doctor a few years ago, decided to accept an excellent job offered at a well established clinic there. Jillie, finding herself to be often alone, dates when she can, but after a nasty divorce a few years back, she is reluctant to settle down with any one man. She often reminds me that she is happy to help me out so that she doesn't have to sit by the phone waiting for a date to call her.

As the afternoon sinks into evening and the light wanes, I switch on the reading lamp beside the window seat and pull the heavy drapes closed. The drapes are another favourite treasure I found at a second-hand shop many years ago. Deep green and richly embroidered with gold and red vines, they block out the dark sky. Mark and I loved these drapes and often proclaimed to each other, "Who would get rid of such beautiful drapes?" We never could find an answer.

Shopping for second-hand things came naturally to me as money was always tight during my youth. Mom and Dad's bookstore did reasonably well in the 1960's and 1970's, but it was not until the late 1980's that it finally hit its stride when they expanded and added a coffee bar. The combination of books, antiques, music, and coffee was an instant hit, and after thirty years in business, the company had finally become extremely profitable. Tourists from the city throng to Kalsson in the summer months leaving behind a healthy infusion of cash in the local economy.

Of course my siblings and I had fled the coop by that time and did not directly benefit from our parents newly acquired wealth, so living on a tight budget was the norm for me. I was used to wearing second-hand clothes and rarely had any items that were new. My bedroom suite was purchased at the Sally Ann, my bike was used, and winter boots were hand-me-downs from Michael. Luckily he was short with small feet and I was tall with large feet.

Mark, on the other hand, had no experience with purchasing things used and found it to be quite distasteful at first. It wasn't until he had found a few bargains at yard sales that he began to see the value in reusing and re-purposing items. As the years went by and Mark became increasingly interested in the impact of lifestyle on the planet, shopping for new items became almost taboo in our household.

He'd loved antiquing with my father and had a large collection of mainly British pocket watches from the Victorian era. I enjoy antiques as well, but not to the same extent as Mark. I did keep his watch collection intact after his accident however as I simply did not have the heart to sell it.

The CD had ended some time ago but Charlie and I linger on, enjoying each other's company. The living room is small and cozy with an eating area at the far end near the kitchen. There is a powder room on the main floor and a spacious bedroom in the loft with a full en-suite.

The past few nights I've been sleeping on the couch, as I find the climb too taxing to negotiate with my diminishing strength. Today I need to find the energy to go up the stairs so I can have a shower and wash my hair.

My stomach growls and I realize I have not eaten since break-fast. Hunger comes as a pleasant surprise as the cancer has all but destroyed my appetite. I have been eating out of necessity rather than hunger or desire, so it is with anticipation that I go to the kitchen looking for something to eat.

I've always enjoyed cooking. Mark and I used to cook meals together as a way of reconnecting after a busy day at work. Both vegans, we would experiment with vegetables, grains, beans, and tofu. We liked to keep fit and healthy which is one reason why his untimely death was even more difficult to accept.

Mark had held such life force within himself, he'd had such energy and zest for living. How odd that his bright flame could be snuffed out in a single heartbeat…in a single beat of the heart.

My own diagnosis of pancreatic cancer years ago left me almost in awe. I was so astonished by the diagnosis and prognosis of no more than a year to live that I could scarcely comprehend it. It seemed to prove once and for all that we are, at best, fragile and unprotected creatures when, on our journey through life, we encounter the wily whim of fate.

I recall the doctor's words, spoken kindly but clinically, "Alexandra," he'd said, "you are terminally ill and you have no more than twelve months to live." I'd sat in stunned silence for several moments, thoughts and emotions rushing and jumbling rapidly in my head.

"I guess that means I'll be seeing Mark again sooner than I anticipated," I responded quietly.

How many times had I wished that my life could simply end? After Mark's accident, I had implored the universe to end my sorrow, to end my relentless suffering. The universe had now answered my prayers, late, but answered just the same.

My oncologist looked startled when I smiled then; a strange, hesitant smile that moved swiftly across my face and disappeared. I stood up in the small, starkly furnished office to shake his hand.

"Thank you," I'd said. I left the medical building and stepped out onto the sidewalk into the sunlight.

"Well, that's a turn of events," I'd said to myself.

In the space of a few moments, my life had dwindled from anticipating another twenty-five years to no more than a year. We all know from the moment we are born that we are eventually going to die. How we live with that knowledge becomes a matter of personal perspective and expectation.

With the instant condensing of my remaining life, I could see how precious each moment would need to be; how fully I would need to be present so that I could savour twenty-five years of living in just one set of seasons.

My life had gone from a grape to a raisin. The grape is much larger when on the vine and the flavour is fresh and lovely but when it becomes a raisin, it shrinks to a fraction of its original size. The taste becomes denser, richer, and sweeter. As I walked down the street from the doctor's office, that was how I perceived my future: shorter but sweeter.

I did not feel unlucky, angry at my body, or fearful of my disease. I believed that the universe had offered me a chance to reunite with Mark sooner than expected. Perhaps, when I too pass into the next life, the terrible, deeply-rooted ache that had shrouded my heart since his death might finally be assuaged.

★ ★ ★

It happened on the evening of our twenty-third anniversary. We had booked a night in a swanky hotel in a lovely, quiet town about two hours drive from home and we had arranged to have a specially prepared dinner served in our suite. Considering how mild the evening was for October, we decided to go for a walk along the lake before eating.

We donned warm coats and scarves and set out as dusk settled over the hotel situated near the edge of the still water. I stuck my cold hand inside Mark's pocket and felt for the smooth heart-shaped stone we had found on a beach many years before. He always keeps the stone with him and now, it was warmed by his body heat. Smiling, he slid his hand inside his pocket too, and entwined his fingers with mine around the heart of stone.

"Your hair looks beautiful tonight," he'd said, his Manchester accent was as strong as ever. "No, it's true," he insisted, pushing a strand of dark brown hair back from my face as I laughed at him.

My hair had long been a joke with us. I, wanting shorter more professional-looking hair, told Mark that if he wanted me to keep it long, as was his desire, he'd have to compliment me on how lovely it was on a regular basis. So for many years now he would, out of the blue and usually inappropriately, comment on how nice my hair looked.

He pulled me into his arms and kissed me sweetly on the lips.

"You know, we've been perfectly matched for hugging and kissing for over twenty-three years now." He did have a point; our bodies fit together like pieces of a puzzle.

"Yes," I'd agreed, snuggling into his tight embrace, "perfectly matched for twenty-three years."

We'd had a rare and beautiful opportunity to experience a truly remarkable love. We'd had our hard times: money problems, death in the family, and the struggle overcoming Gabe, but despite our hurdles or maybe because of them, our love for each other had deepened, intensifying as it became smoother, unified, and more fulfilling with every year that passed.

We had strolled on, hand in hand, along the path that curved then swept away from the lake and up towards the road.

"Shall we go on?" Mark asked. "The light is fading fast now."

"Let's circle back to the hotel using the road. It's getting too dark to return via the lake trail."

"You're a chicken," he'd joked, poking his finger into my ribs. "Afraid the boogie man will get you?"

"Not with you here to protect me," I'd joked back in response.

We walked more briskly, still holding hands, as we listened to the sound of the night owls hooting in the distance. The verge was sandy and I stopped to remove a pebble from my slip-on shoes.

Suddenly, we heard the sound of a car approaching full throttle from around the bend behind us. My shoe, still half off, made me clumsy and I fell to the tarmac. Mark grabbed my hand and tried to drag me off the road but our grasp slipped apart and he stumbled backward.

The car, lights on high beam, bore down on us. At the last instant, it swerved around my prone body, missing me by a few inches, only to slam into Mark. The impact threw him twenty feet down the road where he landed face down on the pavement; a fan of dark blood oozed from his head as his prostrate body lay perfectly still in the bleak light of nightfall. In the palm of his outflung hand he still held the heart of stone.

★ ★ ★

The cupboards are well stocked due to Jillie's diligence and manufactured optimism. I select a can of rice and bean soup and heat it on the hot plate. Luckily, I'd decided to stay grid-tied when I had the photovoltaic panels installed.

I had been using a lot of my battery-stored electricity for heating the cabin as I did not have the energy to keep the wood burning fire stoked all night. With the cells struggling to keep up with the demand as the sunlight hours diminish, I feel relieved to have the local hydro company on standby as needed.

Jillie had baked an organic whole grain loaf of bread for me yesterday and I slice off a pre-cancer size chunk feeling remarkably hungry. The soup and bread taste lovely and I savour the flavours and texture as I slowly finish the meal. It was really very sweet of Jillie to bake the loaf for me.

From time to time I wish the disease would hurry itself along so that I can stop burdening the lives of the people who love me. Still, there are things that I have not sorted out yet, like Charlie for example. I can't bear the thought of putting him up for adoption. I hope the letter I wrote to Gabe in Australia last week reaches him soon; he is the only person I fully trust to love and care for Charlie once I am gone and I sense I will need his help soon.

I never was one who believed in religion. I'd tried youth groups as a teenager and had not been impressed. Mark was loosely raised Church of England, "Whatever that means," he used to say. We had spent our lives not believing in God or Jesus. And the Bible seemed to us to be an elaborate piece of fancy fiction. Rather, we followed our own path believing that nature has its own rhythm and purpose to which we should attune ourselves.

Now as I come nose to nose with my mortality, I realize why people cling to their beliefs like babies cling to their blankets. Dying is damn scary and clinging to anything seems necessary to stay sane. Still, the Trust-in-God because He-has-a-master-plan platitudes don't hold sway with me, even now as I nervously watch my life slipping away.

I don't trust in God. I don't feel that blind faith has helped the peoples of the world. On the contrary, it has caused immense harm and destruction for hundreds of years. I still think it's all crap and I'd rather say: "I have no freaking idea what the hell happens next," and let the chips fall as they may. They're going to fall anyway.

Feeling better, with my stomach full of food, I hoist the seventeen pounds of Charlie cat off the couch and shoo him outside for a private moment. Minutes later, I barely have time to put down fresh water and top up his food bowl, I hear a plaintive meow at the door; I hurry to let him in. When we lived in town, he had a litter box, but since moving to the farm, Charlie prefers to go outside. One less chore for me, but one more worry because of the occasional coyote that wanders across the property.

Gently I rub his ears with my toe, "You're too big to be a coyote's dinner, eh, Charlie?" Reaching down, I pick up the big cat and carefully climb the stairs. I have a quick shower and notice after brushing my teeth that my gums are more puffy and bleeding but this is not unusual for someone with my advanced stage of disease. This is one of many things I have learned while having alternative treatment.

Three weeks after my diagnosis I'd quit my job of twenty-five years as the manager of the medical clinic. I had wanted to concentrate completely on my health and had spent the next months seeking treatments. Despite the efforts of a committed team of health care professionals, my original prognosis of *no more than a year* remained unchanged.

Due to the late diagnosis and the inoperable nature of my cancer, the only options for treatment remained essentially palliative and included chemotherapy and radiation. These treatments might buy me time, but not quality time. So I'd decided to pull out of the Western medicine model and live my life following my intuition and my own research.

This decision had angered my entire family, except for my niece, Amanda. She had supported me from the beginning and had offered me assistance with my research on alternative treatment choices. She had also accompanied me to California and Mexico to provide moral support during my rounds of treatments there.

With my socks still on, I climb into the cold bed. Charlie curls his warm body into the curve of my side and with a groan of contentment, falls into a relaxed sleep. Moments later, I follow his lead.

CHAPTER 2

...each second of life offers the possibility of love...

The next morning I awake to find a warm weight curled up against my back and, for an instant, I believe it is Mark that I feel. But no, it is only Charlie, his body twitching as he dreams in his sleep. I close my eyes and relish the feeling of him. Solid. Warm. Real. I drift at the lip of sleep, drawn inexorably forward into the smudged reality between wakefulness and dreaming.

I have often thought that falling asleep must be much like dying. You slowly fade from wakefulness, releasing control over your body and mind as you are drawn away from yourself (or deeper into yourself) on an adventure that you can't control or direct. You have no sense of time or reality; a total abandonment of yourself to the unknown.

I find myself both attracted to and afraid of this lapse of self during sleep. When Mark was alive, I used to hurry my evening bedtime routine so that we could fall asleep together. Being a thorough flosser, I generally lagged behind and found myself wandering off to asleep alone, long after the sound of Mark's gentle snores filled the bedroom. Now, I fall asleep solo every night; I am still uneasy but I do not fear the adventure ahead that must be faced alone.

The morning dawns brighter than yesterday and with more energy than normal, I get out of bed, slip my feet into slippers and make my way carefully down the stairs. I pull back the drapes swiftly, eager to see if the eagle is visiting. Nothing. No visitor today.

The vegetable patch looks scraggly with frost bitten, limp leaves falling over the edges of the raised garden beds. I had planted a full garden this spring, feeling the energy and renewal that comes with new growth spurred on by the sun.

It had been, as always, therapeutic to dig my hands deep into the dark, fertile soil, to watch the tiny seeds that I sowed germinate, and slowly unfurl into sturdy, edible plants. I had a bumper crop of everything and had given Jillie boxes of tomatoes, zucchini, cucumbers, onions, herbs, and squash all summer and into fall.

I know Mark would be proud of me. Not only was I growing a productive garden, I also mastered the skills required to test the batteries that store the energy from the photovoltaics installed on the south facing roof of the cabin. As well, I installed a rain catchment system that supplied water for the garden. Until recently, I had been heating and cooking with wood. Many of these tasks are vaguely familiar to me from my childhood, having been raised on a farm in a rustic log house built in the Thirties by a Doukhobor family.

I can feel Mark here beside me and have quiet conversations with him, as I learn the ways of living-off-the-land as it was coined in the 1970's. Despite all my reservations, I find the lifestyle suits me better than I would have expected. I have adopted a hermit-like existence that does not include much socializing or time out in the community but I seem remarkably content to sit and watch the seasons pass as I tend the garden, gather the wood for the winter, and harvest the crops.

My parents, both extraordinary gardeners in their younger years, had taught me about planting for our climate, how to control pests naturally, how to mulch, compost and enrich the soil, and how to harvest and store the corps. Without realizing it, I had inherited their green thumbs.

Today I feel an urge to paint. The pale morning light is pleasing so I pull my easel and oil paints from the storage closet under the stairs and set up in front of the window. Chickadees, nuthatches, and the odd robin flit about the feeder I have placed a few feet beyond the window. Although I have never been successful at painting birds, Mark and I always enjoyed birdwatching together. I much prefer to paint abstracts, landscapes, and lately, for the past year or more, I have been inclined to paint trees.

It is lovely to sit in front of the easel with a blank canvas and have the energy to spend the whole day dedicated to my every artistic whim. I stroke the tubes of paint, idly waiting for a colour to speak to me. My hand travels to the tube of deep red that has yet to be opened. Without thinking I grab the tube, open it, and squeeze out a long line of vermillion paint onto my palette. My breath quickens, my heart pounding painfully in my chest.

I have not painted with this intense colour since Mark cracked his head open on the pavement eight years ago. It is not the vividness of the memory that overwhelms me now; it this the fact that I have chosen this day, almost without volition, to use this colour of paint. How inexplicably odd.

After a few hours at the easel, the artist in me is out-maneuvered by the cancer in me. I meticulously clean my brushes and place them away, then take a moment to survey my work. It is good. Very good. Vibrant jabs of colour in red, orange, and yellow hint at a descending sun while deep espresso and chocolate browns sketch shadows and eerie shapes that catch the eye yet are inconspicuous and furtive. I am pleased. The paints spoke to me today. They don't always, but when they do, I run with it, letting the right side of my brain take over and fall into a free-flow of emotion.

Glancing at the antique clock on the sideboard, I realize that Jillie will be by soon for her daily visit. I go to the bathroom to check my face for paint smears. Nope. All is good.

I've been wearing my grey streaked hair in a long, single braid lately. It takes too much effort to wash, dry, and style it so I've not been bothering to do anything at all with it. Jillie keeps offering to take me in to town to get it cut, but I am reluctant. It feels so much like giving up the old me.

Jillie's knock at the front door grabs my attention and I quickly smooth on a berry coloured lipgloss and pinch my cheeks to get a hint of colour before hurrying to the door to let her in.

"Hi, sis," she says, giving me a gentle hug. She is several inches shorter than me and is voluptuously curvy. We share our father's bright blue eyes, but unlike me, she has short, bouncy, blonde curls that wisp gracefully around her beautiful face. She looks so alive and vital compared to my feeble, illness ravaged self. I take her well-manicured hand and hold it to my cheek.

"Thank you for coming," I say. I feel a tear slip down my face. This happens to me often. Emotions arrive, usually unexpected, sometimes unwanted, and always without explanation. Unless I'm with Jillie, I let these emotions have their way, as I see no need to censor them.

"Please don't cry," Jillie says, wringing her hands helplessly.

"I'm not. I just have allergies," I say, pulling away to discretely wipe my eyes and regain my composure.

"Come in. Do you have time to stay for tea?" I ask as I put the kettle on.

Joe Everest, my ex brother-in-law, had found Jillie's high energy, lively, gregarious personality too much to handle after just four years of marriage. In fact, what had attracted him to her in the first place was what drove him away in the end. Joe had been the quiet, stay at home type but for Jillie, this was pure hell. She much preferred to be out with friends each evening, or having endless dinner parties at her house.

Amanda, Jillie and Joe's only offspring, was only three years old when they split up, but Joe had remained an attentive father and Amanda had grown from a well-adjusted child to an intelligent, thoughtful adult.

"Do you work late tonight, Jillie?" I ask as I serve the tea in the double Paragon hand-painted tea cups Mark bought for me for my thirty-fifth birthday. We have migrated to the dining room table and are now seated on the comfortable wooden chairs.

"Yep. I sure do." Jillie opens the cookie tin she has placed on the table. "Look, Alexi, I made you some cookies," she says indicating with a hand gesture.

"You shouldn't be making me cookies, Jillie. You're working too hard as it is with all that overtime at the law office." Unable to resist, I pull the tin closer and have a look.

"They're your favourite...chocolate chip and walnut." I must admit they look delicious. The fresh baked aroma hits me as I pull one out of the tin. I feel my stomach flip flop in protest and bile rises in my throat.

Oh, shit. I can feel the nausea, wave after wave coming on fast. Knowing from experience that I have just seconds before I vomit, I run to the bathroom, slam the door shut and fall to my knees in front of the toilet bowl. Everything I have eaten comes up. My gut aches from the harsh retching and the acidic bile; hot tears burn unabated tracks down my cheeks.

"God damn fucking disease," I wail in a moment of complete despair as I gasp for breath. After a few minutes of deep, calming breathing the nausea subsides. I flush the toilet, using the full flush option, then rising unsteadily to my feet, rinse my mouth and face with cool water at the sink.

Palms on the counter to steady myself, I stare at my reflection in the mirror. No vitality. No beauty. No *anything*. Just an empty shell.

"Where the hell have I gone?" I ask the mirror.

At the door I hear a soft tap followed by Jillie's concerned voice, "You okay, sis?" She is worried and angry, I can tell from her tone. Slowly I open the bathroom door.

"Sorry, Jillie. I never know when that is going to happen." I try to smile, but fail. Charlie comes bustling down the hall with his belly swinging and meows loudly. He brushes against my legs and stares up at me, blinking his eyes in long slow blinks. I pick him up and push my face into his soft fur as his purr kicks into overdrive.

"I'm okay now. Let's go finish our tea before it gets cold."

"You look pale today, Alexi. I'm concerned about you. Let me take you to the clinic so they can make sure you're okay." I can see the pleading look in Jillie's eyes.

"But I'm not okay, Jillie. I'm dying. *This* is what *that* looks like." Putting Charlie down, I take her hands in mine and look directly into her fretful, sad eyes.

"I am content, Jillie. I have made my peace and I am happy here at home with Charlie, instead of cooped up in some hospital ward with tubes sticking out of me and breathing stale, recycled air." I let her hands go.

"Come see what I've been painting today," I invite brightly, leading the way to the canvas that is drying on the easel. Jillie approaches the work and stands with her head slightly tilted to one side. A few moments pass.

"Say something, say anything!" I tease her lightly. "So, what do you think of it?"

"I'm at a loss for words. I really think this might be the best you have ever painted. And all that red. You haven't been using it for years."

"Yeah, not since Mark's accident," I reply quietly.

"It's really amazing, Alexi. I love it." She walks over to me and wraps me in a sisterly hug.

"Hey, what's this about? You're getting mighty touchy-feely all of a sudden." I'm teasing her, but at the same time, I savour the warmth of her love. Despite her gregarious nature with friends, Jillie is notorious for holding back her emotions with family.

"You're so damn talented," she says going on tiptoe to plant a kiss on my cheek. "I gotta go. I'll call you later." Grabbing her purse she heads for the door.

"That is really very kind of you to say, Jillie." She smiles at me then dashes to her car. I close the door and turn the lock.

"Now I'm going to have a good cry," I say to Charlie as tears well up in my eyes. Charlie, who is rubbing his head on my legs, gives a wispy baby meow and I can't help but pick him up again. He feels so reassuring in my arms and I squeeze him tightly before he can object.

I cannot stop myself from reminiscing about that first day when I met Charlie and Gabe. Both came unbidden into my life, both were unbearably beautiful and ever so slightly arrogant. As I recall, it really had been a red letter day.

★ ★ ★

Heidi, apologizing for her lengthy delay in the garden, eventually finds Gabe and me in the kitchen with our drinks.

"I see you two have introduced yourselves," she says gaily.

"Yes, we have," we respond together.

"Say, isn't Mark out of town this week?" Looking cheerfully into the fridge for inspiration, Heidi suggests, "Why don't you join us for dinner, Alexi? I'll make a tofu and veggie stir fry."

"That sure sounds better than the leftovers I have waiting for me at home," I reply. Truth be told, I don't really fancy another evening at home on my own.

Mark had been away more and more these past few years as his employer accepts projects farther afield. We had discussed the issue many times before, but Mark loved his job and didn't mind the travel and time away from home. It was really up to me to find a way to cope. Staying at Heidi's for dinner seemed a fabulous coping strategy to me.

"Now Gabe here is a huge tofu fan," Heidi says, affectionately shoving Gabe in the shoulder as he sprawls on the barstool nursing his beer.

"Really?" I am surprised. He looks more like a meat and potatoes guy to me.

"She's full of it," Gabe replies. "I was raised on three square meals a day with meat in almost every dish. Who'd really want to eat *tofu*, any way?" He said tofu like it was a dirty word.

"I would," Heidi and I answer in accidental unison. That starts us giggling as we pull vegetables from the fridge and begin to wash and cut them for the meal.

"Have you ever tried tofu?" I ask Gabe, once I have regained my composure.

"Nope, but I guess tonight's my lucky night." He doesn't sound convinced.

The three of us chat amiably while we prepare dinner. Gabe explains that he is on his way to Alaska and has stopped for a few weeks to visit Heidi.

"From there on my plans are somewhat unstructured," he explains. He is Heidi's second cousin on her father's side and had finally taken her up on her standing offer to come to Canada for a visit.

I lay out three place settings while Gabe opens a bottle of white wine and fills three glasses. Heidi stays close to the cast iron pan as she cooks the vegetables and tofu in sesame oil. Between bouts of stirring, she whips together a maple syrup sweetened peanut butter and soy sauce to drizzle over the medley of vegetables, tofu, and translucent rice noodles.

Serving ourselves from the stove, we pile our plates high with the steamy, aromatic meal.

"Why don't we sit out in the yard? It's such a nice evening. We could bring the kittens out in their box for some fresh air."

"That's a great idea, Gabe," Heidi agrees. With wine in one hand and a plate in the other, we maneuver ourselves outside to the front lawn. Setting his food and glass down, Gabe volunteers to fetch the kittens.

"He can't take his eyes off those kittens," Heidi says smiling. "He's such a softy with them."

"I feel the same way. They're just so cute," I comment, sipping the chilled Semillon.

"Wow, that's excellent," I say, taking another sip. "I'm not a wine connoisseur, far from it in fact, but this is so refreshing."

"Hey, Gabe. Alexi approves of your wine," Heidi calls out as he re-appears gingerly carrying the big box of kittens.

"Does she?" He inquires, lifting an eyebrow.

"Did you pick this one out?" I ask. The wine is delicious and I savour another mouthful.

"You could say that," he laughs and settles the kittens on the grass. "Harris Vineyards in Hunter Valley, New South Wales is owned and operated by my parents and my brother. I was supposed to take over the vineyard and restaurant business when my parents retired but I never had a keen interest in it. After I got my business degree at UNSW, I knew for certain that I didn't want to pursue that career. That's why I carried on and completed a second degree in the Arts." He lifts the wine to his nose, appreciating the bouquet. "This is a good wine. I'm glad my brother wanted to learn the trade and keep the family business thriving."

Looking closely at the label I am surprised by its delicate artwork.

"I have to admit to buying wine for the label alone. I'd buy this one for sure. Look how beautifully the colours work with the logo and the picture." I hold the bottle out for Heidi to have a look.

"That's my work," Gabe admits, looking rather embarrassed.

"You certainly have contributed meaningfully to the family business with this label and bottle design." Peering at the fine print on the bottle I read about the Harris family tradition of growing grapes and producing some of the finest Semillon in Australia.

"Your family name is Harris?" I ask, though it seems more like a statement.

"Yep, we're the Harris' of Hunter Valley," lifting his glass he says, "Cheers!" Our three glasses clink as we toast.

We eat in comfortable silence for a few minutes, often distracted by the meowing and crazy antics of the kittens who are excited to be outside.

"Alexi is an artist, too," Heidi offers conversationally. I cough, caught off guard by the comment.

"Umm, I'd not go quite that far. Two years at art college does not an artist make." I have never felt comfortable calling myself an artist; it seems too presumptuous and a little insulting to truly talented people.

"Ignore her modesty and protests," Heidi says, laughter lighting up her sky blue eyes. "She's actually really good. I hung several of her original oil paintings in the yoga studio and everybody loves them."

"I'd like to see your work, Alexi," Gabe's gaze transfixes me. I feel my face heat again and I am awkward, falling over my words in reply.

"Umm...well...sure. Sure, why not? Mark's not back for a few more weeks." I don't know why I say that; tacked on like an afterthought with no apparent bearing on the conversation.

"You just tell me when and where and I'll be there." He grins a slow, easy smile that warms the rich brown depths of his eyes and pops the dimple into action. I feel another flush spread across my cheeks. Maybe it's the wine.

"Oh, anytime is okay. But not Monday, Wednesday, or Friday because I have yoga after work, and not Saturday mornings because I'll be volunteering at the annual S.P.C.A. fundraiser. Oh, not Sunday either because I have to help my dad at the bookstore."

"It sounds like it will have to be on Saturday night, then," Gabe says taking control of the situation as I gradually lose possession of all coherent thought.

"Sure, that sounds fine," I mumble into my glass.

"Why don't we go for dinner first? You had better pick the restaurant or we might end up at the rib shack or something."

I'm fairly sure he's poking fun at me, but I'm not certain.

"She's a vegan, Gabe. It's nearly impossible to find a place she can eat," Heidi adds to the conversation.

"Hey, that's not true. I can eat at the Wild Onion, Chung Chang's, the Tex-Mex Cafe, and the Subway. That's not bad for a town of fifty thousand."

"Okay, the onion place sounds good. Let's go there at six o'clock. I'll come pick you up on my motorcycle," he offers.

"No way! I'm scared of those things. Besides, we can walk; it's less than one kilometre from here. I'll meet you here at five thirty." There's no way I'm going to get on his bike.

"Motorbikes are quite safe, you know..."

"Blah, blah, blah," I interrupt him and cover my ears in a childish manner. "I can't hear you," I say screwing my eyes shut and keeping my ears covered.

"Gabe, you'll never convince her." Heidi tucks a golden strand of blonde hair behind her ear and pulls a kitten from the box. "That lady is as stubborn as a mule."

"Listen you two, when I was in high school I used to ride a moped and I crashed that thing three times before giving up on it." There, my explanation should clear up any further discussion on the matter of motorbike safety.

"It sounds to me like some pretty poor motorcycle skills," he jokes nonchalantly.

"Hey, my skills were fine. Motorbikes are just dangerous. Too much power and not enough stability. Nobody can tell me otherwise." Stacking the empty plates, I head back inside the house to the kitchen.

"Here, let me help," Gabe jumps lithely to his bare feet, gathers the wine glasses and the now empty bottle and follows me.

I place the dishes in the dishwasher and tidy up the kitchen. Gabe is quiet but I can feel his eyes following my every movement. Nerve endings tingle and heat moves through me again. Rinsing the dish-cloth out I say, "I'd best be on my way. I have some things to get done at home tonight and then an early start at the office tomor-row." I avoid his eyes as I grab my purse from the barstool and move towards the door.

"It's been nice to meet you, Gabe Harris of Hunter Valley." With that, I flee from the house, waving a hasty goodbye to Heidi, who is still sitting on the lawn playing with the kittens.

"Hey, you forgot to take a kitten," she calls, her laughter chasing after me down the street.

On Saturday morning I feel distracted. I help at the S.P.C.A. fundraising event and answer questions about the organization and the animal adoption process but I find, uncharacteristically, my heart isn't in it today. Back at home I haul several outfits from the closet looking for the perfect combination of casual with flair for my evening with Gabe.

I pair snug black jeans with a white, sleeveless peasant blouse and add a wide black belt and black faux leather low-heeled sandals. A large obsidian oval necklace completes the ensemble. Looking in the mirror, I decide the outfit is definitely pleasant but perhaps lacks any artistic panache. I grab a fuchsia-coloured pashmina and drape it around my bare shoulders.

"That's better," I say to my reflection as I smooth down a wayward strand of hair. It is a mild evening and the sun's rays cast a warm glow over the town as I make my way down the street towards Heidi's house. I arrive punctually at five, ring the doorbell and wait. And wait. I consult my watch, then press the bell again. From inside I hear a faint "come in" so I open the door and step into the cool foyer.

Gabe dashes halfway down the stairs. He is barefoot and shirtless. My small clutch drops from my limp grasp and lands with a plonk on the wood floor.

"Sorry, Alexi." His smile could warm the coldest Kootenay winter day. "I'm not quite ready, as you can see." He gestures towards his naked chest in explanation.

"Uh, yeah. No shirt, no shoes, no service. That's the Wild Onion's motto." I can't draw my eyes away from the well-muscled planes of his torso. Descending to the bottom of the stairs, he comes closer then reaches down and retrieves my purse from the floor.

"You seem to have dropped this," he says placing the bag in my hand, his fingers slipping past mine in a brief moment of sensation. A faintly arrogant smile plays around his lips.

"Umm...thanks," I mumble. I can smell the musky sent of his aftershave.

"Give me two minutes. My shirt is in the dryer still." With a wink and a cheeky grin he bolts back up the stairs taking them two or three at a time.

I peek into the living room and see the box of kittens. Slipping off my sandals, I pad my way barefoot to the box and pick up the runt. He loves the tassels on my pashmina and bats his paws playfully when I jiggle them.

"Hey, my little baby," I coo to him and gently rub his tiny ears. His purr is so loud and rumbly that I can't stop myself from laughing.

"Look at my two beauties," Gabe says, having quietly entered the room in socked feet. He is wearing a burgundy dress shirt and slim fitting jeans that enhances his lightly tanned skin. I can feel myself blush at the off-hand compliment and I feel more like a teenager on a first date than a married woman of eighteen years.

"Shall we go?" Gabe asks. I place the kitten back in the box and cringe in sympathy when he cries piteously.

"Yes. It's a nice evening for a walk." I slip my sandals back on as Gabe pulls on his Blundstone boots. "Too bad Heidi couldn't come along. I guess she's teaching tonight." I make conversation as we leave the house.

"She has two classes back to back this evening so she'll be home late and exhausted," Gabe explains as he walks down the path to the shaded sidewalk.

"Lead the way, Alexi." We set off at a brisk pace, matching our steps nicely as we walk west through the town towards the outskirts of Kalsson.

"This is a really pretty little town. Have you lived here long?" Gabe inquires as we stride along.

"I was actually born here. I've never lived anywhere else. I have not travelled much either, unlike you who has been all around the world. I did go to England once about eight years ago."

"Did you like England? That's one place I have yet to visit," Gabe explains.

"I loved it. I stayed in a little town called Grasmere in the Lake District. Mark, my husband, sent me for a two week painting vacation for my birthday. It was an organized group tour which was helpful as I had never travelled before. There was time allotted each day for participants to explore on their own which I really enjoyed." I smile as I recall that wonderful time.

"You could always go back again. Maybe stay longer and see some other areas like the Peak District. I've heard it's very beautiful also."

"I'm sure I'll get back there someday. Mark is from Manchester and I naturally became more interested in English culture and history after we got married. I'm a third generation Canadian but my great great grandfather was born in London. My dad is a genealogy and history nut and he has traced our ancestors back several generations. I was never that interested until I went to England and felt such a deep and immediate connection to the place. Strangely, it felt like going home." I pause for a moment before carrying on.

"And you? Have you found an unlikely connection to any of the places that you've visited?" I glance at Gabe, aware that he is taking his time to answer. He has slowed our fast pace and turns towards me.

"Here. I've felt that connection here in Kalsson amongst the trees, beside the lake. Beside you." His gaze is steady and open.

"But you don't even know me!" I am flummoxed by his candor and feel unsettled.

"I do know you, Alexi. I feel, here, like I've known you all my life." He places a relaxed fist over his heart. I turn and walk on in silence.

Mulling over Gabe's comment, I don't know if I should run for home, laugh out loud, or feel flattered. In all honesty, it had been that way for me when I first met Mark Hollingberry.

Of course I had felt all the chemical and hormonal fireworks that happen when you are attracted to someone, but deep down, on a subconscious level, I felt my entire being entwining with Mark's right from the beginning.

Within days of meeting, we became life partners. Granted, it had taken us a while to figure it all out, but it was there, right from the first time we met: a bonding of mind, spirit, and soul.

I never questioned or doubted our immediate connection. Although I was young, naïve and innocent, I was not ignorant of the spectacular connection we had formed with each other. From the very beginning, we were soul mates bound by fate and happenstance.

Was it possible that Gabe, an acquaintance of just a few days, could be experiencing a similar connection with me? How could I doubt it when it had happened just the same for me?

"You've gone very quiet, Alexi. Have I offended you?" Gabriel slows my stride by gently touching my shoulder. Turning, I face him, as I come to a standstill.

"Startled, yes. Offended, no. Actually I'm glad you feel comfortable with me because I think I could do with another good friend." Smiling, I loop my arm through his and carry on down the street.

"Come on, I'm starving and we're almost there." We resume our brisk, stride-matching pace. Gabe is quiet and despite our skin touching, I can feel him putting distance between us. I know he does not like the words I have said. A friendly acquaintance was not the relationship he had in mind.

Dinner at the Wild Onion is filled with short, stiff sentences and monosyllables. We had been seated immediately and our server was attentive and courteous. Gabe ordered steak and roasted root vegetables and I ordered the Pad Thai with grilled tofu. The kitchen seems to be taking ages to fill our order.

"Look," I say after several minutes of awkward silence, "why don't we skip looking at my paintings. This is obviously very uncomfortable for both of us. Let's just eat our dinner and call it a day."

"No!" Gabriel's response is short and emphatic. Sighing, he bows his head and slides a hand through his hair. "What I mean is, *no*," he says the word softly this time. "I really want to see your work. I'm sorry I messed up the evening by opening my big mouth." He grins at me, his easy boyish charm sliding back into place. In his eyes I can see shadows but I cannot read them. He looks away, shielding himself from me.

"You may be disappointed. I dropped out of art college after just two years to get married. From then on, I've been essentially self-taught." I feel nervous at the thought of Gabe, an accomplished artist, seeing my work.

"Alexi, I will not be disappointed." He has yet to look at me, but his voice is soft and determined. Our meals arrive and we dig in hungrily.

"Does it bother you as a vegan, which I understand from Heidi means that you don't eat meat, fish, or dairy, to watch me eat meat?" It is a fair question; a question that I have been asked and answered many times over the past fifteen years that I have been vegan.

"Not at all, Gabe. Enjoy your steak. I'm not going to try to make you feel bad about your food choices. But you must return the favour and not tease me about my tofu." I answer truthfully.

I've never been one to preach the vegan lifestyle. All I can hope for is to lead by example. "I don't suppose you'd like to try a bit of my Pad Thai?" I offer, mostly joking.

"Sure. I'll try anything once," he passes me his side plate and I load it with a few choice morsels.

"Wow, that's really tasty," he says, eating it all. "Can I have a bit more?" I laugh and reload the little plate.

"You'd better watch out or you'll end up vegan by the end of the evening." I like teasing Gabriel. He's too serious by far.

After dinner we order dessert. The Wild Onion has a decadent vegan chocolate mousse cake with raspberry coulis that I have ordered several times before.

"If you like chocolate, the mousse is the best option. If you like fruity desserts, the pies are reputed to be excellent."

"Let's share the mousse," Gabe suggests. "I'm full, but you make it sound too good to pass up."

"Sure, we can share it." The waiter brings the dessert with two forks and two coffees.

"Dig in," I say as I lift a forkful of cake to my lips. The raspberry coulis and dark chocolate combination draws groans of pleasure from both of us.

"This is a dessert that *must not* be missed," Gabe says, taking another bite.

"You finish it," I say, pushing the plate closer to him. "I'm too full to eat anymore." Without further urging, he polishes off the remaining cake.

"How do you stay so fit when you're traveling all the time?" I ask curiously, recalling his trim, muscular physique.

"I run every day before breakfast. Once I reach my destination for the day, I do a series of exercises to keep toned. I like to swim also, so I go whenever I can." Gabe takes a sip of his coffee and relaxes back in the chair.

"And you? How do you keep in such good shape?" He regards me assessingly.

"Yoga, walking, a vegan lifestyle...that's about it really," I explain.

"Well, it certainly is working for you," Gabe says, offering up another compliment.

"Shall we head for home?" I ask, feeling the urge to change the subject as the conversation becomes too personal.

The sun had long ago dipped behind the snow-capped mountains and a chill had seeped into the evening air. I pull the pashmina around me and tuck my hands in my jean pockets. We walk quickly to keep warm and arrive at my house fifteen minutes later.

"Come in and make yourself at home. I'm going to get a sweater, then we can go to the studio which is in the back yard." I leave Gabe wandering around the living room looking at pictures of Mark and me taken over the years.

Upstairs, I pull on a soft blue cotton sweater and return to the living room.

"Mark looks like a nice guy. A bit preppy perhaps, but nice," Gabe says peering at a picture taken the previous year.

"He *is* a nice guy." I ignore the preppy comment. "You would like him. Maybe you'll have a chance to meet him before you head to Alaska."

"Yeah, that'd be just great." I have the sense Gabe is being insincere, but I hope I'm wrong.

Leading the way, I head out the back door of the two-story heritage house and walk along the paving stones through the cool, dewy grass to the studio.

The studio – a gift from Mark – was built a few years ago to his specifications and matches the house in style and colour. Designed to allow for ample natural light, it has large windows along each wall. The space has a small fireplace, a kitchenette, and a bathroom. My easel is set up in the best light and a half-finished work awaits completion. On the walls hang more than two dozen of my favourite works. I flick on the lights which are suspended strategically above the picture rail.

"This is fantastic. The studio is absolutely delightful." He draws closer to the painting on the wall. "These are marvelous."

"You'd better watch out or you'll run out of superlatives," I tease, feeling pleased yet uncomfortable by his praise.

Slowly and with concentration, he moves from picture to picture, completely absorbed. The studio is quiet. I can hear the clock ticking on the mantle. It strikes the half hour with a resonating gong and I jump, startled by the sound. Gabriel does not notice and carries on with his perusal.

I move to the gas fireplace and turn it on and then sit in one of the comfortable armchairs near the hearth. It looks like this might take a while I think as I tuck my cold feet up under myself and lean my head back into the soft cushion. Although it is not yet nine o'clock, I feel drowsy as the heat of the fire seeps into my chilled bones; I close my eyes for a moment.

"Alexi." I hear someone calling my name but I can't place the voice. "Alexi." Slowly I open my eyes. Gabe is kneeling in front of my chair and is gently shaking my shoulder.

"I'm sorry," I say dropping my feet to the floor and stifling a yawn. "I don't even recall nodding off." The clock gongs again and I am surprised that it is eleven o'clock.

"No probs." Gabriel smiles at me and sits in the armchair beside mine. "It's so peaceful here. It's no wonder you're able to produce such magical pieces."

"Did you find one that you like?" I ask.

"I like all of them but there is one in particular that stands out."

"I bet it's that one over there," I say pointing to one I painted last year of a stony outcropping protecting a bonsai cotoneaster.

"Nope. Although I do really like that one. Guess again." He seems to be having fun making me guess.

"The autumn trees at the lake side?" I ask.

"Nope."

"We could be here all night at this rate." I sigh and scan all my displayed works. I look at Gabe and try to go with my intuition, not with what other people have liked in the past. He regards me with a steady, dark gaze. His face is illuminated by the flames of the fire and it deepens the colour of his skin, highlighting his dark hair. I cannot read him; his thoughts are unfathomable to me.

"Last chance," he says quietly.

I suddenly point to an unsettling black and red image. I had painted it out of lonely frustration one day while Mark was away on an unusually long trip. The result had been a single tree, charred black, in the foreground with the evidence of a recent forest fire in the background. A single raven in flight is silhouetted against the glowing red sky.

"Yes," he states simply.

"Most people don't like that one." I respond with total honestly. "Even I don't like it most of the time."

"That is because it has such raw passion and anguish. The viewer is almost frightened by it. I love it because it is so singularly desolate. I feel that way sometimes. Like my life is all burned up and I'm just a charred shell of myself." Gabriel keeps staring at the picture, unable to draw his eyes away.

"You don't strike me as somebody that is burned up. More restless and rootless, maybe even searching, but not burned up. There is fire inside of you; a positive, creative fire. I can see it, Gabe." I lean forward and place my hand on his where it lies on the arm of the chair. Startled, he draws his brooding gaze to me.

"I do feel restless these past months...years. It's like my life is skidding by me and I'm not able to appreciate it. I'd like to be able to contribute something to the world but I have yet to find a way."

My lips curve in a faint smile.

"What's so funny?" He asks, slightly affronted.

"When I first met you I thought you were arrogant. Now I see you use arrogance like a cloak; you create a diversion so people can't get a glimpse of the real you. It's very clever, really."

"I am arrogant, Alexi. I got too much, too fast and didn't know what to do with it. I became an asshole, living for the next drink, the next high, the next woman. I became a wasteland. I became *that*," he points emphatically at the blackened stump in the painting. His angst is obvious as he continues.

"By the end of the third film, I had made more money than most people can dream of and I became a person that even I despised. That's when I threw in the towel. I packed my saddle bags and rode out of Sydney on my motorbike. I've not been back since and that was almost three years ago." Gabe looks emotionally drained but continues speaking.

"My family has practically disowned me; my future is bleak despite all of my so-called success. I need to find a way back to a life that makes me happy. I see you, so committed and content with your husband, you house, your painting, your job, yourself...I want to be that committed, that passionate about my life. But somehow the path to that place keeps escaping me. So I keep traveling." Gabe pulls a slim silver case from his jean pocket, opens it and removes a cigarette.

"Do you mind if I smoke?" He asks, placing the cigarette between his lips.

"What the hell! What bombshell will fall from your mouth next?" I am practically screaming as I jump to my feet, grab the unlit cigarette from his lips and fling it into a nearby wastepaper can. "Are you out of your frigging mind?" I can feel my teeth clenching and my body has gone rigid. I press a shaky hand to my forehead and take a few, deep calming breaths.

"Sorry. I didn't think you'd mind." He pushes the offending cigarettes back into his pocket.

"So much for *knowing* me," I snap waspishly. "Seriously, I did not have you pegged as an idiot. Handsome, arrogant, well-educated, sexy as hell...all yes. But just plain stupid? No, I sure didn't see that one coming. *Of course* I mind if you smoke. Why don't I go get a loaded gun and let you shoot yourself now?" I slump back into the chair and stare unseeing into the fireplace. The energy in the room is fraught with emotion. Gabe is confused and uncomfortable.

"Look," I try to explain calmly and rationally, "I work at a medical clinic where I see people day after day killing themselves with cigarettes. It breaks my heart. I like you Gabe and I can't bear to see you harming yourself. I'm sorry about my outburst, but I get pretty worked up when it's regarding someone I care about." Gabe clears his throat awkwardly and runs his palms along the front of his jeans, a gesture that smacks of nervousness.

"I'd better go, Alexi. It's getting late and we're both tired." He gets to his feet and offers me his hand. I take it and rise from the chair to stand in front of him. I want to cry. My beautiful Gabriel has fallen off his pedestal.

"No hard feelings?" He asks, brushing a wayward strand of hair from my cheek.

"No, Gabe. No hard feelings."

A deep sadness settles on my heart.

The next morning the phone rings at an ungodly hour. Peering at the Big Ben alarm clock at my bedside with sleepy eyes I see that it is six o'clock. I pick up the phone expecting to hear my brother Michael's voice on the line. He often calls rather early due to the time difference between Canada and Germany.

"Hello?" I squawk into the receiver, my throat dry from sleep.

"Hi, Alexi, it's Gabe. Did you sleep well?"

"Oh, hi Gabe. You woke me up," I say, rubbing sleep from my eyes before yawning.

"Well, thoughts of you kept me up all night." He sounds cheerful. Excited. "Could we spend the day together? I don't care what we do, I just want to get to know you better and after my blunder last night, it seems prudent."

"Well...I have to..."

"Yeah, I know. You have to work at your dad's bookstore today. I could help you." He reminds me of a puppy dog, all happy and wiggly; if he had a tail, it would be wagging right now.

"Gabe, I'll be doing payroll. There's nothing much you can help me with. It's really not that exciting." I feel mean dampening his enthusiasm.

"Okay. Go help your dad now, then we can go for a drive. You can show me the highlights of the area." He certainly seems determined.

"Gabe, it is six o'clock. My dad doesn't open the store until eleven on Sundays. Also, Mark has the car and you already know how I feel about motorbikes." I throw back the blankets and, still holding the phone to my ear, draw back the drapes. "Oh, it's a beautiful day out," I say in surprise. The forecast had been for rain today.

"I know. I've already been out for a five kilometre run. I could rent a car if you could do the payroll on Monday instead," he coaxes. I sigh heavily into the receiver.

"Well...it's not payday until next Friday." I feel myself acquiescing. "Okay, let's do it; let's play hookey!"

"I'll come get you in one hour and we'll have breakfast on the road." He hangs up before I have a chance to say goodbye. Or to change my mind.

Invigorated, I jump into the shower and wash my hair quickly. I towel dry, brush my teeth and apply a light foundation, a coat of mascara, and a berry lip shimmer. I select deep green cotton capris, a casual but fitted T-shirt in black, and black flip flops. My hair is still wet, so with one eye on the clock, I blow dry it. At five minutes to seven, the doorbell rings.

Gabe is waiting on the front porch. Dressed casually, he dangles a set of keys from his fingers.

"We've got wheels," he says with an ear to ear grin.

The *wheels* belong to the body of a dark blue Ford Mustang convertible. The top is already down.

"Yikes! I'd better get a jacket. It may be sunny but it will be cool with the top down." I dash back upstairs and grab a cotton-lined wind breaker, a pair of sunglasses, and a hat. Back downstairs, I lock the door and place the baseball cap on my head.

"Okay, Gabriel Harris of Hunter Valley, lead on!"

I explain, as we settle into the car, that there are several lovely circuits that we can choose from and we decide to drive east along the shoreline, then cross the lake on the ferry and continue south on the other side.

A small artisan town lies nestled at the base of the mountain thirty minutes drive from the ferry terminal and we decide to breakfast there. We catch the first ferry sailing with moments to spare and after parking the car, we climb the stairs to the viewing area which is open to the elements. The air is fresh and breezy and I zip my windbreaker up around my neck, tucking my hands into my pockets. The sky is clear and shows the pale blue hues of spring; we watch as a jet stream fades in a long streak of vapour across the horizon.

We dock forty-five minutes later and resume our drive along the lake. When we reach Crawford Bay, we stop for breakfast at a tiny café located on the main road through the village.

"You must be famished," I say as he tucks into his bacon, eggs, and toast. "I'm hungry and I didn't run a single step this morning."

"I *am* hungry but I scarcely noticed because I feel high on life today," he says, grinning. "I haven't felt high like this since my days at uni. I used to take it for granted, now I realize how long it's been since I've felt this good." He reaches across the red and white checkered table cloth and touches my hand. "I'm glad I'm sharing it with you, Alexi. Thank you."

"No need to thank me. This is your moment...enjoy it." Our hands linger together a moment longer, then pull slowly apart.

After breakfast, we wander around the small village looking at shops, some of which still have not opened. The hand-made broom store is open, however, and we watch as the craftsman sorts and cuts the straw for the short, wooden-handled brooms he is making. He is very informative and explains the process from raw materials to final product in detail.

Further along the street, a glassblower gives a demonstration of his abilities while a blacksmith forges wrought iron hooks and plant hangers in the adjoining studio. Once we have explored all the artisan and craft shops, we return to the convertible and continue on along the lake to the next town some thirty kilometres away.

The lakeside drive is spectacular; the reflection of the majestic mountains is caught on the still surface of the lake. Occasionally a breeze stirs the image, then it settles to peaceful quietness again. The wind lifts my hair and twirls it around in a messy halo and I try in vain to tuck it up under my ball cap.

"It's just no use!" I wail in mock despair. Gabe glances over at me and smiles but does not comment. He looks splendid in dark sunglasses with his hair wildly untamed, his snug fitting jeans accentuating well-muscled thighs. I decide it is best to keep my mind off him by talking.

"There is a special place I like to go when I'm on this side of the lake. It's just a few kilometres up ahead. Do you want to stop and have a look?" I ask, keeping my eyes on the road.

"You're the boss. This car goes wherever you say." He is smiling again; I can hear it in his voice. There is no sign of the desolate and desperate man of last night.

"There is a point of interest just around the bend. We can stop there first, then we can carry on to my special place." We pull off the road and park near the lakeside attraction and pause to read the placard at the entrance to the house.

The Glass House was built in 1952 by David Brown. It was constructed out of 500,000 empty embalming bottles collected by Mr. Brown during the thirty-five years he spent in the funeral business. He built the house on a whim thinking to create a folly of sorts, but the general public took such an interest in his project, he finally opened the house to the public for tours.

Gabe and I wander through the rooms of the glass structure and then go out to the lake view gardens behind the house. We comment to each other on the whimsical nature of the place as we return to the car.

We then proceed along the lake a few more minutes before exiting off the main highway to travel steeply up a dirt road to a plateau at the base of the mountain where a closed gate greets us. I jump out of the car and open the gate for Gabe and then secure it after he has passed through.

"We're almost there," I say, with a mischievous smile. Following the well-worn track, we continue along a slight grade, then dip into a quiet, open, grassy valley. In the field we can see cows, horses, donkeys, and goats.

"This is an animal rescue farm," I explain. "I've been here many times volunteering. I do whatever I can, which usually includes a lot of stall mucking and fence repairs. The owners of the sanctuary rely on donations and volunteers; it's truly a labour of love for them. Come on. Let's park the car and I'll introduce you to Bill and Teresa Pickering."

As soon as the car comes to a stop, I vault from the seat and rush to the front door of the modest farmhouse and ring the doorbell impatiently. Gabe follows at a more leisurely pace. His gaze wanders over the property while we wait at the door.

From inside the house we can hear dogs barking and a female voice calling, "I'm coming, I'm coming." An older, grey-haired woman with a flushed faced opens the door and a flood of dogs tramples over the threshold barking, jumping, and licking us in a jumble of frantic wriggling bodies.

"Down, boys, down," the woman exclaims, then reaches for me with arms spread wide, a beaming smile on her wrinkled face.

"What a wonderful surprise. It's so good to see you, Alexi," she says giving me a big, warm hug. "Where is Mark?"

"He's working on a project out of town so he couldn't come today," I explain.

"And who is this handsome fellow you have with you, love?" Teresa asks, smiling warmly at Gabe.

"Teresa, this is Gabriel Harris, visiting from Australia. I'm giving him the grand tour of the south arm of Kootenay Lake and I thought he'd enjoy seeing your farm. He's a cat lover." Gabe shakes Teresa's extended hand murmuring a hello.

"Welcome to Pleasant Pastures, Gabe. We love to have visitors. Bill is in town at the feed store, but he should be back soon. Alexi can give you a tour of the farm; she is very familiar with the property." Teresa gives me another affectionate squeeze. "Take the dogs with you, love, they need some exercise."

"Let's see if I can remember their names. The three legged one is Jessie, the Rot-cross is Bruno, the Jack Russel is Kiki, and the black lab is Puddles. And this little one I don't know." I reach down and pick up a minuscule, shaking, Teacup Chihuahua who stares at me with huge, sombre brown eyes.

"That's Tiny. She's the latest addition to the family. We rescued her from a puppy mill a few weeks ago. She's just starting to trust Bill and me. She gets along great with the boys and they are very protective of her." I hold the shivering little creature in my cupped hands.

"Poor little Tiny. You'll be okay now that you're with Bill and Teresa." I kiss the top of her head and gently set her back down amongst the boys. "Hey, Bruno, how are you doing?" I pat the Rottweiler on the back and he slobbers on my hand affectionately in response. The lab has decided to befriend Gabe by sitting on his foot and moaning happily as Gabe scratches him behind the ears.

"Okay, everybody, let's make tracks." I clap my hands and the dogs bound around me in excitement. "We'll see you later, Teresa." I wave and lead the way towards the pastures.

"Right you are, love," she responds gaily, waving back before returning to the house.

We follow the fence line to the narrow gate near the barn.

"Let's go through to the pasture first, then we can tour the barn if you're up for it," I suggest as I open the gate. I let the dogs rush through first. Gabe briefly touches my hand as he follows the pack through the gate.

"Thank you for bringing me here," he says quietly as he passes by me. I am pleased that he is interested in the sanctuary.

"You're welcome, Gabe. Over there, near the apple trees, are the rescued dairy cows. The horses are snoozing in the shade on the other side of the field. Who do you want to visit first?" I ask.

Gabe points towards the horses. "I'd like to see them first."

Walking through the tall grass becomes difficult for Tiny so I pick her up and tuck her in my jacket pocket. She settles in right away, seeming to find comfort in being close to me. The rest of the pack frolic and play-fight in the fresh, spring grass, each of them grinning from ear to ear as happy dogs are apt to do.

The horses, five of them in all, plus two donkeys, are alerted to our approach but remain in the shade, their tails swishing restlessly at the occasional fly. The old chestnut mare nickers a soft greeting and ambles slowly towards us.

She had suffered a shoulder injury at the race track in Vancouver and had been slated for euthanasia but Bill and Teresa had stepped in and brought her to the sanctuary to recuperate. Although she had made a remarkable recovery, arthritis has begun to plague her as the years pass.

"This beauty is named Dolly. She loves to have her withers scratched." I demonstrate for Gabe and Dolly stretches her neck out and wiggles her upper lip showing her teeth. "That's Dolly's way of showing you that you've hit the right spot," I explain. One by one I introduce the horses and donkeys to Gabe, who seems intrigued by their antics.

"I never realized how much personality they have," Gabe says in amazement as Henley, the young gelding, pushes his soft grey muzzle into Gabe's hair and blows out a gentle breath.

"He likes you. See how he is sniffing you? They have an excellent sense of smell and often greet one another by blowing into each other's nostrils."

For the next few hours we wander the property talking about the animals in the pasture and the barn. I give Gabe a brief background story for each animal and try valiantly not to dissolve into tears when recounting the more traumatic histories.

Tiny has stayed in my pocket the entire time but the rest of the dogs have wandered back to the house for some food and a nap, having grown bored with us.

"You sure are a natural with animals, Gabe. You must have had a lot of pets when you were growing up." We have finished our barn tour and are heading back towards the farmhouse.

"Actually, we never had any pets at all. I always wanted a dog but my dad said they were too much work so we never got to have one." There was an undertone of sadness in Gabe's voice.

"Well, that's a shame because you have such an affinity for them."

"Do you mind if I hold Tiny for a few minutes?" He requests quietly.

"Yes, of course you can hold her." Gently I pass the dog to Gabe who holds her carefully in his large hands.

As we reach the house, Bill pulls up in the yard in his bright yellow 1950's GMC truck.

"Hello there, my special gal. What a pleasure to see you." Bill calls through the open window of the truck. He gets out of the cab and dusts himself off with his work gloves, then envelops me in what I call his Papa Bear hug. I introduce Bill and Gabe and they shake hands in greeting. Bill invites us to join them for lunch but I decline the offer with regret.

"We've got to get a move on, Bill. Next time I'll stay for the day and take you up on your lunch offer." We say our goodbyes to Bill and Teresa as Gabe reluctantly returns Tiny to the pack.

As we drive back down the hill to the highway in the now dusty Mustang, I ask, "Did you enjoy yourself?"

"That was just super, Alexi. Thank you so much for taking me there. I will never forget this place or what Bill and Teresa are doing for those animals. It is really quite extraordinary."

We travel on in companionable silence for another twenty minutes until we reach Creston where we stop at the local deli for lunch. After we have finished our soup and sandwich, over beverages we ponder the next leg of our trip.

"If we leave now and go straight home we can get into Kalsson by five o'clock. What time does the car need to be back?" I ask.

"I rented it for a few weeks," Gabe answers, "just in case there are other places you want to show me." He grins impishly at me.

"Well, if time isn't an issue, we can stop at the Wetland Management area at the marshy end of the lake. They have put wood plank pathways throughout the wetland so you can get up close and personal with the birds, turtles, frogs, and insects. It's really a lot of fun. You can also rent canoes and row your way around the hundreds of hectares of marshes."

"It sounds very interesting," Gabe says.

"Mark and I have been contributing financially to this project for years. It is such a valuable endeavor, and the schools use the area for educational day trips for students who get a chance to learn about nature first hand."

"With such a glowing recommendation, I can scarcely say no," Gabe says laughing as he finishes his drink. "Let's go." He settles the bill quickly before I have a chance to reach for my purse.

"I'll pay for gas, then, since you got breakfast and lunch," I offer firmly, feeling uncomfortable with him paying for everything.

"Nope. The least I can do is buy your meals since you are spending your day off babysitting me." His tone does not encourage argument.

"We'll see," I say noncommittally. "On a different note, I figure you must be dying for a cigarette." I laugh at my unintentional pun. "Oops, sorry about that. But honestly, you haven't smoked for hours. Are you going to start getting grouchy on me?" I quirk a questioning eyebrow.

"I'm fine, Alexi. I don't want a smoke." He seems slightly annoyed as we walk back to the convertible.

"Well, that's good. At least now I don't have to throw another fit." I try to ease the conversation back to a lighter tone.

"That's a blessing," Gabe says, smiling as he picks up on my mood. "A person only wants to see that meltdown once in a lifetime." He opens the door for me and waits as I slide into the comfortable, sporty bucket seat before closing it. Leaning forward he rests his forearms on the top edge of the door frame and presses in close so that we are eye to eye. I can see gold flecks in the depths of his chocolate brown irises.

"I must admit, it does feel good to have someone care that passionately about me," he says softly before straightening up and away from the car door. With a boyish grin he pops the brim of my cap down over my eyes. I am too memorized by his scent and recent closeness to conjugate a witty response, or any response whatsoever for that matter.

"Lead the way, oh princess of the day trip," he says in a silly falsetto voice as he climbs into the driver's seat. I can't help but laugh at him. I give him directions out of the small, sleepy town, across the wide, flat valley to the base of the mountains on the far side. As we approach the Wetland Management area, I launch into tour guide mode and begin to educate Gabe on the area's significance.

"The flood plain area at the south end of Kootenay Lake is predominately a marshland and it provides breeding habitat for the rare Leopard frog and the Forster's tern. Duck Lake is contained within the wetland as well as seventeen marshes. The Purcell and Selkirk Mountains rise high above the wetlands to the east and west respectively." I point out the mountains as we approach our destination.

"Those are pretty dramatic mountains," he comments, squinting into the sun for a better look.

"These wetlands provide an excellent area for birds, mammals, reptiles, and amphibians to breed and flourish," I carry on. "They also provide a significant flyway route for migrating geese and other waterfowl," I pause my ramblings, indicating to Gabe that we need to pull off the main road and onto a dirt driveway that leads to the parking lot.

"Listen, I could go on for hours about this place. Why don't we just go enjoy it and you can see for yourself?" Gabe nods his agreement.

We leave the car in visitors' parking and wander down the long wooden ramp to the Interpretation Centre; Gabe again reaches for his wallet but I have my lifetime membership card with me which allows us gratis entry. Since we have missed the final guided canoe tour of the day, we decide to stroll the boardwalk instead, using the maps provided by the centre.

"We may get lucky today and see an American white pelican," I exclaim, excited to be back at the wetlands.

"It's so quiet out here," Gabe says peering into the murky, shallow water at the edge of the boardwalk, hoping to catch a glimpse of a turtle or salamander.

"Yeah, we just love it here. We come as often as possible but it takes up a full day, so we only come once a month or so. Usually Mark brings his camera and I bring my sketch pad and we nestle down someplace away from the busy areas and let nature carry on around us."

"That sounds cozy."

"It really is." We walk on, my flip flops noisy against the boards. I pause and pull them off and then holding them in one hand, we continue.

"There, that 's better! I was scaring away all the wildlife." Now, as we wander along, all we can hear is the rustling of swaying grasses and reeds and the occasional call of a fish eagle, the osprey, high overhead.

"Most of the birds are active early in the day. We're here too late to hear or see much activity."

I sit on the smooth oak planks of a nearby cast iron bench. An attached brass plaque reads:

In Loving Memory of Chappy and Tricks.
Two cats were never loved more. 1982-1997.

"Oh, Gabe, take a look at this memorial. Isn't it just so sweet?" I run my fingertips over the brass plate and think of the beautiful little kitten Heidi keeps begging me to take. I can't help remembering Tetley, our orange tabby cat who died just over a year ago at the age of nineteen. My heart is full of love. My mind full of memories.

"Do you ever experience inexplicable moments that, out of the blue, feel like...I don't know...rapture or ecstasy? As if each second of life offers the possibility of love, of joy, of pure bliss? All you have to do is grab hold of one of those moments and it is forever crystalized into a perfect memory to be cherished forever." I'm not making perfect sense, but he nods just the same.

Drawing my knees up to my chest I rest my bare feet on the polished wooden planks of the bench. I take off my hat and set it beside my flip flops, then run a hand through my hair, letting the breeze ruffle the long brunette tendrils. I clasp my arms around my knees and close my eyes.

Breathing in a long, slow, steady breath, I hold it for a few seconds before slowly releasing it. My mind is soft and dreamy; I am totally relaxed. I hear Gabe sit on the bench beside me. The afternoon sun warms the skin on my bare arms. And I sigh.

"Are you content?" Gabe asks quietly. I turn and look at him, pushing my sunglasses up on top of my head. I nod once. I'm not sure if he means in this moment or in life in general, but for me it does not matter. The answer is the same.

"Yes."

"Me, too. For the fist time in a long time I feel really happy. I think I even know what you meant just now about finding rapture in an ordinary moment. I've been too discontented lately to notice things like rapture." He is looking at me as though he can barely believe his own words. I scoot closer to him on the bench and wrap my arms around him.

"I'm glad you understand, Gabe. I guess I take happiness for granted because I tend to be an easily pleased sort of person. I bet people see how handsome you are, how much money you have, how educated you are, and they assume that you are happy. But then maybe those attributes don't equal happiness. Maybe that comes from our genes or how we are raised or even from our own personal view of the world." I rest my head on his shoulder and feel the firmness of his muscles beneath my cheek.

Gabe relaxes his back against the bench and closes his eyes. The fan of faint tension wrinkles around his eyes smooth. He looks peaceful.

"You sure know a lot about life for someone so young," Gabe comments without opening his eyes.

"I'm not all *that* young," I say, laughing. "After thirty-eight years I'd expect to have learned a few thing along the way." Gabe pulls out of my arms in surprise and looks me over.

"I thought you were in your late twenties. Thirty-two, tops!"

"Sure, keep the compliments coming, big guy. I can always use an ego boost." I am still smiling as I put my flip flops back on and reposition my sunglasses. "We'd better get back to the car. We have a few hours drive ahead of us before we get home."

"Sure, let's go," Gabe agrees. Reaching out, he clasps my hand in his and we retrace our steps back to the car.

It feels odd to be holding a hand that isn't Mark's. Although I know Gabe is only offering comfort and companionship, it feels dangerous and inappropriate for me. I untangle my fingers from his warm, solid grasp and adjust my hat unnecessarily, then tuck both of my hands in my pocket as we carry on. It bothers me that I enjoy Gabe's touch. I didn't expect myself to be drawn to him physically, particularly since I am in love with my husband.

Being on the shady side of the valley at late afternoon towards the end of May brings a sharp nip to the breeze lifting from the marshland. We decide it's time to put the top up on the convertible and the need for sunglasses wanes. Once on the road, we head up the mountain to the summit just before the small town of Salmo where we will eventually loop back down towards the lake, to Kalsson, where we started out.

"Do you mind if I put the radio on?" I ask.

"Go ahead." I search the channels until I find good reception on a classical station. I recognize the piece immediately; it is Solveig's Song by Edvard Grieg.

"Oh, I love this piece," I enthuse. "My mom used to play piano exceptionally well; we grew up listening to her play all the classical composers. Do you enjoy classical music too, Gabe?" I query.

"I'm more of an acid jazz kind of guy. I've not listened to much classical at all."

"I can't say I've listened to much jazz, acid or otherwise," I say ruefully. "Some classic jazz standards have made their way into our collection, but not a lot." I reach for the volume to turn it down, but Gabe stays my hand gently.

"By *our* collection I assume you mean yours and Mark's?" Gabe asks.

"Yes, of course," I return promptly.

"I like that; the way you naturally think in terms of *us* and *we* and *our* instead of *me* and *I* and *mine*. When I was married..."

"What? You never said you were married!" I interrupt him in astonishment.

"Oh, so you're allowed to be married but I'm not?" He sounds more quizzical than irked.

"You never mentioned a wife or ex-wife, that's all." I'm still surprised by his revelation.

"Well, anyway, getting back to what I was saying, when I was married, Lisa and I never really thought about being *us* or *we*. We both got busy with our careers after finishing university and I think we were two *I's* that never became a *we*. I guess that's partly why we didn't last very long."

"How long *were* you and Lisa married?" I question, interested in knowing more about his ex-wife.

"Four years. After we divorced, I got hired to work in the film industry. From then on, I was on a slippery slope towards destruction." He seems despondent. "I think in hindsight that the failed marriage had more impact on me than I allowed myself to believe."

"The good thing about slippery slopes and hindsight is that from them we learn and grow. Because of your good and bad experiences in life, you are developing as a person, learning about who and what you want to be in life. It's really exciting to look at your life, see the things you don't like, and then move towards positive changes."

"Are you always this optimistic about life?" He asks, concentrating on the steep, curvy mountain road ahead.

"Almost always. I see so many sick people at the clinic, it makes me feel grateful every day to be healthy mentally and physically. And I'm grateful to Mark for being the best husband for a girl like me. Maybe I'm optimistic and content with life because I've never had to endure any hardships in my life." I glance at Gabe, then carry on.

"You know, I had a great childhood in a supportive and nurturing home, I found the love of my life before ever getting my heart broken. Maybe my life is so easy, so simple that I *can* be optimistic."

"No, Alexi. I think you are content with life because you attract to it what you want. Good things happen to you *because* of your positive nature," Gabe says with conviction.

"We'll never know, I guess. It's another mystery of life, like the age old question of what came first, the chicken or the egg." We laugh together at our differing opinions.

Dusk has settled firmly over the landscape as the powerful Mustang eats up the kilometres towards home. There is not much to see on this leg of the journey which is fortunate as our scope of vision narrows bit by bit to just the twin headlights of the car. Having reached the plateau, we pass Salmo, a village with a population of just over eleven hundred, and start down the mountain towards Kalsson.

Gabe pulls the Mustang to a stop in front of my house thirty minutes later and turns off the engine.

"Alexi, I had such a good time with you today. Thank you." He turns in his seat so that he can look directly at me.

"I enjoyed the day, too. Thanks for driving and for the meals. It was a real treat." I reach for the door handle, anxious to put distance between us in a car that suddenly feels too confined.

"Let's do another trip. Let me know what day is good for you and I'll be ready." He is grinning like an eager boy again.

"I'll have to think about it, Gabe. I'll call you." Scrambling from the car, I wave a goodbye. Once inside the house, I lean back against the door and close my eyes. It had been a remarkably wonderful day.

CHAPTER 3

...precious words hang expectantly in the air...

November twenty-seventh dawns grey and sombre much like yesterday. Having felt too weak to climb the stairs, I had slept on the couch with Charlie last night. He doesn't care where he sleeps as long as he's tucked up beside me. I put my robe and slippers on and stare out over the frost-covered yard.

From the cloudy sky, the eagle emerges; ghostly quiet he swoops low over the evergreens and then, with a great opening of his wings, drops precisely onto the branch of a tree. He is magnificent and I am transfixed by his presence.

For long moments he waits, barely moving, at the edge of the thicket. Then, he lifts effortlessly into the air and dissolves into the other world. The wild world I know nothing of, just there past the edge of my mowed lawn, in the deeply shadowed forest below the gloomy sky. With a sigh of regret, I move away from the window and begin my daily chores.

Charlie wants feeding and a trip outside, and I must have some nourishment. After tending to Charlie, I prepare dry toast, apple slices, and a cup of tea. That was one lesson I had learned well from

Mark: everything seems better after a cup of strong tea. The toast, made from Jillie's homemade loaf, tastes lovely and I manage to keep it down despite a bitter rolling in my stomach.

I feel at loose ends this morning. Agitated, anxious, expectant. I roam the small cabin, restlessly picking up books and magazines only to put them down again, unable to concentrate. I move to the large selection of CD's and ponder my options. I decide on Erik Satie and prepare to be swept away by the slow, measured notes of the piano pieces for which he is so famous.

This recording was one of Mark's favourites and I smile as I think of him in his study sorting photos or polishing his watch collection. A day never passes that I don't miss him; his smile, his unfailing sense of humour, his smell. Our love for each other had not developed as a long slow burn but rather like a wild prairie fire that once ignited, there was no stopping its progress. By luck or fate, our universes had collided and thereafter our lives were never the same.

★ ★ ★

It is September 1979 and I am just starting my second year of the fine arts program at the local college on the outskirts of Kalsson. I have finished classes for the day and jump into the older two-door Civic I recently purchased with money I earned while working for my parents at the bookstore. After two summers of weekend work, I'd saved enough to buy the car and now life seems full of endless possibilities.

On this day, however, my little car decides to conk out on me as I drive home. Without warning I am without power; the engine has suddenly died. I coast to the side of the street, put my hazard lights on and pop the hood. Peering at the jumble of wires and hoses, I don't see anything amiss. Not that I would likely notice anything anyway, having never looked under the hood of a car before.

The street is quiet and nobody is in sight. I let out a huffy sigh and sit on the curb, waiting for a passerby to help. Moments later, an attractive, young man strides briskly towards me from a bungalow across the street.

"Looks like you could do with some help," he says, smiling warmly. He has a thick accent that sounds British to me, but being terrible with accents, I'm not entirely sure.

"Sunshine here just stopped running," I explain standing up and dusting off my butt with my right hand.

"Did any warning lights show up on the instrument panel?" He asks as he peers under the hood checking the spark plug connections. I notice how nicely dressed he is and worry he'll get oil and dirt on his clothes.

"No, nothing showed on the dash. She's been running just fine." I move closer and look at the engine with him. I can smell his aftershave and notice how blue his eyes are.

"Let's see if she will start up. Do you mind if I give it a go?" He asks politely.

"Knock yourself out. The keys are in the ignition."

He sits in the driver's seat and turns the key but the engine does not turn over.

"Hmm," he ponders aloud, "I think you've got a problem with the distributor cap. You'd best get her towed to your mechanic so they can have a look at it."

"Yeah, that seems like a good plan. You know a lot about cars?" I inquire as he gets out of the vehicle and hands me the keys.

He is slimly built and is just a smidge taller than I am. His nails, neatly trimmed and clean, are definitely not the hands of a mechanic.

With neat, short brown hair it is likely he had it cut by a barber rather than a hairstylist. In Kalsson, along with flared jeans, all the youths wear their hair long and feathered, inspired no doubt by Farrah Fawcett.

"No, not that much, but a similar thing happened to a friend last year and it was the distributor cap that had caused the problems. My name is Mark, by the way." He extends his hand and I reach out to receive the salutation. His hands are warm and dry; his clasp is firm. He smiles warmly; I smile spontaneously in return.

The world around us slows. Tilts. As our hands slip apart, lingering, savouring, my breath and heart flutter. Then the world slowly rights itself and returns to its natural speed.

"I'm Alexandra. Everybody calls me Alexi. Are you from Great Britain?" I query, hoping I'm not wrong. "I'm terrible with accents." I laugh nervously.

"Yes, I'm from Manchester." His smile is beautiful; it reaches his blue eyes and lights them from within.

"It must be a bit of culture shock, coming to a little town like Kalsson," I say laughing again. I feel breathless; my voice is high and airy.

Even the clothes he is wearing gives him away as a foreigner. His jeans are slim fitting and taper to the ankle. Current Kalsson fashion dictates tight fitting flared jeans, white runners, and grey hooded sweatshirts with kangaroo pockets. Mark's shoes are black leather brogues and his Ben Sherman shirt is a short-sleeved blue plaid in a trim design with a neat button down collar.

"It was a shock but people in this town are welcoming. It didn't take long to adjust. Well, except when it comes to style and fashion." He indicates his apparel with a sweeping hand gesture. "I'm about five years ahead of Kalsson when it comes to fashion, it seems." His smile, never out of view for long, is lurking at the edges of his lips.

"Do you think I could you use your phone? I'll need to get the tow truck on its way over before it starts to get dark."

"Certainly. I'll make us a cup of tea while we wait for the truck to arrive." He leads the way down the tree lined sidewalk, then crosses the street to a lovely, craftsman style 1930's bungalow.

"Don't bother to take off your shoes," he says as I bend to remove my white runners.

"Oh, okay." I follow him into the house and he directs me to his office where the phone and directory are.

Mark's office is neat and tidy. It is filled with antique clocks and pocket watches. Many of them are displayed in beautifully crafted wood and beveled glass cabinets. I am curious and snoop around as I hold for the towing company to pick up the line. There is a large drafting style table at the end of the room and I peek at the project lying on its smooth surface. There is a partially completed drawing of a building with notes and measurements in the margins.

A voice comes on at the other end of the line: "Thanks for waiting. How may I help you?" I give my details and inquire about the wait time, then place the receiver back on the cradle.

I follow the sound of clinking china that leads me to the kitchen where I find Mark preparing tea. Placing the necessary items on a tray, he smiles at me as I enter the kitchen and invites me to move to the living room where we can both sit in comfort and watch for the tow truck to arrive.

Placing the tray on the coffee table, Mark sits on the couch and I sit opposite him on an overstuffed armchair.

"This is a nice house you have here, Mark," I say conversationally, my eyes scanning the room and noting the fancy wood mouldings.

"I'm just renting it. I'd like to buy a Victorian house here in town and restore it, but I haven't found the right place yet. Plus, I'm pretty busy at work so finding time to work on a house will be a challenge." He pours the dark liquid into porcelain cups and after adding milk and sugar to both, passes one to me with a sure and steady hand.

He leans back against the couch and sips the hot brew. I follow suit and am surprised by the strong flavour. I had been raised on herbal tea and had never tried black tea before.

"Did I brew it for too long?" Mark asks, noticing my expression. "I always forget how weak you Canadians drink your tea." His eyes are laughing again.

"Uh...No. I like it. It's just that I've never had tea like this before." I take another sip gradually growing accustomed to the taste.

"You can't go wrong with good old PG Tips. I bring boxes of it back with me every time I go home to England to visit. What tea do you usually drink?" he asks as he takes a cookie from the plate and dunks it into his tea before plopping the whole thing in his mouth. I can't hold back my smile, but at least I don't laugh out loud. I have never seen anyone eat a cookie like that before.

"Herbal tea...peppermint, chamomile, raspberry, lemon. You name it, I've had it. My parents raised me and my two siblings to be very health conscious. We're all vegetarians and we grow our own vegetables. We rarely have sweets and we never have caffeine or alcohol in the house."

"That's interesting. I became a vegetarian myself a few years ago. Here, have a biscuit. It's a British thing you know. Tea and biscuits makes everything better."

I take a cookie from the plate. It is thin and plain looking. The word DIGESTIVE is impressed in big letters across it. Interesting. Cautiously I dip the cookie into the tea, carefully balancing the cup on the saucer. As I lift the cookie from the piping hot tea, the bottom, soggy part drops back into the cup and sloshes tea over the edge and onto the saucer. I'm left holding but a fraction of bone-dry cookie in my fingertips.

Mark starts laughing and sets down his tea. "Oh, dear. That's bound to happen to a beginner. Don't worry about it. Try another biscuit." He passes the plate to me and I select another one. A gooey pale brown mass is now floating in my teacup.

"What do I do with the old biscuit?" I ask, showing Mark my tea.

"It will sink to the bottom soon." Once the mass disappeared, I dunk again, but this time I'm very quick and get the entire biscuit into my mouth before it falls apart. Hmm. Mushy texture.

"See, you're a natural! You must have some British blood in you somewhere." Mark is grinning from ear to ear.

"Actually, I do, but it's back a few generations," I join in his mirth once I've swallowed the soft, sweet mess.

"That dunking gene is hard to get rid of," he says in mock seriousness.

Outside, the tow truck pulls up next to my car.

"Wow, that was quick!" I exclaim as I put down my cup and saucer. "Thanks for the tea and cookie...I mean biscuits." I grab my purse and move towards the door. "It was really nice to meet you, Mark." I feel reluctant to part company; he seems like such an interesting person. So different from the local boys at college. Maybe it is because he's older and has a job and has come from Britain.

Mark seems to regret my departure as well. "Why don't you drop by one day and we'll have herbal tea?" He suggests. I leap at the invitation.

"I can come after school any day except Wednesday," I say in a rush.

"School? You're still in school?" He sounds surprised.

"Yeah, I'm taking the arts program at Mountainview College. I'm in my second year of a four year program," I explain, hoping I don't seem impossibly immature to him.

"Ahh, a budding artist. You'd better run along before that tow truck leaves." We wave goodbye as I run down the stairs and across the street to the waiting truck.

It isn't until I finally get home that night, after dropping the car off at the mechanic's and then hitching a ride with the tow truck driver back to my parents' house outside the city limits, that I realize that Mark and I have not set a firm plan for herbal tea. I don't know his last name either. I decide that once my car is fixed, I'll just drop by and hope that he's at home.

"You decided to come home," my mother says in a gently chiding tone, an eyebrow arches as she takes a sandwich from the fridge and removes the plastic wrap. We're in the rustic kitchen, a favourite place for the family to hang out. Taking the offered sandwich I plop my butt up on the countertop and swing my legs to and fro while I gobble up the cheese and tomato sandwich.

I explain how my car broke down and how I had to wait for the tow truck.

"I met this really nice guy, Mom. He's from Manchester and he has really cool stuff in his house... old clocks and watches. Stuff that Dad likes." I rush on, telling my mother, Grace Wainwright, every detail I can remember.

"Are you sure it's safe to go into a man's house when you've never seen him before?" She suggests by her question that it might *not* be a good idea. That is how my parents parent: they lead you in a certain direction, but let you reach the conclusion yourself.

"Ahh, come on Mom. He's a totally cool guy." I hop down from the countertop and look in the fridge for something else to eat.

"Are you still hungry?" Grace asks. "There's some yogurt I made this morning and some apples from the neighbour's orchard."

"Okay that sounds good." One of the perks of still living at home: free meals.

"I'm going to the studio, Mom," I say taking my bowl of yogurt and fruit with me.

As a surprise, my dad had set up one of the outbuildings as a studio for me after I had won an art scholarship in high school. He had added plumbing and a futon bed, so I was able to have my own private space. Last year he added heating so that during the long winter months I could paint comfortably.

I was beginning to feel the need to spread my wings and fly solo, but the time had not come yet and my future was still uncertain. How would I support myself as a struggling artist? Although I love painting, I often wonder if I can make a future for myself without getting a *real* job.

As I sit munching my snack, I think about Mark and what it might be like to fall in love with someone like him. Worldly. Smart. Handsome. And a vegetarian, too. I smile as I lick the bowl clean. *There is no harm in daydreaming is there*? I think to myself.

The next day my car is repaired; Mark's diagnostics were correct. So with a new distributor cap installed, I drive past Mark's house after school, hoping to see lights on inside. I drive slowly down the street and kill the engine as I stop out front.

Oh, shit! I think to myself. Mark is coming out of the front door and is bound to see me. Now I feel foolish for coming by unannounced.

"What the hell, in for a penny, in for a pound," I say to thin air.

"Hi, Mark." I jump from the car and wave gaily at him. His face lights up with a genuine smile.

"Hello, Alexi. I didn't expect to see you today; what a pleasant surprise." He doesn't seem concerned that I've suddenly turned up on his doorstep.

"I just came by to tell you that it *was* the distributor cap that needed replacing." I feel breathless as I stand on the sidewalk looking up at Mark who is coming down the stairs to stand next to me.

"Do you have time to go for a walk with me?" he inquires. "I have to drop these drawings off at work, then we could stop in town for tea." I laugh, recalling my last tea episode with Mark.

"Sure, that sounds great. Where is your office?"

"It's on the corner of Pine and Smythe. Are you okay to walk that far?" he asks as we stroll towards the city centre half a kilometre away.

"Hey, I'm nineteen not ninety!" I state emphatically. "Are you an architect?" I ask, changing the subject.

"No. I'm a draftsman. I work closely with an architect, however, taking his ideas and wishes and creating detailed drawings and plans of the structure that are then passed on to the engineer for final approval."

"That sounds very interesting, but difficult." Mark chuckles at my comment.

"It does take a few years at school and even then the job can be challenging. I really enjoy it, though. I get to travel a bit which gives me a chance to see more of the province." We walk and talk, learning more about each other with every passing footfall.

Our impromptu date for herbal tea in late September 1979 is the beginning of a very beautiful relationship. We meet every day from then on and go walking or stay at his bungalow playing board games and talking well into the night.

By late October, we have advanced to holding hands and cuddling on the couch. I introduce him to my parents at the bookstore one quiet Sunday and they welcome him immediately, seeming to like him as much as I do.

It isn't until the middle of November that Mark mentions that he will be flying home to England for a three week holiday over the Christmas break. Without warning my eyes fill with tears that slowly slip down my cheeks.

"Hey, I'll be back," Mark says softly, as he holds me in a warm hug. "It's just three weeks. You won't even have time to miss me."

"Yes, I will. Three weeks is *forever*," I cry, my tears falling even faster now.

"Don't cry, Alexi." Gently he tilts my chin up and kisses me lingeringly on the lips.

It's my first kiss; our first kiss.

It is pure magic.

I lean against his frame and nuzzle my face against his open collar. I can smell the clean, fresh lemon scent that is Mark. Lifting my head I raise my lips to his for another touch of magic. As our lips meet, the world around us slips quietly away.

Sometime much later, reality begins to seep in around the edges of our embrace and we gently pull apart from one another.

"You're right," Mark whispers in my ear, "three weeks is forever."

It is several days later when Mark tells me that he has cancelled his trip home and will be spending Christmas in the Kootenays. I am overjoyed by the news. I fear I could never have survived twenty one days without him.

I am in such a festive mood that I decorate my studio with a tiny Christmas tree, red and white lights, and glittery decorations. I keep the heater on day and night so that I can enjoy my own space in comfort even as the snow outside begins to pile up.

Mark and I spend many hours together in my studio listening to music, mostly British pop bands that he likes, such as The Jam and The Clash. I am far more familiar with classical music having been raised in a household that favours such composers as Chopin, Bach, Schubert, and Liszt. We eagerly learn from each other as we explore these musical genres.

On Christmas Eve my parents, siblings, and Mark gather at my family home to decorate the tree while snacking on all our family favourites. We turn up the volume on the stereo and sing along with the Christmas carols. My older brother, Michael, has come home from university where he is finishing his PhD in biochemistry. He has the brains in the family. Jillie, my younger sister, still lives at home and is in her final year at high school. She is the beauty in the family with her bright blue eyes and curling blonde hair.

Mark is warmly accepted by both Jillie and Michael and he does not seem to be homesick at all, this being his first Christmas away from home. Mom made mulled apple cider and I sip a hot mugful as I sit on the couch watching the evening unfold.

"Are you having fun, Alexandra?" Mark asks. I nod. Closing my eyes, I lean against Mark as he sits beside me on the couch.

How different my life would be right now if my distributor cap had not been cracked. Dreamily, I open my eyes and gaze at Mark. He is so dear to me. Deep within my heart and entwined with my soul, I feel him becoming a part of me.

I know it for the first time and I know it to be absolutely true: *I love him.* I have no reservations; I have only an all encompassing belief that we belong together. Forever.

Smiling, I hold tight to this new revelation. It will be my secret for a little while longer.

Mark smiles at me and tightens his arm around me as it drapes over my shoulders.

"I'm so happy right now," I whisper. "Thank you for being here, Mark." I feel this moment, drenched in perfection, will be with me for a lifetime.

"I'm happy, too." He smiles reassuringly at me and then lifts his mug for a sip of cider.

Due to the winter road conditions, Grace invites Mark to spend the night and she quickly makes up the hide-a-bed in the living room once everyone else has retired for the night.

"Thank you, Grace," he says as he turns back the covers. Mark and I say good night, exchanging a soft kiss and reluctantly I retreat to my bedroom.

The clock ticks loudly on my bedside table. I am unable to sleep due to excitement about my recently acknowledged love. I leave the warmth of my bed and grab a thick terry cloth robe.

I creep quietly to the living room and in the glow of the fireplace I can see Mark lying awake in bed, his head propped up on a pillow.

"Hey," I whisper in greeting as I edge closer to the bed. "Mark, it's me." He turns and raises himself up on one elbow.

"What are you doing down here? I thought you went to bed?" His handsome features are softly lit by the Christmas tree lights.

"Come with me," I say quietly, reaching to take him by the hand. "Come on, let's go." He tosses on his shirt and pants over his boxers, trying not to make a noise.

We slip out the back door and run swiftly through the icy air towards my studio. The moon shines pale on the snow-covered ground. We slip off our boots before jumping onto my futon bed, snuggling together for warmth. I pull a thick down comforter over us.

"Should we be doing this?" Mark asks as I wrap my arms around his neck and press my body urgently against his.

"Yes," I respond simply. I pull back from Mark so I am face to face with him.

"I think it's time that I tell you how much I care about you, Mark. I can't remember my life before you and I can't imagine my life without you." I trace my fingertips over his firm lips. "I love you." The precious words hang expectantly in the air.

I see a single tear slide down his cheek and I wipe it away with the tip of my finger.

"I love you, too, Alexandra." His eyes, even in the dim light of the studio, are bright with emotion. Simultaneously we move together, our lips touching, our passions igniting as fire spreads through our bodies.

On this night, body meets body, soul meets soul, and our spirits entwine as we discover the physical plane of our love.

Not long before the first light of dawn appears, Mark pulls me firmly into his arms, then proceeds to kiss me thoroughly.

"Merry Christmas, Alexi." Tenderly he cups my face in his hands.

My smile is filled with love, "Merry Christmas to you, Mark." We kiss again, our lips bruised and tender from our lovemaking.

"I must go back to the house before somebody gets up." Mark prepares to slip from the bed.

"No, don't go yet," I whisper holding him against my naked body. He delays his inevitable departure for a few more minutes as our lips meet again and again.

"I must go, darling. I'll see you later." He leaves the studio quickly and I, filled with unimaginable love, laugh joyously. It is indeed a Merry Christmas.

I persevere with school until the end of my second year of college, but find, since Mark's marriage proposal on Valentine's Day, that my interests have been diverted. All I can think about is getting married, buying a house and settling down with Mark. I decide not to enroll for the third year of the four year art degree.

Like many young couples contemplating marriage, we had a few obstacles to overcome. Where and when would we get married? What would I do for work? Could we afford the house we dreamed of on just Mark's salary? All valid questions with no obvious answers.

I have been staying at Mark's house most of the time, hating to be apart from him more than absolutely necessary. My parents are excited about our engagement and seem pleased to welcome Mark permanently into the family.

After several weeks of discussion, Mark and I decide to wait until fall, then elope to San Francisco to be married. Neither of us desires a big church wedding and we want to use as much of Mark's savings as we can for buying a house.

Meanwhile, I start searching for employment opportunities in Kalsson. Several job postings come up each week at the employment agency, but the jobs do not appeal to me, being either in the service industry or in retail.

One day in early September, my employment counselor calls me to her office to discuss an opportunity in the medical profession. This catches my interest but I fear my lack of experience will be a hindrance.

My counselor explains that due to a current lack of MOA's, Medical Office Assistants, the local medical clinic would be willing to train the right candidate. It would involve working part-time in the clinic and part-time studies at college. Once the courses are completed the candidate will receive a diploma and become a full-time member of the staff at the clinic.

"That sounds perfect for me," I say with enthusiasm. "How do I apply?" I am eager to begin the process. She explains that she will forward my application, resume, and reference letters to the clinic manager.

"If they are interested, they will call you in for an interview," the counselor explains. "The closing date is in two weeks."

I wait patiently for a week, then gradually begin to lose hope. I have not told Mark, planning to surprise him if I get the job.

Finally, two days before the closing date, I get a call from the clinic manager inviting me to come interview for the job. I dress carefully and tie my hair back in a smooth ponytail. Crossing my fingers, I head for the clinic.

The interview goes extremely well and at the end, the manager offers me the job.

"Welcome aboard," she says, shaking my hand. "We'll see you on Monday at 9:00 o'clock sharp. Wear a white uniform, white shoes, and please wear your hair braided or up in a bun. We want you to look professional even while you're in training."

Nineteen eighty is an exciting year for us. I start my new job, we marry in San Francisco as planned, Mark carries on happily at work, and for my birthday in December, Mark gives me an orange tabby kitten whom I name Tetley.

The following year, I complete my courses and receive my MOA diploma; I start full time at the clinic as expected. I love my job, finding the fast-paced, responsibility-laden position rewarding. The clinic provides office space and facilities for ten doctors, including three specialists. As my knowledge in the field increases, my job becomes easier and less stressful. I can see potential for growth and set my sights on office manager after my second year at the clinic.

We continue living in Mark's rented bungalow while we wait patiently for the perfect heritage house to come on the market. It is not until the spring of 1983 that our search ends and we finally fall in love.

Perched near the edge of the lake at the quiet end of town sits the Victorian beauty that has eluded us for so long. Run down at the heels, she will need much work to restore her to her previous grandeur, but we are ready.

We had been buying books, tools and fixtures for the past two years in preparation for this moment. Now we can finally get started. Our offer is accepted, the house passes inspection, and the down payment is transferred to the bank. At long last we have a house of our own and a shiny new mortgage.

So begins ten years of hard, determined work as we push on month after month wiring, plumbing, replacing windows, re-roofing: the list of things to do is daunting but Mark and I love it. We work well together on the project and rarely have cross words or differences of opinion. Eventually, we are able to ease back a bit and enjoy the house more while working on smaller, interior projects like painting every room and restoring the three fireplaces.

Mark's parents have come to visit us several times during the past decade but it isn't until four months before my thirtieth birthday that we finally make it across the pond to England. We fly together to Manchester where we visit Mark's family for a week. Then, as an early birthday gift, Mark puts me on a bus and sends me to the

Lake District to enjoy two weeks of painting with a small group tutored by a professional painter. At the end of the two idyllic weeks, I return by bus to Mark and his family in Manchester and we fly home from there. This is the first true holiday we have taken since our honeymoon.

Before getting married we had discussed having a family. It seemed both of us were happy to remain childless until such time that we changed our minds. As the years pass, I wait for my biological clock to tick loud enough for me to hear it. No such ticking can be heard, even as I approach – then edge by – the prime reproduction years.

My siblings both have kids but Mark and I seem to be happy status quo. We discuss adoption as a possible option as I near an age that could cause a difficult pregnancy and increased risk to the fetus but as I enter my late thirties, it becomes apparent that we prefer to remain a twosome.

It is during the late nineties that Mark begins a project at work that involves building an ecologically friendly house on a farm. He becomes fascinated with the idea of building *green* as it is coined and begins to voice a desire to build an environmentally responsible house for us.

This matter becomes the first divergence of our paths since we got married. Our heritage house, only just fully restored, fills me with joy and I cannot bear to discuss selling it after all we have invested in it. I don't want to start all over again. Mark on the another hand is excited by the idea of a new project.

We are at odds over this unshared vision of our future for many years and Mark always acquiesces to allow my desires to take precedence. Nonetheless, he plans, studies and dreams of an off the grid straw bale house located outside of town on a few hectares where we could grow our own vegetables and fruits.

Despite the fact that I always manage to talk Mark out of the project, I feel a constant niggling concern that I am blocking his ability to capture his dream. I war with myself, wanting both what I want – to stay in our beautiful Victorian jewel – and wanting to facilitate Mark achieving what he so desires.

It creates a noticeable tension within our relationship; we seem incapable of resolving the tension without one or the other of us forfeiting something extremely important to each of us individually. It is a conundrum that defies a solution.

Where some marriages might dissolve slowly over time from such a divergence of desires, ours becomes stronger. We struggle with the problem by being honest, being respectful of each other's desires, and by remaining open to finding a solution that might in itself be a compromise.

It remains clear to us, even at the most difficult times, that being together is the most important part of the equation. How and where we live will always be less important than simply choosing to be with each other. After all, this commitment to each other was the foundation of our wedding vows:

> *From this day on, as we declare our love for each other,*
> *we will always and forever choose to be together.*

Year after year our vows stand firm.

When Gabe enters my life, there is again a disconnect in our marriage, except for this time, Mark is unaware of the reason and the root cause is of an extremely devastating nature. I decide to keep my relationship with Gabe a secret; it is the only secret I have from Mark. This reluctance to share fully casts a shadow and a burden on our marriage.

It is during the year following Gabe's departure that the foundation of our marriage is truly shaken. I am completely at fault for the stress we sustain during this tumultuous year. Mark, left in the dark, can only struggle to grasp the fraying edges of our relationship and try to hold them together.

Riddled with guilt, confusion and an enormous sense of loss, I strain to find a way, any way, to make sense of my riotous emotions. Then, one year to the day after Gabe leaves town, I make a difficult but necessary decision.

After work, on a Wednesday afternoon in early June 2002, I walk to the apex of the bridge spanning the lake and peer over the railing; my heart is heavy but resolved. The inky black water of the lake sixty feet below moves sensuously with a deep, slow current. The moment has arrived. There is no reason to delay.

CHAPTER 4

...make a new path and step on it with both feet...

The shrill ring of the phone jerks me rudely from sleep. Trying not to disturb the easily-disturbed cat, I reach for the cordless phone at my bedside.

"Hello?" I answer sleepily.

"Hi, sis." I recognize Michael's voice despite a poor quality line from Germany.

"Hello, Michael. How are you and Elizabeth and the boys?" I haven't spoken to Michael for a few weeks and I realize how much I have missed talking with him; how much I miss having him around.

Michael had been offered a fantastic research opportunity at the University of Munich, so he and Elizabeth had moved to Germany when the boys were in their early and mid teens. Now they are young men with active lives of their own.

"We're doing fine. Busy. Always busy. Henry is still working like crazy on his thesis and hopes to submit it in the spring. And Nick is more interested in girls than focusing on his studies. Still, his grades are pretty good and once he finishes his science degree, things will get more challenging as he starts specializing in his field."

Michael had passed all his smart genes on to his two boys who happily follow in his Biochemistry PhD footsteps. My sister-in-law, a fashion editor for a trendy German magazine, has her hands full living with these three self-proclaimed science nerds.

"I'm glad to hear you're all doing well."

We continue to chat for another half hour, talking about my painting, my health, our parents' health, weather; all the usual stuff. When we hang up, I snuggle under the warm covers and pull Charlie (who protests just for show) into my arms for a cuddle.

I wonder idly if I'll see the eagle today. With any luck the weather will be bright and I can take a walk up to check the post. Maybe Gabe will have responded to my letter. I can't imagine the postal service of both countries being that efficient, but still I can hope.

With Gabe increasingly on my mind, I readily recall those extraordinary days of late May and June when Gabe and I drifted gradually together.

★ ★ ★

The day after Gabe and I had ventured to Creston and back dawns with light rain and a brisk wind. I bundle myself up in a jacket heavier than usual for late May and walk to work, hoping that the puddles don't leave dirty splash marks on my shoes and skirt. Today promises to be a long one; first I'll do my regular 9-5 shift, then I'll go to the bookstore to do the payroll for my father's company. I'll be lucky to be home by nine tonight.

My day at the clinic goes smoothly with just a few hiccups typical of a Monday: I run out of toner for the printer; I have a doctor leave early after learning of a family emergency creating a domino effect on patient appointments; I have to call in a plumber to fix a leaking toilet. At five o'clock, I collect my jacket and head for the bookstore, a fifteen minute walk across town.

"Hi, Dad," I call as the bell chimes above the front door and I enter the store.

"Hi, yourself," he returns with a smile. My father is a tall, slimly built man and at seventy years of age, he doesn't appear to be slowing down or ready for retirement. Always a dapper dresser, he is sporting a royal blue jacket over a white shirt with a bow tie. His dark hair is liberally dusted with grey, but he remains handsome despite the wrinkles fanning out from his startlingly blue eyes. The deep grooves bracketing his mouth speak of a man who likes to laugh and does so often. His smile is warm and welcoming as ever and I scurry behind the counter for a hug.

"I missed you yesterday," he says, turning his attention to sorting through a pile of used books.

"Yeah, I went over to Creston and didn't get back until quite late." I hang my coat on the back of the chair and settle in front of the computer, preparing to do the payroll.

"Oh, I though Mark was out of town until early June on that project in Alberta." Dad sounds confused.

"He is. Actually, I went with a relative of Heidi's. Do you remember Heidi Hefler from the yoga studio?" I ask.

"Sure. She's been in the store a number of times," he recalls.

"Well, her second cousin is in town for a few weeks visiting from Australia and I offered to be a tour guide for the day."

I pull out the payroll book and begin to enter details into the software program. What with the antiques, the bookstore, and the café, the business employs five full-time and three part-time staff, plus my father and myself.

"That sounds like fun. Did she enjoy herself?" My father asks as he sorts books into piles for cataloguing later.

"He. And yes, he did. We went to Crawford Bay for breakfast, then to Bill and Teresa's sanctuary, then into Creston for lunch and topped the day off with a stop at the Wildlife Management area. It was quite a full day." I describe the day trip enthusiastically, recalling it with enjoyment.

"I bet Mark will be sorry to have missed out on that," Dad comments.

"I know. It's too bad he was out of town," I agree.

By nine fifteen I finally arrive home and am undressing, ready to sink into a hot bath when the phone rings. I dash into the bedroom and grab the phone.

"Hello?" I expect to hear Mark's voice as he often calls in the evening when he's working out of town. I can't stop a small thrill of tension in the pit of my stomach when I hear Gabe's deep voice.

"Hi, Alexandra. How was your day?" A flush spreads over my body and I run my palm across the bare expanse of my abdomen trying to calm the fluttering sensation I feel there.

"Umm...it was okay. I just got home. Actually, I'm just about to get into the tub," I say stepping cautiously into the steamy water.

"Hello? Hello? Are you there, Gabe?" There is such a long pause I begin to think I've lost the call.

"Yeah, I'm here. I'm just trying my best not to imagine you naked, lying in a tub of scented bubble bath," his tone is playful but there is an undercurrent of sensuality that makes me nervous.

"Gabe," I say exasperatedly, "do I have to remind you again that I'm a happily married woman?"

"No. You don't have to remind me." I can hear him sigh at the other end of the line. "Just tell me about your day and I promise to behave myself."

"Okay." I slip beneath the water, careful to keep the phone from getting wet. I begin to detail the events of the day and before long, Gabe is laughing at my obvious embellishments.

As the water cools and the clock's hands edge past ten, I climb out of the tepid water and towel dry, swapping the phone from hand to hand.

"Gabe, I really have to go. It's getting late."

"Can I come by to see you tomorrow after you're home from work? You don't have yoga until Wednesday, right?" He certainly has memorize my schedule, I think to myself.

"Sure. Why don't you come over for dinner around six?" I hear him groan.

"More tofu, ugh!" He is taking the mickey as Mark is fond of saying. "I'll see you at six, then," he agrees and hangs up the call.

The next day I get home from work by five fifteen and immediately make a start in the kitchen. I open a bottle of white wine and have a few sips while preparing our dinner. The peal of the doorbell alerts me to Gabe's arrival and I dry my hands on a towel as I go to greet him at the door.

"Hello, Gabe. Come in and help yourself to some wine. I selected it because of its beautiful label," I say with a wink as I rush to the stove to stir the steaming pot of curry. He laughs and pours himself a glass.

"I'm just finishing up here. Dinner should be ready soon." I carry on chopping and stirring.

"It smells good," Gabe says, sitting at the large, country-style island centered in the U-shaped kitchen.

"This is a quick and easy curry dish I like to make when I don't have much time. You'll love it; there's not a single scrap of tofu in it." I have set the table in the formal dining room thinking that I have not had an opportunity to use it for several weeks.

I serve the meal up from the stove and bring two heaping plates of spinach and garbanzo bean curry over basmati rice to the table.

"Dig in. It's a fairly mild curry; I wasn't sure how hot you'd like it."

"Oh, I like it pretty hot," he says with a wicked glint in his eyes and a cheeky grin that reveals his dimple. I roll my eyes heavenward in response to his smart ass comment.

We talk about my work and I regale him with stories meant to entertain and amuse. The wine flows throughout the meal and by the time we have finished eating, I feel a warm buzz taking over my body.

"Let's have dessert in the living room," I suggest after we have loaded the dishwasher with our plates.

Taking the chilled, spicy chocolate mousse from the fridge, I spoon the smooth, creamy dessert into small crystal bowls and garnish it with dark chocolate curls.

"Wow, those look too beautiful to eat, but I'm going to try it anyway." He spoons up a mouthful. "Mmm. Delicious." The hint of hot chilli and cinnamon come as a delightful surprise to the taste buds. We savour the dessert in silence until the bowls are empty.

"That was a tasty meal, Alexi. Thank you."

"Oh, I love cooking. Mark and I are always experimenting with new recipes on anyone who is willing to be our guinea pig." I wave off his thanks in a casual manner.

Feeling a chill in the air, I turn on the gas fireplace and return to the couch, drawing my feet up under me. I close my eyes and relax into the silence.

"You're not going to fall asleep on me again, are you?" Gabe inquires. I smile but don't open my eyes.

"That's up to you," I answer, knowing it sounds a bit flirty but the wine has made me not care. "You'd better tell me some good stories about being on the road, or about your youth. You decide. Just don't bore me to sleep!" I know that Gabe has started to adjust to my sense of humour and will not be offended by my joking.

"Where shall I begin?" Gabe pauses for dramatic effect, tapping his cheek with his index finger, a look of contemplation on his face. "I could tell you about the time I was chased by a kangaroo through the park. Or about the time my brother locked me in the wine cellar for a day."

And so the evening progresses, one youthful tale of peril and adventure after another. I am far from sleepy and find myself riveted by his storytelling. The man has a gift when it comes to spinning a good yarn and I can't remember the last time I laughed so frequently.

When the antique clock strikes midnight I know I must call the evening to an end, despite the fact that I am enjoying Gabe's company immensely.

"Gabe, I must kick you out. It's getting really late and I have a busy day at work tomorrow." I stand up, teeter a bit, right myself, then carry the crystal bowls to the kitchen.

"That wine went to my head," I say, my words slurring slightly, as I tipsily escort Gabe to the front door.

"Luckily I walked over so I don't need to worry about driving under the influence," Gabe says pulling on a black leather motor-cycle jacket. He prepares to leave, opening the front door half way before turning back swiftly and kissing me unexpectedly on the lips.

"Thank you for a lovely evening, beautiful," he says, then steps briskly over the threshold and closes the door firmly behind him.

"You'd better run, you coward," I exclaim to the closed door, my fingertips touching my bemused lips.

I don't hear from Gabe again for three days. On Friday night after arriving home from yoga class, I finally get a call from him.

"I thought you decided to leave town," I say after his initial salutation.

"Nope. I'm still here." He is smiling; I can tell from the buoyant enthusiasm in his voice. "I'm going to drive to the Okanagan tomorrow for the weekend and I want to invite you to come along. Oh, and by the way, Heidi wants me to tell you all the kittens have homes now except for our runt. She wants to know if you want him or not." There is a long pause in the conversation as my brain muddles through the consequences of both offers.

Before my brain has formed a response, my lips say, "Yes and yes. Yes to the invitation and yes to taking the kitten." I stop abruptly, wondering to what I've just committed myself.

"Well, great and great." Gabe laughs. "I'll tell Heidi. Maybe you can pick him up next weekend so that you two have time to settle in together for a few days before you're back to work."

"That's an ideal plan. That's exactly what I'll do. What time shall I be ready tomorrow morning?" I ask, scarcely believing I've agreed to go away with Gabe for a weekend in Kelowna.

"Five."

"What the hell? A girl needs her beauty sleep, you know!" I like to get up and get going in the morning but this is ridiculous.

"Are you fishing for a compliment?" Gabe asks, chuckling.

"If you'd been paying attention, Gabe, you'd know by now that we vegans never fish. See you at five." This time I hang up the phone first before he has a chance for a smart comeback.

I can hear a doorbell ringing insistently and I pull a pillow over my head trying in vain to block the aggravating noise.

"Go away," I cry, half asleep. Wiping grit from my eyes I glance at the clock and can see from the glow of the dawn sky that it is five minutes past five.

"Oh, shit!" I jerk awake in an instant and, grabbing my black robe, run downstairs tying it as I go. I fling the door open without using the peep hole, knowing it is Gabe waiting impatiently on the other side. My hair hangs in wild, tangled disarray over my shoulders and I try in vain to twist it into submission.

"Well, hell-o," he drawls, letting out a low whistle, "I love the look. It's perfect for a long drive in the convertible." I glance down at myself and notice the front edges of the robe are gapping open. Hastily I tuck myself into the robe more securely.

"Oh, shut up and come in, you great big lout." I open the door wider to admit him and a blast of cool morning air hardens my nipples to granite. Oh, great, I think to myself, that's just what I needed.

"I'm sorry I'm late but I overslept. I'll be at least an hour. I still have to pack an overnight bag and I forgot to have dinner last night so I must eat before we go," I explain crossing my arms protectively in front of me as I notice Gabe's glance drop to the neckline of my robe.

"No probs," he says cheerfully. "I'll get breakfast on the table while you pack and shower. Then we can hit the road after we've eaten."

As I shower, I wonder what he'll make for breakfast. The poor guy has probably never cooked a vegan meal before. Once out of the shower, I dress quickly in casual jeans and cotton shirt, then apply a light coat of makeup. I pack a small travel case and throw in my cosmetic bag before returning downstairs half an hour later. I find Gabe in the kitchen singing a U2 song in a reasonably good baritone.

"Breakfast is served," he announces, interrupting his song when he sees me enter the kitchen. "We have a tofu scramble with vegetables and some cheesy stuff I found in the fridge. And of course, toast. The coffee is ready when you are." Gabe serves up a plate for me with a flourish.

I dig in hungrily and am surprised by the delicate flavour of fresh tomato, basil, and coarsely ground pepper.

"This is really good, Gabe. I didn't know you were handy in the kitchen."

"You will find that I'm handy in other rooms of a house as well," he states with mock boastfulness.

"There's that arrogant attitude again," I say, sighing exaggeratedly as I help myself to more toast. "Seriously, though, when did you learn to cook?"

"My mother taught me when I was just a boy. She always said it would come in handy. I guess she was right after all." He reaches for his coffee and flashes me a dimpled grin.

As we eat, we discuss plans for the weekend. The drive to the Okanagan Valley is about four hours and involves two mountain passes plus kilometres of beautiful scenery. Once in the valley, there are several smaller communities surrounding Kelowna, the largest city in the region.

Kelowna is situated idyllically on the Okanagan Lake which boasts activities such as jet skiing, dinner cruises, wake-boarding, and swimming. Of course only diehard enthusiasts will venture into the lake in May as the water temperature is too cold yet for comfortable water sports.

Gabe is particularly interested in the wide selection of vineyards in the region and wants to visit as many as possible. He has booked us in at the Luxury On the Lake Resort, a lavish hotel on the lake's shore near the heart of the city.

"That's a bit pricey," I say when he tells me where we're booked. "We could stay at..."

"Let's see if we like the place first," he interrupts. "If we don't like it, we can find another hotel, okay?"

"It's a five star resort, Gabe. What's not to like?" I respond as I wash the breakfast dishes and put them away. I hate to leave dirty dishes in the dishwasher over the weekend.

Fifteen minutes later we're packed into the convertible and opt to leave the top up this time, due to the cool, early morning temperature. Gabe turns the radio on to the classical station I had selected in Creston and the strains of a Beethoven symphony fill the car.

"I'm starting to really like this music," Gabe says as we leave Kalsson behind. "It can be melancholy, or joyful, or soothing. You never know, even within one piece, what you're going to get. It's very engrossing." We listen intently to the sweeping strings of the master of symphonies until the piece ends with a thundering crescendo of notes.

"That was wonderful," Gabe says with enthusiasm. We remain quiet for a few minutes as the car eats up the kilometres.

"So what did you do all week, Gabe?" I break the silence as I turn towards him in the bucket seat.

"I went over to Bill and Teresa's, actually. I had intended to help them with barnyard duties, but once I got there, it became clear they preferred to use my business knowledge to help them manage that aspect of the sanctuary instead."

"Oh, that was nice of you to offer your time." I'm surprised. It seems there is more to the man than meets the eye.

"Bill had purchased a computer to help Teresa with the donations and expenses but they had both struggled trying to set up the program. It took some time, but I got them up and running late yesterday afternoon. That's why I called you so late last evening; I had just arrived back in town."

"That sure should take a load off of Teresa's shoulders. She never did like all the bookkeeping required to run the sanctuary. She'd rather be tending to the animals." I reach out and touch Gabe's arm. "That was very thoughtful of you, Gabe."

"When we get back, I'm going to go over to the farm again and this time I'll put some work in on the fences. Bill mentioned he has a few big jobs pending that require some muscle, so I'm also going to help him with that."

"Maybe I could come help, too," I suggest eagerly. "I'm pretty strong." Gabe grins at that but says nothing as his eyes stray to my lean muscular arms.

"Don't you have to work at the clinic on Monday?" He asks.

"Yeah, but I've got lots of sick days banked; I could get my co-worker to cover for me for a day or two." In actual fact, I've never taken a sick day since I started at the clinic. It would be for a very good cause after all.

The kilometres speed by and we chat amiably about Gabe's travel adventures. Having been on the road for almost three years, I remark on the possibility of him heading home to Sydney soon.

"I guess I can't run away forever," he says in a resigned voice. "I'll have to go back eventually. I just need to figure out what I want to do with my life when I return."

"Compared to you, Gabe, my life is really very boring," I comment. "I work, I go to yoga, I paint. Nothing really exciting there, but somehow it just suits me. I've never been drawn to the grand adventure lifestyle; I've never heard the call of the open road. I'm too much of a home body, I guess."

"I never had a place as an adult that felt like a home," Gabe comments. "At uni I lived in a shared dorm and then when Lisa and I got married, we bought a sleek, modern condo that she really liked, but it never felt like home to me. When we divorced, we sold the condo and I bought a stylish townhouse in a nice part of the city but I never fully unpacked and Lisa took all the furniture in the settlement. That's what greets me when I get back: an empty house with unopened boxes and no furniture." He sounds dejected at the very thought of it.

"It doesn't take much to make a place a home, Gabe. A few pictures, a couple of cherished objects, your special books. You could make your place very welcoming in no time with just a bit of effort. Then you'd enjoy being there more." I try, as I'm wont to do, to solve the problem. "Sometimes a quick coat of paint in a colour you like helps to make a place your own."

"You're such a doer, Alexi. I like that about you. You're always doing something, trying to make your world or someone else's world a better place." Gabe's compliment warms my heart.

"I guess I like to solve problems. That's one reason I like working at the clinic; I get to solve a lot of problems. It's rewarding to take something that isn't working and find solutions to make it work."

At Rock Creek, a small community half way to Kelowna, we pull into the gas station to use the washroom and fill the car with fuel. I pick up a bag of trail mix in the convenience store and while Gabe cleans the bugs from the windshield of the Mustang, I take the opportunity to pay for the gas before Gabe returns to the service counter.

"Let's go," I say, buckling up my seatbelt in the car.

"I need to pay for..."

"I paid already," I say cutting Gabe off in mid sentence.

"Oh...great, thank you." He slips into the seat and starts the engine. We talk and joke as the kilometres of forest interrupted by hectares of farmland fly by.

The more I get to know Gabe, the better I like him. Once you get past the crazy beautifulness of his physical self, you begin to see the deeply thoughtful, kind, and intelligent person that lies beneath the surface.

I can certainly understand how his family wants more from him – for him – than a vagabond lifestyle, but I can also see how his travels are leading him to the place he needs to go. We all need to trust, support and be patient while he finds his footing. My father loves to say that Rome was not built in a day, and for Gabe, this is clearly a case in point.

I lean my head back against the headrest and close my eyes feeling drowsy after the early morning departure. I won't fall asleep I tell myself; I'll just rest my eyes.

"We're here, Alexi," Gabe says gently smoothing a strand of hair out of my eyes. "I hate to wake you up, you look so peaceful."

"Geez, I'm really making a habit of falling asleep on you," I smile at him, then cover my mouth as I yawn.

"I don't mind, Alexi, although I hope it's not an indication that I'm a boring conversationalist!" His fingertips have lightly trailed down the length of my hair, stopping at the tips, then reluctantly, let go.

"Shall we go in?" I ask, opening my door. "I bet it's too early to register and get the room key."

Gabe gets out of the car and pulls the luggage from the trunk.

"They told me we can pick up the key as soon as we arrive."

"Great. Let's take a look at this place." I know my pocket book is going to squeal when I pay for my room, but it certainly is a beautiful hotel. Mark and I always pick modest three star hotels when we stay in Kelowna but I guess it won't hurt to splurge this one time.

The *key* which turns out to be a plastic card, opens the door to reveal a spacious, tastefully appointed modern room with a small, separate kitchenette on the right and a living room on the left.

"Where is my room?" I ask, feeling a bit uneasy.

"This is a two-bedroom suite. One bedroom is here," he opens a door that leads to a large bedroom with a sitting alcove and fireplace. "The other room is here." He leads me to the other side of the living room. This bedroom is smaller, but has a better view.

"You pick the one you want," Gabe offers.

"They're both lovely. This one has a great view of the lake but the other one has that gorgeous fireplace. Hmm. Decision, decision. Why don't you take this room with the lake view? You can even see the vineyards from here. See, over there on the far shore?" We stand shoulder to shoulder surveying the distant landscape. He places his arm around my shoulders and pulls me close to his side. He smiles down at me.

"Thanks for coming along. I know we're going to have a great time."

"Kelowna is always fun," I respond. "Mark and I have been here many times over the years and always find interesting things to do." I quietly move out of his embrace then take my bag into the other bedroom.

"I'm going to freshen up, Gabe. I'll just be a few minutes. What do you want to do first?" I splash cold water on my face in the en-suite, then dry myself with a fluffy white towel as I return to the bedroom.

"I've hired a driver from the hotel to chauffeur us to the vineyards for the afternoon, but I think we should have lunch first. Are you getting hungry?" He is leaning against the doorjamb of the room, his ankles crossed nonchalantly.

"I'm starving," I say, realizing it's been hours since breakfast. "I know of a great little café a ten minute drive from here. Shall we go there?" Gabe nods his agreement. I open my cosmetic bag, remove a brush and groom my travel disheveled hair.

"Here, let me, Alexi." He moves swiftly across the room, taking the brush from my fingers and with long, sure, gentle strokes, he begins to brush my hair.

It feels wonderful; too good, in fact. Heat flushes my skin and in the mirror, I can see my cheeks are turning pink.

"Here, Gabe," I say taking the brush back. "I can finish." I twist my hair up on top of my head in a loose knot and secure it with a small clip.

"There. I'm ready for lunch now." I put the brush away quickly.

"Come on, then, beautiful, let's make tracks." He leads the way back to the car and we drive along the lake to the Calico Cat Café, the triple C as the locals call it.

The menu has many options for both veggie and meat lovers so Gabe and I have no difficulties ordering lunch. He selects a BLT and I opt for a grilled root vegetable wrap with toasted walnuts.

"I'd never have thought to use nuts in an entrée. They always seem more like something you'd use in baking," Gabe comments as I munch my way through the wrap.

"Vegans get pretty creative when it comes to adding protein to their meals. Of course, we have to watch our B12 vitamin too, because you only get that vitamin from meat sources and from yeast. These days soy milk is fortified with it so that makes it easily available to anyone who drinks it." I always enjoy sharing information with people who are interested in a vegan lifestyle.

"What other sources of protein do you use besides tofu and nuts?" Gabe inquires before biting even teeth into his sandwich.

"Well, there's beans...black, garbanzo, soy, pinto, kidney, azuki...the list goes on. Then there's grains like quinoa, wheat, and kamut. And there's split peas, falafel, seeds...we really have a wide range of protein to choose from."

"It's hard to believe that I'm forty-one years old and I have never met a vegan before you. You're my first," he says with a grin.

"Depending on who you ask, about two to three percent of the North American population calls themselves vegan," I inform Gabe. "It's not a lot, but that number is growing a little every year."

"Why did you become vegan, Alexi?" Gabe seems earnestly interested in the topic.

"It's better for the animals, it's better for the environment, it's better for me. It's a win win solution for everyone. I have a T-shirt that says *Save Everything, Go Vegan*. That pretty much sums it up."

"Interesting. Very interesting," he muses, leaning back in his chair, a beverage in his hand.

Once we have finished lunch, we return to the resort to meet our driver. Gabe and I settle into the back seat of the Mustang and relax as Thomas, our chauffeur, easily negotiates the early afternoon traffic. Thomas suggests several popular vineyards across the lake on the west bank of Kelowna which recently became a separate district of its own.

The gently sloping hills of the newly named West Kelowna get only morning sun and tend to produce aromatic and balanced Pinot Noir, Pinot Gris, and Gewurztraminer wines, Thomas explains. This area, home to more than a dozen wineries, is referred to as the Golden Mile.

In comparison, the eastern slopes of the valley are sandy-soiled and receive full sun exposure. This Black Sage Bench area produces a grape with a much bolder flavour. Because of the combination of mountains, lakes, fresh air, and intense sunlight, many grape varietals flourish in the Okanagan Valley and the nearby Similkameen Valley.

Thomas, an expert on the local industry, suggests a route that includes five vineyards all within the Golden Mile with another three vineyards on the east side for later in the day. We agree to the plan and he drives us across the floating bridge connecting Kelowna with West Kelowna. We drive up the steep slope of the west bank, then turn off the main highway towards the lake. A long, deep bench provides ideal space for the vineyards.

We stop first at Kinglet's Nest, a relatively new vineyard named after the small songbird prevalent in the area. A newly constructed timber-frame and wrought iron sampling room boasts an unimpeded view over the vast rows of grape vines down to the wide expanse of the shimmering lake below.

"This is fantastic," Gabe enthuses as we seat ourselves on the comfortable bar-style stools that line the countertop of the sampling area. The engaging and informative staff ply us with samples of several reds, two whites, and finish with a sweet, Botrytis affected dessert wine.

An hour later, we walk back to the car arm in arm while engaging in friendly banter over which wine we enjoyed the most. Thomas is surprised and pleased to receive a small box of exquisitely, hand-made ice wine chocolates we purchased for him at the winery's gift shop.

"Thank you both, that was very kind of you," he says as he accepts the gift. He drives us half a kilometre due west to the next winery.

The afternoon melts quickly into evening and I can feel the effects of the wine samplings slowly accumulating. Gabe has been teasing me as I get more and more 'foxed' as he coins it. Being fairly new to the game of wine tasting, I have yet to learn the art of tasting the wine, then spitting it out. Due to my lack of knowledge in this regard, I have become much more inebriated than Gabe and this seems to amuse him to no end.

By six in the evening the tasting sessions are over for the day and Gabe and I are both feeling hot, tired, and hungry. Thomas returns us safely to the hotel and Gabe quietly passes him a healthy tip. We enter the cool oasis of our suite and I flop on the couch in the living room.

"Gosh, that was fun," I say as I flip my sandals off and sprawl comfortably as I release my up-do and allow the heavy tresses to fall to my shoulders.

"Say, don't they have a pool at this resort?" Gabe nods. "Do you feel like going for a dip before dinner?"

"Good plan," Gabe responds readily.

We change into our bathing suits and bundle into thick, cotton robes and flip flops provided by the hotel before taking the elevator down to the mezzanine.

The heated pool and jacuzzi are situated outdoors amongst lavishly planted and gently terraced gardens. Stripping off my robe, a rush of cool evening air hits my heated skin and I dive into the pool in a fluid arc. Gabe, slower to gain entry into the water, stands at the edge of the pool, looking splendid in his blue and white bermuda shorts. His physique has the long, lean lines of an aerobic athlete; a runner or cyclist, not the short, bunched muscles of a weightlifter.

Slicing the edge of my hand along the surface of the water, I send a wide fan of spray in Gabe's direction, drenching his body. He yelps and jumps back, his abdominal muscles contracting with the effort.

"Come on, chicken. The water's warm." I laugh at him as he dips a toe tentatively into the pool.

"It doesn't feel all *that* warm," he says, hesitating a little longer.

I drench him again with another bout of spray.

"Stop that, you crazy woman!" He shouts, cannon-balling off the pool deck, splashing me thoroughly in the process.

"Last one to the end of the pool is a rotten egg," I call as soon as Gabe has surfaced from his ungainly leap into the pool. I strike off in a fast crawl, but find that Gabe easily overtakes me in the race. I arrive several seconds behind him, laughing and spluttering. I hadn't a chance against his strength and speed.

"You're a rotten egg." He laughs and splashes my face with water.

Grabbing his wrist, I try to stop his shenanigans. Now, eye to eye in the deep end, Gabe pulls me against his solid frame while kicking his feet to keep us afloat.

The evening shadows have fallen and the garden lights, liberally placed amongst the plants, twinkle magically with soft, glowing light all around the pool. Everything is quiet and still; the surface of the water is inky and shimmering.

My heart flutters in my chest. I can feel Gabe's smooth skin where my hands rest on his shoulders. Strands of wet hair stream across my eyes, my cheeks, my mouth. I arch my back and dip my head into the water effectively smoothing the wayward wisps back from my face. I can feel Gabe's arms around my waist, holding me firmly. His eyes are black. Intense.

"Gabe, you best let me go," I breathe the words into the dark silence of the tranquil night.

"I can't." He pulls me closer, his lips nuzzling my brow line, moving down, over my cheek to the edge of my lips. He hovers there and I feel his longing without actual contact.

Slowly. Slowly. Slowly, his lips sink onto mine, his tongue gently invites itself into my mouth. He tastes like wine. And Gabe.

I am immobilized by sensation; water licks my skin while a light breeze that feels like a thousand butterfly wings dances over my exposed shoulders. Gabe's tongue, inquisitive, coaxing, laps at the inside of my mouth, drugging me mute. I feel myself collapsing into him; swallowed up by the pure strength and beauty of him. Cut free from everything that I am, I know that I am in danger of drowning.

With heroic effort and steely conviction, I pull myself out of his arms, out of the water, and run, streaming as I go, to the poolside lounge chairs where I wrap the thick robe around my aroused and conflicted body.

Gabe swims to the edge of the pool beside the lounge where I remain standing, shivering. I am completely out of my depth with this man.

"I'm sorry," he says quietly. He stays in the pool and I suspect he'll need to remain in the water for a few more minutes yet.

"Did you hear me? I am such an idiot and I apologize." I nod, acknowledging his words.

"I'm on new ground with you, Alexi. Before, I used to take everything I wanted. I didn't ask, I just took. With you, I only want to take what you are willing to give. I seem to forget myself and become… greedy." I sit on the chair and silence swirls around us. I rest my head in my hands and look for words.

"I want to give everything to you, Gabe, but I can't. I have already given myself, my word, my vow, my promise...to someone else. I can't break that commitment – not for you – not for anyone. Not for any reason. This is who I am; take it or leave it."

Gabe pulls himself out of the water and dries himself quickly before pulling on his robe.

"I know that's who you are and I'm sorry that I crossed the line." He sits beside me on the lounge chair and gently bumps my shoulder with his.

"Friends?" His voice is a mere whisper.

"Yeah, friends." I nod. A long sigh slips from my lips. I feel as if I've just barely escaped unscathed.

"You know, Alexi, I was not a very nice person for a lot of years. Following my divorce from Lisa, I began to associate with a bad crowd of guys from the movie industry. It didn't take me long to lose my way in the deluge of alcohol, drugs, and groupies that was the norm for my new *friends*. I cringe to think of how devastated my parents must have been to see me so completely out of control in my own life." Gabe's words are coming, half strangled with emotion, from deep within himself. It sounds like a confession; he feels a need to be absolved of his past sins.

"I am not the person to ask for forgiveness. You need to forgive yourself for screwing up; for hurting your family; for being less than you are capable of being. All those old thoughts and actions are not *you*. It's ancient history. Forgive yourself and move on. Make a new path and step on it with both feet firmly planted. It will take courage; fighting demons always does, but it will be worth it. You're worth it, Gabe."

He leans against me, absorbing my words. Minutes tick by, the temperature dips, and my fingers grow icy cold.

"Come, Gabe, we need to go back to the room before I freeze." Taking his hand, I pull him off the lounge and we return to the suite together, then separate quietly as we go to our bedrooms to get dressed.

"I'm starving; we'd better think about getting some dinner inside us." As usual, I'm hungry again.

"Shall we order room service or do you want to go out?" Gabe asks as he browses through the hotel's menu options.

"Let's go out. We can walk down to the centre of town, it's only about four blocks, and eat at a family owned Mexican restaurant that I've heard is good. Do you *like* Mexican food?" I ask, realizing that I don't know if he enjoys it or not.

"Sure. That sounds fine to me," he responds quickly.

"I'm going to grab a jacket," I state as I walk barefoot to the bedroom. "The evening is cooling off now that the sun has gone down behind the mountains. Did you bring a jacket, Gabe?" I had not noticed him wearing one.

"Yes, mother hen. I have a jacket." He's laughing at me, *again*. Gabe is back from that dark place that he sometimes goes to.

While in the bedroom, I brush my damp hair, then smooth it back into a long, swingy ponytail. I apply a lip shimmer, then pull a deep blue, linen jacket from the closet. It looks good with the jeans and white blouse I have on. I spritz my favourite perfume on my wrist, neck, and hair and enjoy the sweet, cotton-candy-like notes of the fragrance.

"Are you ready, Alexi?" Gabe calls from the living room.

"Yep, let's go." I button the jacket and join Gabe.

"Wow, you smell nice," he says as he hooks a finger through the loop on his leather jacket and swings it casually over his shoulder.

"Thanks," I respond, suddenly wondering if I have applied too much scent.

We walk along the waterfront promenade until we reach the city's core then we turn up a vehicle-restricted alley to the secluded restaurant. The place is full and we, along with a dozen other people, have to wait outside in the cool evening air for a table.

"Lucky we brought our jackets," I comment rubbing my hands up and down my sleeved arms to warm them.

"Here, you can wear this." He drapes the leather and tobacco scented jacket over my shoulders before I can form a protest. Immediately I feel myself warming up as I snuggle into the extra layer of clothing.

"You'll be cold now," I say looking a Gabe's muscular but bare forearms.

"I'm tough. Don't worry about me." He smiles at me and I can tell he'd never admit it even if he was freezing. It's such a guy thing.

"Well, thank you. I feel much warmer now."

Fifteen minutes later we are finally seated at the back of the lively, bustling restaurant and although the service is slow due to the busyness of the place, our waitress is pleasant and helpful. We place our order and sip lime margaritas while listening to the mariachi music blaring from the speakers overhead that lends authentic flair to the experience.

Our appetizers arrive shortly and we both enjoy a bowl of spicy black bean soup. Our entrées are equally as tasty and quite filling. Gabe decided to try a vegetarian dish, just for the fun of it, and found the enchiladas to be very flavourful despite the absence of meat. I have a bean, vegetable, and guacamole burrito that, although messy, is delicious.

We agree to skip dessert and instead return to the room and open the bottle of Fortified Vintage Foch I had purchased at Kinglet's Nest earlier in the day. We had learned during the tour that the Marachel Foch grapes, picked at an extremely ripe stage, are fermented then fortified with neutral spirits to produce a Port-style wine that has aged at least one year in oak barrels. The resulting wine, possessing aromas of coffee, mocha, chocolate, and dark fruit notes is said to pair beautifully with dark chocolate so we had also purchased a box of ninety percent pure chocolates from the gift shop.

After a quick call to housekeeping, the hotel kindly provides us with elegant, crystal glasses. Gabe opens the bottle and pours the so red it's almost black Foch into them. The colour in the glass is rich and beautiful, the aroma enticing. Each taking a glass, we clink the crystal rims and raise the liquid in a silent toast.

"I wish I could talk intelligently about wine," I comment as I sit on the couch with my feet tucked up. Gabe has opened the box of chocolates and he passes them to me before selecting one for himself. I savour its smooth, velvet like texture as it mingles with the lingering flavours of the Foch.

"Wine snobs are boring," Gabe points out. "All you need to know about wine is do you enjoy it or don't you? Only drink what you like. Everyone has a different palate, so one wine doesn't suit all. You need to look at the occasion as well. A light lunch on the patio on a hot summer day might suggest a light, fruity white wine, while a heavy meal in the middle of winter might want a rich red wine. It's all a matter of what you feel like having. Now this one," he says, raising his glass, "this one is lovely. I can see why it won several awards."

"I agree. You don't need to be an expert to enjoy this Foch." Our conversation trails off and comfortable silence fills the room.

"It's your turn," Gabe says after a few minutes.

"My turn for what?" I inquire, selecting another chocolate from the box.

"Your turn to tell stories about your past."

"Well, there's not much to tell. As you know, I was born in Kalsson thirty-eight years ago. My parents were both born and raised in Vancouver on the west coast and after getting married and having Michael, my older brother, they decide they wanted a less urban environment in which to raise their family, so, like many people during the sixties and seventies, they decided to migrate to the country." I pause for a sip of wine, then continue.

"After an extensive road trip through the province, they settled on Kalsson because it pulled at their heart strings like no other place they had visited. They bought a small farm and started growing vegetables and living rather rustically. A year later, I was born and then two years after that, my sister Jillie came along." I pull a soft, knitted afghan from the back of the couch and drape it around my shoulders, then carry on with my tale.

"My dad inherited some money from his uncle soon after Jillie was born and my mother encouraged him to open a bookstore in town. Being an avid book collector, it didn't take much persuading to get him to accept the idea. My mother stayed at home caring for us kids and tending the farm and Dad opened the Book Worm on Grand Street. The store did okay but those first ten years were financially difficult." I glance at Gabe; he seems engaged still so I keep speaking.

"As a child, I was not aware of things such as money. I was only aware of all the fun we had playing with the farm animals and with each other. We had lots of chores to do, like milking the goats, collecting eggs from the chicken coop, hauling water to the house from the well, and helping Mom tend the garden."

"Haul water? Didn't your house have plumbing?" Gabe sounds shocked.

"Nope! No electricity, either. And no phone. We used kerosine lamps for light, wood to heat and cook, and we borrowed a neighbour's phone when we needed it. It was all very rustic and simple."

"And you said there wasn't much to tell," Gabe chides me jokingly.

"Oh shush. Do you you want to hear more or not?"

"Yes, please." He tops up our glasses and settles back, ready to listen to more of my life story.

"Our house was built in the early Thirties. The entire area had been settled by a sect of Russian immigrants called Doukhobors. Because they rejected all secular government, Russian orthodox priests, church rituals and such, there was a mass exodus of Doukhobors from the Russian Empire to south-eastern British Columbia and southern Alberta at the end of the nineteenth century."

"Interesting. I've never heard of Doukhobors," Gabe comments, then encourages me on.

"These pacifists were harshly oppressed in Russia by both the tsarist state and by the church. They suffered persecution from the eighteen hundreds until eighteen ninety-seven when the government agreed to allow the Doukhobor people to leave Russia. Many settled in the Kootenays, particularly around Grand Forks, Castlegar, and the Slocan Valley. After years of farming these areas, some Doukhobors assimilated into the general population while some moved to other areas of Canada."

"It must have been challenging for them to leave their homeland and start new lives here in Canada."

"I'm sure it must have been," I agree with Gabe. Shall I go on?" I ask. He nods.

"An old Doukhobor homestead on an acreage became available for purchase and my parents jumped at the opportunity. The house and outbuildings were constructed from logs cut from the local forest and the pastures were developed by hard work. When the farm came into our hands, it had been abandoned for several years. It was a labour of my family's love to restore it to a functioning, liveable homestead."

"Remarkable," Gabe comments, shaking his head.

"I think what might have drawn my parents so instinctively to this place is because, like the Doukhobors, my parents are vegetarians. They share a respect for the land and for the animals."

"Maybe the feng shui or qi of the land attracted your parents," Gabe suggests.

"It could be. Certainly vital energy has always been abundant on the farm. We all can feel it. It truly was a wonderful place to grow up."

We lapse into silence again. I yawn and glance at my watch. "Oh, good lord, it's almost midnight. Why did you let me prattle on?"

"It's not prattle, Alexi. I love your story. I want to hear more. Are you up for it?"

"Well, okay but only if I can have a top up of the Foch." He obliges me. I pick up the story again, recalling my early years when we had been schooled by a neighbour who had a teaching degree and three children of her own to educate.

"Our study hours had often deteriorated into play-time and chores took priority over our schooling. To suggest that our formal education had been spotty would not be an insult; rather, it would be very accurate indeed. What we learned instead of a normal curriculum was about living with our hands in the soil and our hearts with the land." I stop talking, remembering the feeling of being that young, that free.

"When we finally entered secondary school, the social adjustment was difficult; it wasn't until graduation drew near that I had finally been accepted by a group of peers that excelled in the arts like myself. I had found my niche. My clique."

"Cliques are difficult; everything seems impossible when you're on the outside looking in," Gabe muses.

"That's so true. Things got much easier for me, however, once I was accepted by the other artists. In my final months at school, I won an award for my paintings and my dad set up a studio for me. The Book Worm was doing much better by this time because Dad had expanded the business to include the sale of classical music and antiques." I sip my wine, my mind full of memories.

"With money flowing a little easier, it was possible for my parents to afford extra classes for me with an excellent art teacher. Once the studio was finished, I painted all the time, getting better and better. That's why I decided to carry on and go to art college. Then, shortly into my second year, I met Mark. At the end of my second year, I dropped out of college and got married."

I glance over at Gabe and notice his eyelids have fluttered shut. His long, dark lashes lie against his cheek and the half filled glass dangles dangerously in his loose fingers.

"Hell-o," I call gently. "Hello, Gabe." He jerks awake, almost spilling the last of his Foch.

"You fell asleep on me this time," I chide. "I told you my life story was boring. It put you out like a light."

"I'm so sorry, Alexi. I remember everything you said right up to when you got extra lessons with your art teacher." He looks embarrassed.

"It's okay, Gabe. You didn't miss much of the tale." I stand up, feeling sharp pins and needles in my feet. "Ouch! Even my feet fell asleep," I joke as I hobble towards the bedroom.

"Good night, Gabe. That was a wonderfully self indulgent day. I'll see you in the morning." I enter my room and firmly close the door behind me just as he says, "Sweet dreams, Alexi."

Sunlight hits my eyelids; I groan sleepily and throw an arm over my eyes to block the intruding rays. I can smell the aroma of fresh coffee and I peek over my arm to see Gabe standing in the doorway of the bedroom holding two mugs of coffee.

"I could get used to this kind of service," I say, smiling as I push myself into a sitting position, a pillow supporting my upper back.

"Organic coffee with brown sugar and soy milk. Just the way you like it." Gabe passes me a mug, then perches on the edge of the bed, facing me.

"How do you know how I like my coffee? Lucky guess?"

"Nope. I recalled how you'd ordered at the Wild Onion when we had dinner together."

"Very astute of you, Gabe." I can't help but feel impressed. We sip quietly for a few moments.

"Great coffee," we say in unison, our words bumping into each other. We laugh.

"What shall we do today? More wine? Art galleries? Museums? Lake side walks?" I list a number of potential options.

"Do you want to do more wine tasting?" Gabe inquires.

"I'm easy. I can come here anytime, so you should be the one to decide." Gabe ponders and sips and then ponders some more.

"Let's check out the museum. I noticed they have a Native art exhibit on right now. That should be intriguing. Then, if we have time, we could catch a couple of art galleries. Shall we breakfast first at the hotel?" He asks solicitously.

"Sure, that all sounds just fine. What time is it, anyway?" I ask. Gabe glances at his chunky Swiss Army watch.

"Ten fifteen."

"Oh, I've overslept!" I finish the last mouthful of coffee and set the mug on the nightstand, then flip the covers back, careful to avoid hitting Gabe with the duvet. I notice he is freshly shaved and fully dressed.

"What time did you get up?"

"Six thirty. I went for a run down the lake to an area called Mission Hills."

"Oh, that's a long run."

"Just over an hour. When I got back, I showered and then went out looking for soy milk. Luckily, the corner store down the block had some."

Feeling like a lazybones I head to the bathroom for a quick shower. "I'll be ready in fifteen minutes," I call over my shoulder as I close the door behind me.

"Take your time, beautiful. I'm in no rush," Gabe responds.

The Native art exhibit is fascinating. The museum staff prove to be well informed about the instillation and guide Gabe and I though the extensive collection of mainly Haida, Coast Salish, Nootka, and Tlingit works. Several large totem poles have been temporarily erected especially for the exhibit. Masks, jewelry, baskets, and Bentwood boxes are all displayed to their best advantage in a large circle around the totem poles. Our guide, Linda, briefly explains to us the belief systems of the Aboriginal peoples of the West Coast.

"In the beginning, the first descendents of the Creator, who is from the upper world, had special ability to transform from human to animal form and back again." We move slowly through the exhibit, listening intently as Linda carries on.

"Eventually these original ancestors of the Creator lost the ability to transform and remained in their human form. The coastal Aboriginals of today can trace their lineage back through the centuries following the symbols and crests used by their clan, to find from which animal form they have descended." She pauses to allow us time to look at the intricately painted red and black Bentwood boxes.

Carrying on, Linda explains, "Each animal is believed to have special and unique character traits and powers. The bear, for example, symbolizes strength, family, and courage and is treated like a noble guest, particularly in the Haida culture. The beautiful and rare Kermode Bear, the black bear with a recessive gene that makes it white, is revered by the coastal Natives."

"Oh, yes," I say enthusiastically, "I've seen pictures of those lovely Kermode Bears. They're also called *Spirit Bears,* aren't they?"

"Yes, that's right." Linda answers my question and then continues.

"The eagle has a close relationship with the Creator and can travel from the physical world to the spiritual world. While the raven sends messages down from the Creator, the eagle takes messages and prayers to the Creator. Eagle down is scattered to welcome guests of honor, while mature feathers are worn only by tribe members of importance. The eagle feather transmits to the wearer its strength and grants the ability to speak truthfully from the heart." Linda pauses again, allowing time for us to absorb all that we are learning and to ask a few questions.

Gabe and I are staggered by the wealth of information we receive from the guide. She continues to describe the most notable symbols of Native lore, including the hummingbird, the wolf, the salmon, the thunderbird, the frog, and the sun and moon.

Linda explains how in a culture that has no written language, totem poles, masks, songs, dances, and stories are used extensively to pass important family history from one generation to the next. Legends and notable events are recorded on the totem poles that are often raised during Potlatch celebrations.

The poles, hand carved from Western Red Cedar trees, can be used in several ways. For example, one pole on display is short, stout, and flat-topped. It is an example of a longhouse post and would be used for an interior wall to support the roof, along with three matching posts. House frontal poles are placed against the exterior of the house and typically arch over the doorway. Memorial poles commemorate the dead while mortuary poles contain the remains of the dead in boxes that are incorporated into the pole's design. Potlatch poles demonstrate a clan's wealth and power and are erected during great ceremonies that last several days and include feasting and the extensive giving of gifts.

The museum has a tall, exquisitely carved memorial pole on display and Linda, starting at the bottom symbol, describes each pattern and its relevant significance to the clan member who carved it. This particular pole, carved by a member of the northerly Tlingit clan, depicts the story of a great chief and his transformation from the raven. A frog, symbolizing wealth, touches its tongue to the back of a wolf and in so doing, passes on knowledge and power. The wolf, a great hunter, is an intelligent, family-oriented, loyal figure and is believed to help support those on a healing journey; his representation on this pole suggests a history or lineage of great hunters within the clan.

Several hours later, Gabe and I complete the exhibition and we enthusiastically thank Linda for her detailed and personal tour. In the gift store we take time to look a the jewelry, masks, paintings, and books for sale. Some of the jewelry, made from argillite, a hard slate like rock found only on Haida Gwaii, a grouping of islands off the North Coast, has been hand carved into symbols of Native lore.

"Look, Gabe," I call excitedly. "Here's a silver and argillite pendant. See how it's fashioned to depict man transforming to the eagle?" I hold the large, intricately carved pendent up so that Gabe can see it.

"That is really stunning." Taking it from my fingers he offers it up to my neck, but I laugh and pull away.

"It looks great, but it's way too expensive for my budget." I'd already looked at the price tag and, although I'm sure it's worth every penny, I can't afford it. I put it back in the showcase reluctantly. Gabe purchases a small silver necklace depicting a wolf for Heidi.

"She is, after all, the only family I have in Canada so the wolf seems the appropriate choice," Gabe says as the sales clerk wraps the little gift.

"She'll love it," I respond, having already closely examined the carved teardrop shaped pendant suspended from a fine silver chain.

"Come, let's track down some lunch. I'm hungry again." Gabe casually hooks his arm around mine and leads me back towards the car.

"Why don't we go to that café there, across the street? We can leave the car parked where it is." The café in question, Jezebel's, is a deli style eatery and would likely have food that we both could enjoy.

"Sure, that's a great idea. You go on ahead and order for me and I'll go plug the parking meter."

I reach for my purse. "Do you need some change?" I have my wallet out but he shakes his head.

"I've got a pocket full of the stuff," he says smiling as he jingles the coins in his jeans pocket.

Ten minutes later Gabe joins me. I have ordered a turkey club with a side salad and fries for Gabe and a warm pasta salad with roasted garbanzo beans and balsamic drizzle for myself.

"I thought you'd left town without me," I tease, "you were gone for so long."

"You missed me, did you?" His reluctant dimple appears as he gives me a devilish grin.

"You must walk terribly slowly."

"I was window shopping on the way back from the car. There's no law against..." his retort is cut short as lunch is served to our table.

"Did you enjoy the exhibit?" I ask as we tie into our lunch.

"It was phenomenally educational. I really admire the connection between the clan culture and the environment. The First Nations people show so much respect for their elders, the animals, and the land. It's so far removed from mainstream thinking; at its core, it's about respect...honour...appreciation. Our culture could learn a thing or two from paying attention to their ancestral wisdom."

"I agree. We've all become so disconnected from nature what with cell phones, television, the internet...we're so easily distracted and we do everything at warp speed. I'm not sure our culture can even *feel* anything anymore." We eat in silence, pondering what we've learned and feeling a bit in awe of it all.

"I'm intrigued by the concept of transformation. It's a pleasing idea, thinking of passing through the millennia as one creature or another. Biblical ideas about the afterlife have always left me unconvinced but this idea of...*transforming*, it resonates with me. I like it."

"It does certainly offer an interesting perspective on dying...on leaving our human form behind," Gabe concurs.

When we have finished the meal and the plates have been removed from the table, Gabe consults his watch.

"I think we need to make a move for home. We've got a long drive ahead of us and an early start tomorrow. I'll go settle the bill..."

"No, Gabe," I say quietly. "This was my treat."

"Thanks, Alexi. This café was a good choice."

We return to the hotel and pack our few belongings and drop the card key at the front desk. When I reach for my wallet, Gabe informs me he already paid for the rooms at the time of booking.

"We can settle up later," he suggests casually.

The trip home seems long and I keep drifting close to sleep. Vaguely I am aware that Gabe is playing with the radio controls, then I hear him put in a CD. I recognize Robbie Robertson's delicious voice and smile contentedly. It is one of my favourite albums; self titled, it is his first solo recording. Usually I sing along word for word, but at the moment sleep is beckoning me and I, ever the obedient servant, follow.

"Hey, beautiful, wake up." Gabe gently wrestles me from my nap. I yawn and stretch. We have stopped at the Rock Creek gas station again to fill up. I realize a trip to the loo would be prudent and get out of the car only to feel the nip of the evening mountain air against my skin.

"I had a strange little dream while I was napping," I say to Gabe once we're on the road again. I have lots of dreams, many of which I can easily recall in vivid detail.

"Tell me about it," Gabe encourages me. I gather my memory of the dream and begin.

"I was swimming against the current in a beautiful, shallow stream. Although I was myself, I swam like a salmon, darting upstream low along the rocky creek bed. I could see up though the clear water and spotted a Spirit Bear dipping his massive clawed paw into the water trying to grab me." I pause for a moment recalling the feeling of fear.

"I continued to swim as fast as I could and I got past the bear unharmed. Further along, I could see a raven at the end of an old, fallen log protruding out over the stream. He was watching me and again I feared for my life. He hopped down from the log into the shallow water and grabbed me in his powerful beak. I struggled and struggled but couldn't break free from him. Then, an eagle suddenly swooped down from high above and snatched me from the raven.

My fear vanished. The eagle gently set me on a limb of a tree and flew away, spiraling higher and higher until he disappeared from sight into the bright blue sky. Then I woke up." The images remain intense and real in my mind.

"What do you think it all means?" Gabe asks.

"I'm not sure. Something to do with struggling with obstacles... being saved in a time of fear. Likely it's all that Native lore running wild in my subconscious brain," I laugh, feeling foolish for sharing the dream with Gabe.

The rest of the journey goes by quickly and we arrive back in Kalsson by dinner time. We decide to part company so that we can each get a few things done before leaving for Bill and Teresa's in the morning.

Gabe and I had been slaving away for several hours in the humid drizzle digging post holes in the back field when Teresa arrives with a basket packed with sandwiches, cookies, and cool drinks. The dogs followed her and they now mill about looking for treats and hugs. We chat for a few minutes with Teresa, then she hands Gabe the basket.

"I've got to get back to the house so I'll leave you to it. I'm busy catching up on my bookkeeping. That software you installed makes it so much easier, Gabe." Teresa enthuses. "Come on, pups, let's head home." The dogs follow her, playfully leaping through the long grass. Tiny is tucked safely in Teresa's apron pocket.

"Let's see what we've got," Gabe says as he carries the basket over to the base of a large, fully leafed out chestnut tree and settles on the dry grass that has been sheltered from the damp by the dense foliage.

I remove my work gloves and wipe the perspiration from my forehead with a bandanna. I feel tired, hot and sticky but I don't mind because I know we can do the job much faster than Bill, who, although very fit, is in his late sixties.

The homemade sandwiches are large but we eat several before slowing down and sipping the apple juice Teresa has delivered.

"She makes wonderful cranberry walnut cookies. Here, try one." I pass the Tupperware filled with a dozen or more cookies to Gabe.

"Forget one! I'm going to have a few." Gabe helps himself to three big cookies.

"Are these vegan? They taste just like normal cookies." Gabe munches his way through the first cookie. I laugh.

"They are normal, they just don't have butter or milk in them. See, I'm eating one right now." I make a show of biting into one of the cookies. "Teresa knows I'm vegan and is very good at modifying her recipes when I come over to help," I explain, brushing crumbs off myself.

"May I say how cute you look in your braids and dungarees?" Gabe flashes me his dimpled grin as he passes his comment.

"And you, fine sir, look very strong when you're digging post holes." I bat my eyelashes playfully at him. In truth, he'd looked pretty amazing, his T-shirt sleeves straining to contain his muscular arms. The moment begins to feel awkward and I busy myself putting the remains of the picnic back into the basket.

We finish up the day at dusk, putting the final post in place just as the mosquitos become intolerable. Bill would run the hot wire to the posts later. Tomorrow we planned to help Bill replace some support beams in the barn.

"All hands on deck," Bill had said.

Teresa made up two spare bedrooms in the farmhouse and Gabe and I crash right after dinner, both of us exhausted from the physical labour.

We breakfast with Bill and Teresa at seven the next morning and get an early start on the barn. Gabe and Bill talk technicalities while I visit with the goats, pigs and sheep. Once the details have been established, Bill and Gabe direct me to assist them in hoisting a massive timber into a vertical position using a dead man's winch.

The job is challenging and somewhat nerve-racking as the new post is positioned on the recently poured and cured concrete pad. Once in place, the bigger challenge of maneuvering the support beam to rest on the post begins. Breaking for lunch is voted down and the boys and I continue to use brains and brawn to finish the job.

By late afternoon, famished and knackered, we sit on a bale of hay in the barn surveying the completed job.

"That went so well," Bill says enthusiastically. "Thank you both for helping. It's sure great to have that beam in place and ready for next winter's snow load."

"Don't thank me," Gabe says. I'm more than happy to help you provide a good home for the animals."

"Ditto," I respond. "No need to be thanking us after all the things you and Teresa do yourselves." Standing up, I brush loose stands of hay from my dungarees. "Let's go find some food; I'm hungry and thirsty."

Talking and laughing, we head to the house, wondering what delightful meal Teresa has cooked up. Shortly after dinner, we depart and begin the long trip home.

Back at the house later that evening, I wearily climb into bed after a long hot soak in the tub. The king size bed seems empty without Mark and I pull his pillow into my arms so that I fall asleep with his scent on my mind.

The next day at the clinic is busy. A young female doctor has been hired recently to alleviate the heavy patient load on the existing doctors. I help her move into her new office and set up her computer and networking passwords, then I give her the grand tour of the facility. Doctor Emily Stainsby, eager and energetic, seems like an ideal candidate for the position. She, like her father, wanted nothing more than to be a small town family practitioner and for her, today that dream is realized.

I treat Emily to lunch, then leave her to settle in and peruse her patient files for the next day. Smiling to myself, I return to my office to attend to the accounts payable files. The afternoon flies by and at five o'clock, I've finished the last entry in the accounting program and turn off my computer.

On my way home, I stop at the grocery store for a few items, then walk briskly to the house. I have time for dinner and a quick shower before leaving for the concert. Mark and I had purchased season tickets for the Arts To You series. This collaboration between local business and government was intended to bring the arts to the people of the interior, in their own communities. Mark and I used to laugh and call it *music for hicks from the sticks*. Nonetheless, the concert series had become tremendously popular and sold out every season.

The group slated to perform tonight, the Stanford Quintet, named after the lead violinist and concert master, would play Franz

Schubert's Quintet in C, a dynamic work that is a favourite of mine. Mark had been disappointed to learn that he would miss the performance because of his work commitments. I had offered Mark's ticket to friends and family but with no takers, I now have a spare ticket in my purse.

Despite the fact that I am attending the concert alone, I decide to dress up anyway. Occasions for formal attire are rare in Kalsson, so many concert-goers take the opportunity to don their best threads and put on some bling.

I select a below the knee, black, pencil skirt that hints at the classic 1940's style of Christian Dior and couple it with a three quarter sleeve tunic that nips in at the waist and flares slightly at the hips. Black, faux leather pumps complete the ensemble for a stylish, retro look. I clasp a single strand of pearls, a gift from my mother for my wedding day, around the column of my throat. Twisting my long, wavy hair into submission, I secure it in a chignon with a silver barrette. With little time to waste, I dab my favourite perfume on my neck and wrists before grabbing my black and silver clutch and rush for the door.

The theatre is only minutes from home and since the evening, though leaning heavily towards dusk, is still warm, I decide to hoof it rather than call a taxi. I walk along the street with a long swinging gait as I look forward to the evening ahead. I turn right onto Bartlett Street only to see Gabe striding along the sidewalk in my direction. When he sees me, a smile breaks across his face.

"Hell-o, beauti-ful," he says with enthusiasm as he scans me from head to toe. "You look like you just stepped out of a fashion magazine. What's the occasion?" I can feel heat surge through my face.

"I'm going to a concert over at the Imperial Theatre. Would you like to come? I have Mark's ticket spare since he's still out of town." I can't quite believe I just invited him to come with me.

"Is it that classical stuff we listened to in the car?" He asks, but doesn't seem to care about the answer because he has already turned around and started walking with me towards the theatre. "Won't I be turned away?" He wonders, looking down at his Levi's and white cotton shirt.

"Yes, it is classical. Schubert. And no, you're not going to be turned away, even though you are a smidge under dressed." Suddenly the evening seems much brighter to me and I feel a little jump in my step.

"You sure are tall with those shoes on," he comments, noticing that I can almost look him in the eye now.

"Yep, nearing six feet. That's why I don't wear heels very often." Stopping curb side for a red light, I stick my neatly shod foot out and waggle my ankle from side to side. "They do look rather spectacular with this outfit, if I must say so myself."

"Oh, yeah. You look good, that's for sure." He tosses me a dimpled grin before we step off the curb in unison as the light turns green.

The line up at the theatre is long and we talk amiably while we wait.

"Heidi's teaching tonight," I point out conversationally. "I offered her Mark's ticket a few days ago but she couldn't cancel her class on such short notice."

"I'm glad our paths crossed tonight, Alexi. I'm excited to be going to my first classical concert. It's Schubert, you say?" He lifts an interested eyebrow.

My reply is interrupted as the theatre staff ask for our tickets. Once inside the ornate red velvet and gilt theatre, we find our seats easily.

The program notes outline not only the history of Franz Schubert and the pieces to be performed but also gives a biography of each member of the quintet as well. Gabe reads the information, commenting here and there as he points out items of interest.

The musicians file in one by one and take their seats on the stage and begin to tune their instruments: two cellos, two violins, and two violas. The concert master, Phillip Stanford, gives a brief introduction to the piece, then silently counts the quintet into the first movement.

The musicians give a wildly abandoned rendition of Schubert's work and are received with enthusiastic applause at the end of the last movement.

"Did you enjoy the performance?" I ask as we leave our seats during the intermission in search of a beverage in the elegant lounge of the theatre.

"Marvelous. Just marvelous. I didn't expect to like it as much as I did. Have you heard that piece before?" Gabe inquires as he hands me a glass of sherry.

"We have it on CD, but it's always so much better live." The bell chimes as we finish our drinks indicating that the intermission is over and we return to our seats, ready for the second half of the concert, which includes quartet No. 13, the Rosamunde, and No. 14, Death and the Maiden.

Again, the performance is electric and the audience gives a resounding applause and standing ovation for the musicians as the final notes of the evening fade. We funnel slowly out the front door of the theatre into the cool evening air, the crowd dispersing once it reaches the street.

"Shall we go for a drink?" Gabe asks, taking my arm in his.

"Roasters Coffee Shoppe is open late; we could go there. I have to get up early for work in the morning so it'll have to be decaffeinated."

"Come on, then, before you turn into a pumpkin." As is his habit, Gabe is laughing at me again.

The coffee shop is busy with a post-concert crowd and we stand in line outside to get a table. Once inside, we seat ourselves at a small, round bistro-style table near the window. Gabe places our order for decaf soy lattes at the counter, then rejoins me.

"It certainly is busy in here tonight," Gabe comments as more people squeeze into the café.

"Roasters has been very popular ever since it opened a couple of years ago. It's trendy and offers all kinds of different coffee drinks. It took a bit of a toll on Dad's store, but fortunately, his customers are very loyal so it didn't impact him too severely."

The lattes are served to our table by a teenage barista, and Gabe and I sip the hot beverages in silence.

Emily, the new doctor at the clinic, stops by our table to say hello and introduces us to her husband. We chat for a few minutes, then they move on when a table becomes available.

"You must know everybody in town, what with living here all your life and working at the clinic."

"It's true. I do know a lot of people. That's how small towns are; everybody knows everybody. It can be a blessing and a curse; comforting but stifling, too."

We finish our drinks and Gabe walks me home despite my half-hearted attempts to dissuade him.

"Thank you for a lovely, impromptu evening, Alexi," Gabe says as he delivers me to the front door.

"I'm glad you enjoyed yourself. It would have been a shame for the ticket to go to waste."

"Good night, then," he says softly, leaning in towards me, then hesitates. He let's out a long, slow breath and straightens away from me, then steps off the porch without another word.

"Good night, Gabe," I call, my words bouncing off his retreating back.

The next days at work are long and difficult and by Friday evening, I can feel myself needing some time to relax. I call Heidi to see when I can come pick up the kitten and we decide on late morning. This gives me a chance to catch up on housework and still leaves time to go to the pet store to pick up all the things kitten will need. We still have Tetley's old litter box, food bowls, and scratch post, but I want to get kitten some new toys and, of course, food and litter.

Saturday I struggle home from the shop with cloth carry-bags bulging. It doesn't take me long to set up Tetley's old eating area in the pantry and the litter box goes in the mudroom at the back of the house. With the new toys spread around the living room invitingly, I feel ready to bring kitten home.

I fish the cat carrier out of the crawl space in the mudroom and after dusting it off, line it with a soft towel. I walk briskly to Heidi's house, excited to be picking up my kitten at last.

"Hello, Alexi. How are you?" Heidi smiles warmly as she ushers me into the house. "Poor little mite is beside himself. All his siblings have been picked up by their new owners so he's pretty scared and lonely."

In fact, he is howling his head off and climbing up the side of the box frantically.

"Oh, dear. Looks like I'll have my hands full for a few days while he settles in." I pick him up and cuddle him to my chest, cooing softly. He quietens instantly.

"Gabe said to say 'hello', by the way," Heidi says helping me load the kitten into the carrier. "He's off visiting some artist he met yesterday. He's a West Coast Aboriginal and has a studio where he carves masks and stuff like that. Gabe was really keen to check it out."

"Well, I best be on my way before trouble here starts howling again. Say 'hi' to Gabe when you see him." I take my leave, waving goodbye to Heidi.

I walk home slowly to avoid jarring kitten who has decide, unfathomably, to take a nap. Once at home, I open the carrier and wait for him to come out in his own time. Half an hour later, he creeps out and begins to check every nook and cranny on each floor of the house. Eventually returning to the living room where I have been patiently waiting, he stares at me for a few moments, then, with total confidence, climbs my jean-clad leg and arrives with a triumphant meow on my lap.

"Hello, my little angel," I coo softly and scratch him under the chin with my index finger. His purr is loud and immediate. Circling on my lap like a dog, he finally plonks down with a soft sigh and squeezes shut his still smokey-blue eyes. My heart is full of tender emotion as I stroke kitten's soft, bright burnt-orange coat. He is delightful, even in sleep.

The phone rings and I quickly grab the handset before kitten is disturbed from his nap.

"Hello."

"Hi Alexi." Marks's voice, so familiar to me, sounds dejected from the moment he speaks.

"Hey, my love. How's it going out there? Are you coming home soon?" I know my tone is hopeful.

"I'm stuck here for a few more weeks, Alexi. The project is coming along, but we keep hitting bureaucratic red tape that's slowing us right down. I should be home by June ninth, with any luck." I can feel tears welling in my eyes.

"Are you there, Alexi?"

"Yes, I'm here." There's a catch in my voice and I dab a tear away. "I miss you. I was really hoping you'd be home soon."

"Hey, darling, don't cry. I miss you, too." Mark's voice has gone soft and quiet and I know he wants to be home with me.

"Mark, guess what I got?" I try determinedly to stay positive and decide to spill the beans.

"What did you get?" he asks inquisitively.

"A kitten! He's an orange tabby and he's just an angel. He's on my lap right now. Heidi had a litter of kittens that she rescued and this one is the runt so nobody took him. I had to save him."

"But I thought we weren't going to get another moggy right now?" Mark sounds confused.

"I know, but I get lonely by myself all the time and he really needs a good home and I miss Tetley..." I can feel the tears threatening again.

"It sounds like it was meant to be. Does that kitten have a name yet?" Mark asks, apparently accepting the change in plans in stride.

"Charlie." The name pops into my head from thin air. "Yep, his name is Charlie. You're going to fall in love with him, Mark. He is such a cutie." I tickle Charlie's toes and he spreads his tiny paw wide without opening his eyes, a smile plays on his kitten lips.

"I love him already," Mark answers. "I can't wait to get home and see you both."

We talk for another hour and when we finally hang up, I feel much better. Only a couple more weeks; I can manage, especially with Charlie keeping me company.

Saturday night is busy at the Hollingberry household. Charlie, when not sleeping, has a penchant for getting into and onto everything. He seems capable of scaling sheer walls and leaping great distances. Perhaps the name Spiderman would have suited him better. He turns out to be not just a cute little kitty, but a determined one as well. At the first light of day, I finally get some rest when Charlie decides it's time to sleep.

The doorbell rings at nine-thirty, waking us both. Slipping on my housecoat, I grumpily make my way down the stairs to the front door. Peering through the peep-hole I see Gabe standing on the porch, hands in his pockets, whistling a Midnight Oil tune. He looks rested, refreshed, and relaxed; I feel a stab of envy as I think of my sleepless night.

"Good morning," he says brightly as I open the door. Charlie, pushing past my legs, climbs straight up Gabe's jeans without preamble.

"Ouch, you little bugger," Gabe gasps, pulling, with difficulty, the cat off himself. He cradles Charlie in his arms and steps across the threshold at my invitation. "How are you this morning?"

"I'm exhausted. That little charmer you're holding kept me up all night. I only got a few hours sleep, just before dawn. He may look like pure gold, but he's a rotten tomato!" There is no bite to my words and a smile curves my lips as I move down the hall into the kitchen and put the coffee maker on.

"Would you like a cup?" I offer as I get the soy milk and sugar out.

"Yes, please. It smells wonderful." Gabe has yet to put Charlie down; they seem enthralled with each other.

"I wanted to see how the little fella was settling in. He seems as happy as a clam." Gabe tickles Charlie's belly and gets ten needle sharp claws stuck in his hand for his efforts.

"Ouch! You're dangerous!" Gabe repositions the kitten in the crook of his arm so that he can pick up the mug of freshly percolated coffee I have set on the counter for him.

"Did you name him yet?" Gabe asks as he gently hugs the runt to his side.

"I'm calling him Charlie."

"That suits him completely," Gabe says, smiling. "Hello, Charlie." The kitten gnaws on Gabe's knuckles feistily, his eyes lively with devious kitten energy.

"What are you up to today?" Gabe inquires, disengaging his hand from Charlie so he can pick up his mug again.

"I'm going to sleep all day!" I say, laughing.

"Ahh, come on. It's so beautiful out; let's go for a walk. Heidi told me about a trail to the top of the bluff on the other side of the lake. Maybe we could hike up there today?"

"It is a pleasant outing. It takes well over an hour to get to the top. Once you get there, it is spectacular with wildflowers and lake views in all directions." I can feel myself perking up as the coffee kicks in and thoughts of a day-hike swirl in my brain along with the caffeine.

"You go get dressed and I'll make you some breakfast. Charlie can help me." He puts the kitten on the countertop and begins looking through the cupboards. I don't comment, but cringe at the thought of the cat on the kitchen island. My studies as a MOA have left me well versed in bacteria and harmful pathogens. I shrug. What doesn't kill you makes you stronger as my dad was wont to say.

Gabe serves whole wheat pancakes with almond butter and maple syrup with a fresh fruit side salad.

"Wow. You've outdone yourself, Gabe. I haven't had pancakes this good for ages." My mother, famous for her pancake breakfast extravaganzas, would have had trouble holding her own against Gabe's delightful golden-brown cakes.

"I hope Charlie will be fine on his own while we're out," I say as we share the last remaining pancake.

"He'll be okay for a few hours. Has he figured out the litter box yet?" Gabe wipes a speck of maple syrup from the corner of my lip with his finger. Startled, I pull back from his touch.

"Oh, he's great with that. No accidents so far," I respond with a calm I do not feel. "I guess he can get by without me for a bit." I reach down and stroke Charlie as he pushes his tiny, soft kitten body against my legs. I know I will miss him even though we'll only be separated for a few hours.

Dressed in cotton shorts and a T-shirt, I put on my lightweight hiking boots, adjust the straps on my daypack that is filled with water, snacks, and a first-aid kit, and pull the brim of my baseball cap low over my eyes.

"Let's get going, Mr. Harris. Time is wasting." All signs of tiredness have left my newly energized body. We drive the short distance to the trailhead, park the car, and begin the steep ascent to the top.

Foster's Bluff attracts hikers from all around the area and the trail tends to become congested in July and August. Being late May, foot traffic is quiet and we hike the trail undisturbed. We can hear the guttural vocalization of a solitary raven calling deep in the woods; chickadees, flying close to the trail, make easy conversation with themselves; high in the trees, tiny nuthatches, already paired for the season, busily comb the forest for bugs to eat. I hear the call of a bird I don't recognize and I feel a stab of longing for Mark, who, being a self-taught expert on birds, would have been able to identify the call immediately.

The scent of spring and pine resin is heady after the long grey days of winter and I inhale the stimulating fragrance with reverence. I feel myself enveloped by the arms of Mother Earth. She is rich with wondrous, amazing creatures, and overflowing with delightful plant specimens eagerly reaching upward to the sun. I love this feeling of awareness. Awareness, in every fiber of my body, of the dark, loamy soil beneath my feet, the tall, ancient trees towering above my head, the insects, birds, and animals that silently accept me into their midst. It is a magic elixir that lifts my spirits to a higher plane of consciousness. I feel overwhelmed with emotion and wipe a single tear from my eye.

"You're very quiet," Gabe notices, slowing his pace so that I almost bump into him on the narrow trail. "Are you okay?" I nod and move past him, taking the lead. We toil on along the steep forest trail until sometime later we break free of the tree line and step out onto the rocky bluff that is our destination. The sky is pale blue interrupted only by pure, white whipped cream clouds. The vista up and down the lake and across the water to Kalsson is spectacular.

"That view is worth the hike," Gabe says, sitting on a large boulder. "It's just breath-taking. And look at all these flowers." Using his hand to shade his eyes, he scans the landscape in admiration. The orangey-red Indian Paintbrush nestles against the purple of Lupine and the delicate yellow flowers of Arrowleaf balsamroot. The bluff is awash with vivid colour.

"Oh, look!" Pointing, Gabe indicates a Red-tailed Hawk circling on the thermal breeze created by the heat of the midday sun.

"Lovely," I respond, watching as the hawk's feathers splay upwards at the tips taking full advantage of the zephyr.

We find a level spot beneath a deciduous tree that provides dappled shade and sit down for a rest, a snack, and a drink. I place a large bag of trial mix between us to share, then pass Gabe an apple and a bottle of chilled herbal tea. The small, frozen gel pack I placed between the beverages in my knapsack has worked well and the drinks are still cold.

We munch and drink in silence, watching nature busily carry on around us. A large ant crawls onto my pack and Gabe reaches out to kill it, but I stay his hand and shake my head. He nods and smiles in understanding. The ant carries on his investigations until he finds a speck of apple that has fallen to the ground. Bingo. The happy ant struggles with his prize but manages to drag it across the forest floor to a rock under which he and his prize disappear without a trace.

"He's going to have a great lunch," Gabe says. "Wait till he finds this!" Gabe places his apple core beside the rock where the ant disappeared. I sense that inside Gabe there lurks a man on the verge of blossoming.

Lying back on the hard ground, I cradle my head in my hands with my cap pulled low over my closed eyes. The sun slips behind a cumulus and a breeze picks up. I shiver, waiting for the sun to pop back out from behind the dollop of white clouds. I drift lazily at the doorstep of sleep but am too aware of my surroundings to step over the threshold.

A fly buzzes by, a chipmunk leaps and bounds amongst the drooping boughs of an evergreen overhead, an insect crawls up my arm. I swipe at it with a lazy hand without opening my eyes. I feel the bug on my arm again and this time I turn my head to view the culprit.

The culprit is Gabe, grinning from ear to ear as he trails a piece of dried grass over my skin.

"I'm not going to let you fall asleep on me again," he says leaning back on his bent arm and continues to torment me with the blade of grass.

"I didn't," I say indignantly. "I was fully awake."

"You may still have been awake, but not for long. I know your propensity for falling asleep at the drop of a hat."

I glance at my wristwatch and am surprised by how late it has gotten.

"We'd better head back, I don't want to leave Charlie on his own for too long." I get to my feet and repack the snack items into the daypack. I reach out my hand and help Gabe to his feet as he groans in protest.

"Do we have to leave already?" He complains as he dusts twigs and leaves off his jeans.

"Yes, we do grumpy pants. It'll take us over an hour to hike down to the car." We check the apple core before we leave and see that Mr. Ant has invited his thirty best friends to the feast. We chuckle at that and begin our descent from the bluff.

Halfway down the trail, the footing becomes loose and shaley. I steady my pace and move slowly over the unstable soil with Gabe following a few feet behind. We have almost reached the end of the tricky section when my toe catches on a tree root bulging up through the dirt. My right ankle buckles and snaps as I fall to my side, skinning my knees and outstretched palms.

Shaken, I lie still, as pain shoots through every part of my prone body. Loose pebbles pummel me as Gabe scrambles to my side.

"Don't move, Alexi," he commands sharply. I feel his hands gently probing my body for broken bones.

"I'm okay," I say, spitting dirt out of my mouth as I slowly bring myself to a sitting position. Everything is bleeding: my lip, my hands, my knees. My ankle throbs and gingerly, careful not to scrape my open wounds, I remove my right boot and sock.

"Oh, boy. That doesn't look good," I say as I take stock of my swollen, bruised ankle. "I wonder if it's broken?" I ponder out loud. Gabe has pulled the pack off my back and is going through the first-aid kit looking for bandages and antibiotic ointment.

"We'll get you bandaged up then off to the hospital for X-rays," he says as he applies the bandage to my knees and hands.

"This will sting," he warns me before he dabs an antiseptic wipe on my split lip. "I'm sorry about that," he says as I wince in pain. "There, I'm all done." Gabe's chocolate brown eyes are full of concern as he helps me to my feet.

"Lean on me so you don't put weight on that ankle," he says putting on the pack and lifting my left arm up and over his shoulders. Supporting me with his right arm, I try a few tentative steps down the hill.

The pain that shoots through my ankle is excruciating and I gasp in agony. Tears sting my eyes but I blink them away and try another step.

"Lift your foot up," Gabe suggests. "I'll help you hop on your good leg." We try this for a few minutes and make slow but steady progress. My left arm, stretched in an awkward position over Gabe's tall shoulders begins to ache and we stop for a rest. We carry on again, but our progress is slowed by the pain in my neck and shoulder. Gabe stops me, then moves down the hill a stride, and turns his back to me, shrugging off the daypack.

"Hop on," he says indicating that he'll piggyback me. The daypack hangs loosely by one strap over his shoulder.

"Gabe, I'm too heavy. I'll hurt your back."

"Bollocks!" Gabe retorts emphatically. "Get on. It will be much easier and faster this way." With a sigh, I climb ungracefully onto Gabe's back when he lowers himself into a squat position.

"This is nuts," I exclaim as he lifts me, his arms looped under my knees for support.

"Lean in close, Alexi. It will help me keep my balance as we go down the hill."

Inch by inch, with pure strength and determination, Gabe makes his way down the mountain, never faltering despite his encumbrance. I can feel the effort of his back muscles against the plane of my torso, his breathing labored, his heart thudding in exertion.

For the first time in my life, I wish I had been born a petite, fine-boned person instead of the Amazon that I am, a testament to my fourth generation Germanic roots on my mother's side. Stopping to rest at frequent intervals, we manage to safely reach the trail head in forty minutes.

At the car, Gabe helps me into the seat, careful not to bang my ankle. Due to my connection with the clinic, I get immediate attention at the emergency department and am whisked away in a wheelchair for an X-ray which upon development, reveals no broken bones.

The ER doctor explains it is a very bad sprain that will require rest, ice, and crutches for five days. So much for my previously unblemished sick day record at work I think to myself. Still, it could have been worse. I could have broken my ankle.

Gabe drives me home and settles me on the couch with my leg elevated and surrounded with ice packs, then he goes hunting for Charlie, who surprisingly did not turn up when we got home. Minutes later, Gabe comes back downstairs, a grin on his face.

"He's sound asleep on your pillow, Alexi. He's just the cutest thing you ever saw."

"He must have worn himself out playing," I suggest with a sigh.

"Yeah, about that. He did break a ceramic mug of some sort that was on the window ledge in the bedroom. I'll go clean it up later once he wakes up. No need to tweak the tail of the dragon, so to speak."

"Darn, that was one of Mark's favourite Toby jugs from England. It was rare and expensive. He'll be disappointed." I sigh and adjust the ice packs. "Not a very successful day, all in all," I say feeling a bit dejected. "And now I get to sit around for five days with nothing to do."

"I'll come stay with you," Gabe offers. "I can cook, look after Charlie, and keep you company. What do you say?" Gabe seems determined to help. "After all, you wouldn't have hurt yourself if I hadn't coaxed you into hiking up to the bluff."

"What will Heidi say? You're supposed to be visiting her, not me!"

"She'll say, 'go help Alexi, Gabe.'" His eyes are alight with teasing laughter.

"It would be nice to have someone here," I respond, thinking how difficult it will be to look after Charlie when I am barely able to move.

"Is that a *yes*?" Gabe asks hopefully.

"Yes, it's a yes. Thanks for being willing to help out." I feel oddly relieved not to be facing the next few days alone.

While Gabe goes back to Heidi's place to pick up a few personal items, and tell Heidi about my accident, I call my co-worker and organize relief for my position for the coming week.

"Don't worry," Jody says confidently. "We can manage a few days without you. Take care of yourself and get lots of rest."

"Thank you, Jody. I'm sorry I had to call you so late and on a Sunday no less. Call me if you have any problems at the clinic. I'll be home just hanging out with my new kitten, Charlie."

We chat for a few more minutes, then end the call just as Gabe returns to the house, a small duffle bag in his hand. Charlie charges down the stairs on his short, little kitten legs, meowing demandingly. Gabe sweeps the runt up into his arms and chucks him under the chin.

"Are you ready for some dinner, Alexi?" Gabe asks entering the living room, the kitten still in his arms.

"I'm pretty hungry, all right," I reply. "I'm not sure if there's much in the fridge. Maybe we can have..."

"Don't worry about it," Gabe says, cutting me off with a smile. "I'll throw something together. Do you want me to get you anything before I get started in the kitchen?"

"I do need some help getting off the couch. Can you hand me the crutches, please?" Gabe puts Charlie down and brings me the crutches. Awkwardly I lift my stiff and swollen ankle off the pillow and try to heave myself to my feet.

"Yikes! That hurts." I tumble back onto the couch.

"Here, I'll help," Gabe pulls me effortlessly into a standing position and passes me the crutches from where they have fallen against the sofa.

"Thanks, Gabe." I place them under my arms and, with clumsy co-ordination, make my way to the bathroom. Using the facilities was not easy or pain free but it was absolutely necessary. Pouring a glass of water from the bathroom tap, I swallow two anti- inflammatory painkillers before making my way slowly into the kitchen.

"No way," Gabe says when he sees me coming to help in the kitchen. "You go elevate that leg like the doctor said and don't forget to take your medication."

"Man, you certainly are a bossy old sod," I whine meekly as I turn and head for the couch again.

"I'll bring dinner to you when it's ready. Now, do you want a drink while you're waiting?" Gabe follows my slow progress into the living room. Geez, this guy was more attentive than a waiter at a five star restaurant.

"Sure, I'd love a cup of PG Tips. I like it really strong with sugar and soy milk, please and thank you." Gabe arranges the ice packs around my ankle once I've seated myself on the couch again, then whisks off to the kitchen to make the tea.

Charlie, who had been climbing his multi-level, carpeted, kitty jungle gym, wanders over to me, parks himself near my good foot, and stares intently at me. I pat my lap and wait while he contemplates distance, height and speed. One ear wings back, listening to Gabe singing in the kitchen, then shoots forward again. Calculations complete, decision made, Charlie leaps off the carpet and I catch him as he scrambles over the lip of the couch. Note to self: double the height, same distance, good speed. Circling several times in a dog-like manner, he lets out a soft sigh and drops into a tight ball of orange fluff on my lap. His purr is deep and rumbling and I relax, enjoying the moment.

Gabe brings me the tea minutes later and I silence potential conversation with a forefinger to my pursed lips. I point at Charlie and Gabe smiles in understanding, nodding his head. I mouth the words *thank you* as he hands me the mug, a brightly coloured ceramic affair with the words I Love San Francisco splashed garishly on the side. This mug, a gag gift from Mark, hailed from our honeymoon trip almost twenty years ago. By force of habit I move the mug a quarter turn to the right to avoid the chipped rim before sipping the tea gratefully.

I can hear Gabe clanging pots and pans in the kitchen and wonder once again what he'll dream up for dinner. My question is answered over an hour later when he brings in a tray holding two plates of lasagna, green salad, and multigrain dinner rolls.

"That looks appetizing, Gabe. Thank you for cooking yet again."

"No probs, Alexi. I really enjoy cooking in your kitchen. You've got all the mod cons, that's for sure." He passes me a plate of food, cutlery, and a napkin, then takes one for himself and sits cross-legged on the floor beside me placing his plate on the coffee table.

"Are you okay there, Gabe? That can't be very comfortable."

"I'm fine. I like eating informally. I was going to open a bottle of wine but I don't think it's recommended while you're taking painkillers."

"I shouldn't, that's true, but you can open one for yourself if you'd like," I offer. "Or you might want to try some of Mark's micro-brewery beer that's in the fridge."

"No thanks."

The lasagna is delicious and I realize how hungry I am as I take another bite. Charlie, still asleep on my lap, seems unaware of my carefully balanced plate hovering over his head.

After Gabe has cleared away the dinner plates, he returns to the living room and sits beside me on the couch, watching Charlie as he dreams in his sleep.

"Well, what do you want to do now? Shall we play cards? Board games? Watch a movie?" Gabe lifts a quizzical eyebrow and waits for me to mull over the suggested options.

"Let's read to each other. I have a pile of books Dad brought for me from the bookstore that I've been meaning to read and haven't had the time."

"Sure, that sounds like fun. Where are the books?" I explain where to find them and Gabe returns to the living room a few minutes later with a small stack of paperbacks in his hands.

"Okay. Let's see what we've got to choose from. Well, there's *Pride and Prejudice*, a story everyone should read at least once. There's *On Mystic Lake* which appears to be..." he trails off, reading the back cover, "...women's fiction." He sounds dismissive.

"Hey, I love Kristin Hannah's stories. Don't knock 'em 'til you've tried 'em!"

"Okay, okay. Don't get your knickers in a knot, I was just teasing you." He takes the next book and looks at the front and back covers. "Here you have full on chick lit which you'll never – ever – get me to read. The last book is....ah ha, a true classic." He smiles, turning the slim volume over in his hands, rubbing his thumb pad over the embossed title.

"*The Unbearable Lightness of Being* by Milan Kundera published in..." Gabe flips over a few pages, "Nineteen eighty four. It has been translated from French to English."

"Have you read it?" I ask, intrigued by his reaction to the novel.

"Yes, several times, but I'd love to read it again. With you."

"Done deal. Who reads first?"

"I will." He settles beside me, careful to leave Charlie undisturbed. He opens the book, clears his throat and reads the first sentence in a clear, steady voice. I close my eyes and, leaning slightly sideways, nestle my head against Gabe's chest so that not only can I can hear the story but I can feel it as well.

The novel is not an easy read and requires full engagement of the reader's mind. Gabe negotiates the written words well and reads concisely without error.

When it is my turn to read, I apologize before I even start, "I'm not very good at reading aloud but I'll do my best." With Gabe's encouragement, I pick up where he left off and feel my confidence build as the pages fly by. Around midnight, I feel myself grow weary and close the book, stifling a yawn.

"I'm all done in," I announce. "Time for bed." Gabe takes the book and places it on the coffee table and then helps me to my feet after I have carefully shifted the sleeping puss onto the couch.

Grasping the crutches I gingerly negotiate the edge of the coffee table and work my way to the bottom of the stairs.

"Hmm...this could be tricky," I say, pondering my dilemma.

"Not really," Gabe states taking the crutches out of my hands and scooping me up into his arms. "Hang on," he says, then easily carries me up the stairs.

"You're just showing off now," I tease, my arms circling his neck for extra security. He deposits me gently in the master bedroom and returns moments later with my crutches.

"Where shall I sleep?" He asks with a marked lack of cheekiness.

"You can use the guest bedroom that's just across the landing. The bathroom is down the hall on the left. There are clean sheets on the bed and fresh towels in the linen closet. Let me know if you need me for anything." He raises a cheeky eyebrow and smirks; the bad boy is back.

"Good night, Alexi." Gabe pulls me into his arms for a brief moment before pressing a kiss to my forehead. He abruptly turns on his heel and leaves my room.

"Good night, Gabriel," I whisper to thin air.

I awake early on Monday morning to a soggy grey dawn. My sleep had been restless, finding it difficult to achieve a comfortable position with my leg elevated on a pillow. Before bed I had a quick spit bath, as my father liked to call them, and I missed my typical long, hot soak in the tub.

Charlie had wandered into my room during the night and had curled quietly up against my side on top of the quilted coverlet. I welcomed the warm comfort of his tiny body but had feared I might accidentally roll on him in my sleep. As it turned out, we both survived our second night together with much more amity than we had our first.

I creep out of the king size bed and pull my housecoat on before picking up the crutches to slowly make my way to the bathroom. The bathroom is large, with a double sink vanity and a deep soaker tub which nestles up against a large picture window that frames a prefect and private lake view. I never tire of the vista and treasure it as my favourite room in the house. The colour and decor had been a challenge but Mark and I had agreed on deep chocolate brown with hints of mint green. The results, surprisingly feminine despite the dark colour, had surpassed our expectations.

Moving to my sink, I splash water on my face, pat it dry with a fluffy cotton towel, and apply a moisturizer. Sitting on the high-backed antique chair located next to the tub, I examine my ankle and note the puffy, blue-black tissue extending from my calf down to the top of my foot. It feels very uncomfortable and I take a dose of medication, hoping to quell the pain.

The trip downstairs is slow as I take one tread at at time, careful to avoid putting weight on my ankle. Once at the bottom, I use the crutches to move down the hall into the kitchen where I can hear Gabe singing his heart out as he makes breakfast.

"Good morning, Gabe. Did you sleep well?" He smiles and nods; the dimple makes an early morning appearance.

"Hey, beautiful. And you? Did you sleep okay? How's the ankle this morning?" He drops to one knee in front of me and pushes aside the hem of my housecoat to examine my ankle; he runs a feather light touch from the top of my foot to my knee. An involuntary shiver skates across my skin.

"It's fine," I respond quickly, moving to the far side of the island with shuffling haste.

"I'm glad to hear it," he smiles as he moves back to the stove.

"What are you cooking? It sure smells good." I hitch my sprained leg over the seat of the barstool to take the weight off it and lean on the countertop for support.

"Breakfast burritos," he states. "They're almost ready. Coffee?" I nod eagerly in response.

We eat breakfast in the kitchen and discuss plans for the day.

"If you and Charlie don't mind, I think I'll hobble over to the studio and paint for a bit."

"I can stay and babysit Charlie and then later I'll go pick up some groceries. The fridge is looking pretty bare." Gabe clears away the breakfast plates then refills Charlie's bowl and freshens the water dish.

"Are you sure you'll be okay?" I ask, feeling a little guilty for abandoning him; I get to paint and he gets to run errands.

"Go. Have fun. We can meet back here around lunch time. You'd better prepare a list for the grocery store so I get the brands you like to eat."

I grab a pen and notepad from beside the phone and jot a list of items.

"Here, that should cover it." Using the crutches, I move to my purse in the hall closet and pulling out several bills from my wallet, I hand them to Gabe.

"I don't want to take your..." I cut Gabe off abruptly.

"Do not argue. Just take it." Reluctantly he pockets the money.

"Would you mind picking up a parcel for me at the art supply store? It's prepaid and the shop is close to the grocery store. Here's the spare key for the house."

"No worries. I can pick up anything you need," Gabe responds casually taking the key. Charlie decides to join us in the kitchen and makes a beeline for the food bowl, packing away a tidy amount of dry and moist food before sitting down to clean his face with the side of a tiny, white paw.

Gabe and I exchange a smile as we watch the little tyke meticulously groom himself from head to tail like a pro.

"I forgot how adorable kittens can be." Gabe says, the smile still evident on his face.

"I'll see you two later, then," I say shuffling down the hall and making my way laboriously up the stairs to the bedroom where I dress in casual, flowing hemp pants and a fitted red V-necked shirt. I slip on a pair of Birkenstock's and carefully make the trip back downstairs and out across the yard to the studio.

The backyard had been terribly neglected when we bought the house and it had come as a complete surprise how much delight I'd derived from restoring the grounds to their full potential. I had not realized how much I missed digging in the soil. With a plan mapped out on paper, I had armed myself with rich top soil, a variety of plants and a few huge granite stones. I had created undulating and mounded beds, then planted them heavily with shade plants.

Ferns, astilbes in a wide range of colours, hostas, and a variety of ornamental grasses grew readily in the shade of the grand old chestnut tree that dominated the centre of the yard. The boulders, placed randomly amongst the plantings, look natural and create a welcoming oasis. A low hedgerow marks the end of the garden and a black wrought iron gate leads to the sandy beach of the lake shore.

A dense cedar hedge on both sides of the property provides privacy and completes the picture of perfect tranquility.

Paving stones, set in the lawn, lead from the deep veranda, past the stone patio, and over to the studio. I tread the stones with care as the crutches sink a few inches into the grass. Once inside, I open a few windows to allow fresh air to flow through the studio. Taking out my brushes and palette I seat myself on a padded wooden stool before a blank canvas.

I close my eyes and breathe deeply the mixed aroma of oil paint and clean lake air. I wait expectantly. My eye wanders over the plethora of available colours and my attention is drawn to the burnt orange.

I enjoy this moment of suspense; this moment when, from thin air and wild imagination, a picture forms in my mind and my hand takes the invitation from my heart and soul and lays down layer upon layer of paint until, from nothing, comes an image straight from my innermost self. Unguided. Unguarded. It is a simultaneous stripping bare the soul and an opening of the heart.

Today I feel light and playful. My brush strokes are fast and sure. Colour flies onto the canvas; thicker here, thinner there. A form takes shape; sharp detail is added while the background is subtly defined, redefined. I put down my brush and palette and arch my back, releasing the muscles that have tightened while I worked. I flex my fingers and lift my arms over my head in a slow stretch. The clock on the mantle strikes twice and I am shocked by the lateness of the hour. I stumble to my feet, reaching for my crutches just as there is a quiet knock at the studio door.

"Hi," Gabe says says, entering the room. "I'm sorry to disturb you but I thought you might like some lunch."

"I must apologize, Gabe. The time just got away from me today."

145

"Let's have a look," he says moving towards the easel. I *look* at the painting for the first time and smile in delight.

"Oh, Alexi." Gabe stares in wonder at the canvas. "That is unbelievable. You have captured every single nuance that is Charlie."

It is true. The orange tabby kitten, sitting half in shadow on a dark hardwood floor, has paused in his preening, a white and pink padded paw lifted half way to his face, to gaze expectantly at the viewer. The eyes, still the smokey blue-grey of a youngster, have such an innocence about them that it evokes an immediate and emotional response from the viewer.

"Yes, that's Charlie, all right." I feel contented but drained. "Let's go back to the house. As usual, I'm starving." Slipping the padded crutches into my armpits, I move slowly towards the door. My breath catches as a wave of pain sweeps up my ankle into my calf. Wincing, I move forward again.

"Hey, are you okay?" Gabe opens the door for me and pauses when he notices me grimacing again. Dropping to one knee, he examines my ankle with a delicate touch.

"Oh shit, Alexi, your ankle seems much worse." Sure enough, my ankle looks more swollen than before. "Maybe sitting for so long let the blood pool and increased the swelling. We'd better get that leg elevated and iced right away." Gabe's voice is full of concern.

Without a single word he scoops me into his arms, leaving the crutches behind, and carries me into the house. Depositing me on the couch, he grabs the ice packs from the freezer and positions them around my leg that is elevated on a pillow. He returns to the studio to retrieve the crutches and places them close by me.

The doorbell chimes and I groan in irritation, not wanting to get up.

"Don't move a muscle. I'll go answer it." He hurries off down the hall. I can hear greetings being exchanged and recognize the tone of my parents' voices.

"Hello, Alexandra," my mother says, entering the room. "Your friend, Gabriel, has just introduced himself to us. I bumped into Jody from your office and she told us about your little accident. Your father and I decided to come by and see how you're doing." She has arched a delicate eyebrow that has a voice of its own. It is a voice I am all too familiar with and it is clearly saying, "Why didn't you call us?"

"Hi, Mom. Dad. This is a pleasant surprise. What are you two doing here? Who's minding the store?"

"Let's not worry about that," Dad says gruffly. "Here, let me take a look at that ankle. Did you get X-rays yet?" I nod as I move the ice packs off my ankle so that Dad can have a look.

"That doesn't look good, Alexandra. Maybe you should see the doctor." After his inspection, Dad drops his reading glasses down so that they dangle on his chest from a fine, silver chain that is looped around his neck.

"I saw the doctor yesterday. He said rest, ice, and anti-inflammatory drugs. I'm doing all of that. Gabe has been a tremendous help to me."

"I've not done much, really," Gabe says, clearly not feeling accolades are necessary.

"What did Mark have to say about it?" Dad quizzes me, a frown furrowing his brow.

"I haven't told him yet. He'll likely call tomorrow; that's when we would normally call each other. I'm fine. Don't make a big fuss." My parents, loving as they are, can, at times, still treat me like a child.

My dad makes a harrumphing sound and lets out a breath of air. Mom is wringing her hands in an uncharacteristically nervous way.

"Why don't you stay for lunch?" Gabe offers, sensing some tension in the room. "I know it's late, but if you're hungry, you could join us. Alexi and I were just about to eat."

"Uh...well..." My dad stumbles to a halt and glances at Grace. Regaining her composure she responds politely.

"Edward and I would be delighted, Gabriel. Thank you."

"Sit down and keep Alexi company. I'll get lunch on the table in a few minutes." Gabe whistles tunelessly as he goes to the kitchen.

"Well, he's certainly a handsome man," Grace says quietly.

"Oh. Yes, I guess so. I hadn't really notice." I pluck non existent fluff off the cushion I'm propped against, avoiding eye contact with my mother.

"You'd have to be completely blind not to notice that man," Edward declares. "He's got the looks and presence of a movie star."

"Like I said, Dad, I haven't really noticed. We've been hanging out a bit and now he's offered to help me with Charlie while I'm on crutches."

"Who the hell is Charlie?" Edward demands in a sharp tone.

"That is Charlie," I say, pointing as the kitten wanders sleepily into the room right on cue.

"You got a kitten?" Dad asks at the same time as Mom says, "He's so cute."

Charlie sniffs Dad's pant legs, then moves on to Mom's nylon clad legs.

"Watch him, Mom! He likes to climb up legs." Grace, a cat lover since childhood, reaches down to chuck Charlie under the chin.

"He's just precious. Where did you get him?" She asks.

"Gabe's cousin, Heidi, rescued a whole litter. Charlie was the runt and nobody wanted him, so I had to rescue him."

"You are such a softie, Alexandra," Grace says, smiling. She lifts Charlie onto her lap and strokes his fuzzy kitten coat. He purrs in response, then circles like a dog before plonking down for a nap.

From the doorway, Gabe clears his throat to gain our attention.

"She is a softie, all right. That's one of the things I love about her. She fell for that kitten the moment she saw him," Gabe is speaking to Grace but is looking at me with a gentle smile playing on his lips. He winks at me, then announces that lunch is ready.

An hour later, after we have finished lunch, Gabe and Grace go out into the garden for a stroll then disappear through the gate at the bottom of the yard while Dad stays behind to keep me company.

"Alexandra, I'm going to say this to you loud and clear: you are playing with fire where that man is concerned. He is trouble any which way you look at him." Dad looks distressed as he paces back and forth in the living room.

"Dad, you've got it all wrong. Gabe and I are friends. Nothing else. I'm married to Mark, remember?" I feel too old to be getting this kind of lecture from my overly reactive father and my words are laced with agitation.

"Mark my works, Alexandra. Distance yourself from this man or you will destroy everything." Dad's words are dark and foreboding. I remain quiet, thinking how odd it is that he and mother have taken such an immediate dislike to Gabe.

"He's not a bad guy, Dad. I think he's really nice, actually."

"That's my point. He's a nice guy, he's attractive, Mark's away...do I need to fill in every detail for you, Alexandra?"

"No, Dad. I get your drift. You're worrying for nought, however. I'd never hurt Mark like that." I find Dad's remarks troubling and

I feel a headache looming. I push my hair back from my throbbing temples.

Grace and Gabe return from their lakeside walk smiling and chatting amiably and I can only guess that he has used his arsenal of charms to ingratiate himself to my mother as there is no sign of her earlier agitation.

Later in the evening, after my parents have left, Gabe and I continue reading the novel we had begun the night before. Reading aloud has become easier for me and the words flow nicely from my lip as I read page after page. By midnight we both feel tired and I close the book with a yawn.

"Time for a shower, then bed," I state, getting awkwardly to my feet. "Thanks for all your help today, Gabe. It was really nice of you to make lunch for my parents."

"No worries. I enjoyed meeting Grace and Edward. They are such interesting people. I had a lovely chat with your mother in the garden. She sure knows a lot about plants," he points out with a smile.

"You charmed the socks off her," I say, grinning. "I bet you never put that dimple away for a single second when you went for your walk."

"I don't know what you're talking about," he says with a sheepish grin. I punch him on the arm playfully.

"You do so." I shake my head, tisking as I go. "You good-looking men are all the same."

Gabe grabs my arm and swings me to face him. I stumble and lurch into him, dropping the crutches against the wall with a thunk.

"You think I'm good looking?" He asks earnestly.

"Of course I do. Have you never looked in a mirror?"

"I don't like looking in mirrors. They reveal too many flaws in my character." Pressed up close to him, staring into his deep, expressive eyes, I cannot imagine what he is talking about.

"Uh...well...hmm," My words are incoherent. I press my hand against his chest and push away from him, putting some distance between our bodies but not before I feel a stirring of longing. A longing to remain in his arms, pressed close to his heart.

My father's words echo in my mind as I feel and fear the fire of which he so recently spoke.

Over the next few days I notice my ankle becoming less swollen and more comfortable. I can put weight on it but still use the crutches despite sore, chaffed armpits. Gabe has been an enormous help, keeping Charlie and me fed and entertained. I find myself enjoying having a houseguest but realize that my time with him is coming to an end.

We finished the novel last night and amidst a shower of tears, I agree with Gabe that it is indeed a remarkable novel.

"The only problem with that story," I said to Gabe once he had closed the book after the final chapter, "is that it is unbearably sad, not unbearably light." I had cradled Charlie in my arms and wept silently when Gabe read the part where the hero, Tomas, euthanizes Kerenin, the cancer-riddled dog that had been a faithful friend to both Tomas and his wife, Tereza. Gabe had moved close to me on the couch and had held Charlie and me in his arms until my storm had passed, then he had gone to the bathroom and brought me a box of tissues.

"You'd best mop up," he'd said with a gentle tone, offering me a handful of tissues. I dabbed at my smeared mascara and blew my nose noisily, which startled Charlie from his nap.

I had gone up to bed shortly thereafter and had slept well enough, but this morning the mirror reflects my red, puffy eyes. And that's what I get for being a sentimental silly I chide myself as I dab on makeup in a futile effort to appear rested.

Today, the first day of June, looks promising. From the bathroom window I can see Gabe out on the sandy shore, skipping stones on the smooth, calm surface of the lake. I watch for a few moments, realizing, not for the first time, that I have become inexplicably fond of him. A sense of sorrow overwhelms me and I turn away with a sigh of regret.

Charlie enters the bedroom with his striped orange and white tail straight up in the air and presses his soft body up against my bare legs. The tactile tip of his tail snakes up and around my calf and feels like a soft kiss. I feel my spirits lift as I pick the little runt up and inhale his baby kitten fragrance. His purr is loud and immediate, as always. I plop him on the bed while I dress in jeans and a short sleeved sweater, then pick him up again and walk carefully and crutch-free down the stairs. The moment feels like a triumph.

In the kitchen, I feed Charlie, then busy myself making French toast; I want to surprise Gabe with breakfast when he returns from his walk. Twenty minutes later, he appears at the back door looking invigorated and smelling of pine needles and the fresh outdoors. We exchange greetings as he enters the kitchen.

"Sit," I invite, gesturing to the stool. "I've made breakfast for you." I smile as I serve up two stacks of hot French toast topped with nut butter, maple syrup, and sliced banana. I pour him a mug of coffee, then doctor one for myself. I pull up a second stool and sit beside him.

"Dig in while it's hot," I suggest, doing just that.

"I didn't expect you to be up so early, otherwise I would have made you breakfast so you can stay off that ankle." Gabe looks concerned.

"My ankle is much better, that's for sure. Here, have a look." I pull up my pant leg so he can see that indeed my ankle does look much improved.

"Hmm. Nice," he offers with a twinkle in his eyes.

"I came down the stairs without the crutches and it didn't even hurt. I think I'm almost fully recovered. I bet Heidi will be happy to have you back at her house again." I smile, but it feels feeble.

"Hey, are you kicking me out, Alexi?" Gabe quirks a questioning eyebrow.

"Well, not so much kicking really. More like nudging. I'm extremely grateful for all your help and your company, but I'm sure you're keen to get back to your own life..." I trail off, looking into the depths of his eyes.

I can read them now, I think to myself, surprised at the revelation. I can read uncertainty, indecision, and sadness then I can see a decision being made. A veil drops; I can read nothing more.

"Okay, I'll leave tomorrow. Today, I thought we could go paddling on the lake in the canoe I saw stored behind your studio. Do you have life jackets?"

"Oh, Gabe, that would be so much fun! I haven't been out on the lake yet this year. We've got life jackets in storage; I'll get them out once I've tidied up the kitchen." I quickly clear away the breakfast dishes, humming as I work.

My mood has vastly improved as I imagine the golden day that lies ahead of us. The sadness is still there, but it has shifted into the background, lurking quietly for the moment, at the edge of my thoughts.

With the life jackets belted and buckled around our torsos, Gabe and I pull the canoe down to the water using a two-wheeled canoe cart. Gabe encourages me into the boat first then takes off his boots and tosses them into the boat, wading barefoot into the icy water. He has rolled up his jeans to avoid getting soaked and I can't help but notice how comical it looks. I smile to myself, treasuring the moment.

Picking up the paddle, he pushes off from the sandy shore and begins a steady, powerful paddling rhythm.

"You must have done this before," I guess, noticing how confidently he handles the boat.

"I rowed all through university, both in a sculling boat and a sweep boat. I've always enjoyed rowing but this is the first time in a few years that I've been on the water. It sure feels great to be out here."

Gabe paddles across the lake, then, staying close to the shoreline, works his way north east. We catch a glimpse of three mule deer furtively eating the newly leafed undergrowth a the lake's edge. Farther along, we see a Belted Kingfisher flying rapidly just above the surface of the water calling to his mate, or perhaps guarding his territory, with a sharp, ratcheting sound.

Pulling the canoe up on the pebbled shore of a secluded beach, we remove our life jackets and set about exploring the crescent-moon-shaped bay. Sitting down in a sunny area, I doodle in the sand with a stick I found earlier, while Gabe stacks rocks to form a small inukshuk, reminiscent of the Inuit people's famous design which, I recall from our tour at the museum in Kelowna, represents the human form and provides a welcome to travelers.

Tiring of our games, we lie back on the warm sand side by side; I shield my eyes with my forearm and listen to the lake lap near our toes. Some time later Gabe rolls to a sitting position to face me and reaching into his pocket he removes a small red velvet box. I sit up as well, wondering what he is about to give me.

"Alexi, I want you to have this. I bought it for you in Kelowna and I have been waiting for the right time to give it to you." He opens the box and removes the necklace that I had admired at the gift shop.

"You know I love it, Gabe, and I truly appreciate the gesture, but I cannot possibly accept it." I try to place the necklace back in the box, but Gabe insists.

"Please, I want you to have it. Please accept it as a token of my affection for you." He clasps the necklace around my neck, his fingers warm and lingering on my nape. Wordlessly I acquiesce.

"Thank you, Gabe. It was very kind of you to get this for me." I touch the pendent, loving the heavy warm weight of it nestled between my breasts.

"I want you to know that if you ever need anything from me, Alexi, anything at all, I will always be there for you in any way that I can." His hands cup my face gently, his thumb pad brushes away a few grains of sand stuck to my cheek. He is so close that I can smell the notes of his musk scent; his eyes are dark pools. Unguarded, vulnerable, raw.

"Thank you, Gabe. That means a great deal to me. I hope I will never have to burden you with my problems." I place my hands over his, squeezing my eyes shut against the tide of emotion that threatens to swamp me.

Pulling his hands slowly away from my face, I clamber to my feet, avoiding the use of my injured ankle. I hand him a life jacket and buckle up my own. The time has come to head for home.

The ride back is cold; the sun, obscured by thick, fluffy clouds, fails to warm our skin as a breeze sets up along the surface of the water. Gabe's muscles strain against the current as he rows us back to the Lake House. Pulling the bow of the boat up onto the shore, he offers his hand to assist me as I step out of the canoe onto the beach.

"Thank you, Gabe. That was great. Thanks for doing all the rowing." My smile is genuine, nonetheless I feel melancholy lurking in the wings of my consciousness. It had been so close to a perfect morning.

"No probs. I love rowing so the pleasure was all mine." We load the canoe back onto the cart and Gabe pulls it into position behind my studio and covers it with a deep green tarp.

"I'm going to stop by the studio for a few minutes, then I'll come up to the house. We need to decide what to do with the rest of the day."

"Sure, I'll see you soon, then." Gabe picks up his boots and the life jackets and walks barefoot along the paving stone path to the house. I can see him flexing his shoulder muscles and I hope that he is not sore from the rowing.

In the studio, I check my e-mail. I'd anticipated a response from one of the art galleries in Vancouver, but no word yet. With any luck, my request to display a few of my paintings would be accepted by one or two. Mark and I planned a trip to the coast in August and hoped to take the canvases with us. So far, none of the galleries has responded. Still, it has only been a few weeks since I sent my portfolio out. I remain hopeful and optimistic.

After lunch, Gabe and I play card games and snack on popcorn, which we find out Charlie enjoys also.

"I've never seen a cat so crazy about popcorn." I laugh out loud as Charlie tries to pull the bowl towards himself with his paw. I toss a kernel up in the air and watch as Charlie leaps energetically to catch it, then gobbles it down and looks for more.

"Yep, he's crazy all right," Gabe agrees with a smile. We both fall silent and suddenly I wonder what Gabe is thinking.

"You know, Alexi, I must say that staying here with you and Charlie in your beautiful, tranquil, Victorian home has been one of the best experiences of my life." Gabe gazes at me earnestly. "It's really been special. Getting to know you has been a pleasure." I can feel heat building in my cheeks at Gabe's compliment.

"It's been the same for me, too. I've loved having you stay with me at the Lake House. I sometimes feel like we've known each other forever and yet it's only been, what..." I struggle to count the days correctly in my head.

"Yeah, I know. It feels like a lifetime but it's only been just a few weeks." Gabe agrees. We sit quietly saying nothing. Thinking. Feeling. Fully aware of ourselves; of each other. Our connection is undeniable. Strong. Poignant.

"Let me take you out for dinner tonight as a thank you for all you've done for Charlie and me these past days," I offer, suddenly feeling the need to escape the four walls of the house.

"That would be fun, thank you. Shall we go to the Wild Onion for old time's sake?"

"Sure. Why not?"

After I've freshened up and changed into jean capris and a sweater, Gabe drives us in the Mustang to the restaurant as I fear my ankle will not yet tolerate a long walk.

While we wait for our appetizers to arrive I can't help but smile as I recall our first meal at the Wild Onion. At the time, I'd been on the verge of dumping Gabe and running for home. The connection that he described back then makes complete sense to me now. His presence feels so right in my life that I wonder how I will survive when he gets on his motorbike and leaves town.

"You're very quiet, Alexi," Gabe observes, finishing the last of his appetizer.

"I'm thinking about what you said before, just after we first met."

"I say a lot of stuff that's just pure shit," he responds, seeming to be impatient with me. With himself.

"No, not to me you don't," I reply calmly. "To me you speak a lot of truth and I appreciate your candor." Our fingers hesitantly intertwine on the table top, then pull away.

We finish the meal in relative silence, each of us deep in our own thoughts. Occasionally I glance at Gabe who seems to be drawing away from me in scarcely perceptible increments as the evening progresses.

"What's wrong, Gabe?" I inquire softly, trying to catch a glimpse of the thoughts behind his closed expression.

"Nothing. Are you ready to go?" He slaps a few bills on the table, despite the fact that it was to be my treat, and pulls his leather jacket off the chair and steps back, waiting for me to follow him. The man obviously has his knickers in a twist. His long stride is quick and I stumble as my newly-healed ankle protests under the stress of trying to keep up.

"I'll meet you at the car," I call to Gabe as he rushes from the restaurant. His pace slows immediately and he turns back, taking my arm to give support.

"Sorry, Alexi. I'm such an ass..."

"No, Gabriel. You are a man with something on his mind. That doesn't make you an ass. Maybe right now isn't the time to say what's bothering you, but when the time is right, I will listen." I place my cupped palm on his cheek for a moment, starring into his troubled eyes, then remove my hand. "I will listen."

He nods and, walking slowly, assists me to the car. The ride home is dead quiet and it isn't until we get inside the house that he speaks again. Going to the fridge, he selects a bottle of wine, opens it, and fills two crystal glasses.

"Cheers," we say in unison as we clink the rims. Settling side by side on the couch in the living room, we sip our wine and wait. Finally he speaks.

"I should never have come to stay at your house, Alexi."

"But I thought you said you enjoyed your..." Gabe cuts me off abruptly.

"I loved being here with you and Charlie but it's all wrong. I try to pretend that you're not married, that you and I could have a future together and that's when I realize that I..." He looks away, faltering mid sentence. "That's when I realize that I must leave *now*." He drains his glass quickly then moves through the house hastily gathering up his possessions and stuffing them into the duffle bag. He pulls on his jacket and returns to the living room. Slashes of vivid colour wing up his cheekbones; a storm of emotion swirls about him.

"Goodbye, Alexandra." At the front door he shoves his feet into his boots as I trail behind feeling bewildered.

"Good night, Gabe. Drive carefully and call me in the morning, okay?" He gives me a curt nod and leaves the house closing the door firmly behind him. The latch clicks loudly as I turn the dead bolt. Deafening silence fills the house, surrounding me. Desperately lonely, I climb the stairs slowly. In the guest bedroom the bed has been stripped, the sheets placed neatly in the corner with the bath towels. I throw the laundry in the hamper and remake the bed.

In the master bedroom, Charlie is fast asleep beside my pillow. I slip off my shoes and climb wearily onto the bed with him, curling myself around his small warm body.

This is how Mark finds us, hours later, when he arrives home unexpectedly in the pre-dawn hours. Stripping down to his boxer shorts and T-shirt, Mark joins us on the bed, pulling my grandmother's age-softened quilt over our bodies. He wraps his arms around me, spooning me into his embrace. Still half asleep, I pull his left hand over my shoulder and up to my lips; I kiss the back of his hand, pressing my cheek against it as tears seep from my eyes in a slow, steady stream.

"Shh. It's okay, honey, I'm home now." Mark pulls his hand free from my grasp and smooths the hair back from my face. I cry myself back to sleep sandwiched between the warm, comforting bodies of Mark and Charlie.

CHAPTER 5

...crystalizing, it becomes a memory...

Even though I feel desperately weak, I am determined to check the post this morning after I've had a cup of tea and some toast. The wind is strong today, whipping around the edges of the cabin with a relentless howl. An eddy of leaves whirls and dances outside the living room window and Charlie is captivated. His ears are pricked forward, his pupils dilated; his tail snaps from side to side in excited agitation. Silly goose, I think as I smile to myself. He never tires of such antics no matter how old he gets.

After breakfast, I bundle up in a winter coat, hat, scarf, boots and gloves before venturing out into the frosty, demanding November wind. I set a determined pace and walk through the faint skiff of snow, up the driveway to the mailbox at the top of the hill. The box is full of mail and I eagerly scan each envelope looking for an Australian postmark. Dejected, I stick the bundle of mail into my pocket. Nothing. Still nothing from Gabe.

I dreamt about him last night. It had been many years since I dreamt of Gabe, yet this morning I had a distinct recollection of him. Of that last week when he had stayed at the Lake House; that week when Mark had returned home from work several days early. Of that time when I found, no matter how I tried, I could not stop crying.

★ ★ ★

The Monday following Gabe's departure from the Lake House I return to work on an ankle that feels nearly healed. With every hour that passes, I wonder if I should call Gabe, but I steadfastly resist the urge. By three o'clock, I'm a distracted, miserable mess. All I can do is think about Gabe and wonder why he has not called me.

Finally, on Wednesday afternoon, Gabe calls and asks that I meet with him after work. He is a few minutes late for our meeting at the parking lot behind the clinic and when he arrives, I hop quickly into the passenger seat of the Mustang. Gabe looks tired and drawn despite his God-gifted features.

"Hi, Gabe. I missed you." I rest my hand on his as his palm curls around the gear shifter.

"Hey, beautiful. How are you?" His voice is soft and low.

"I'm okay. Mark came home a few days ago."

"Yeah, I know. Heidi noticed his car was parked in front of your house. It could only mean that he was back." Gabe pulls the Mustang into the late afternoon traffic and drives across the bridge to a quiet, secluded park at the water's edge.

"Come. Let's sit on the sand." He leads the way to a spot on the beach that the sun has yet to neglect. Sitting down, I remove my sandals and draw my knees up under my chin. I stare across the calm water of the lake to the distant shore – a vision of blues and greens.

"Why did you need to see me, Gabe?" I ask after a few moments of silence.

"Look at me, please, Alexi." I turn and look at Gabe as he struggles to articulate his feelings. Earnestly he carries on. "I need you to know how I feel about you. I've never felt this way before – so completely and compellingly connected with another person." Leaning forward, Gabe cradles my face in his hands. His thumbs trace the arch of my brows, his fingertips trail down my face, down the column of my throat until, with feather-like gentleness, he touches the pulse in my neck, his thumb pads coming to rest at my supra-sternal notch. Slowly he releases me from his caress.

"I need to tell you…I love you." Of its own accord, my hand smacks across his lips, effectively rendering him speechless.

"No!" I rip my hand away from his mouth. "Do not say that. Do you hear me? Do not tell me you love me." My voice cracks on the last words. I drop my forehead onto my raised knees and wrap my arms tightly around my legs. Sobs rack my body as I fight for control. But the tears win. The deep, aching love I have for Gabe wins. The flood gates open then and emotions pour out of me. Unstoppable.

"I cannot see you ever again, do you understand? I have a beautiful life – I love Mark – I have no right…no reason…to be falling in love with you." I shove the heels of my hands into my eye sockets, trying to stem the flow of tears.

"Shh…" Gabe takes my huddled form into his arms trying to soothe my frantic emotions. For a moment, I lean against his strong body, savouring the feel of him, the smooth, warm texture of his skin, heated by the last rays of sun. A calm settles over me. Moments pass as I gather the strength to stand up.

"Take me home now, Gabe. I cannot return your love." Gabe nods. He pauses, before getting to his feet, to brush a hand quickly across his eyes. I have the impression that he has not cried for some time. Perhaps he never has.

The next day, Heidi drops by the house after work to see Charlie and she mentions that Gabe has taken the Mustang and set off for

Alaska. He plans to come back before the end of summer to return the car and pick up his motorbike, she explains. This news does not surprise me, yet I am shocked as feelings of desperate loneliness wash over me.

Mark, aware that I am not my normal self, has shouldered the blame, certain that his long absence has caused my melancholy. He has gone to great lengths to cheer me up but I erect a wall between us that he is unable to scale.

June flows to July and July to August and Mark soldiers on, trying in vain to right his self-proclaimed wrongs. Our intimacy disintegrates to nothing and even holding hands becomes distressful for me. Charlie has become my choice for comfort and he helps me in his quiet kitten way as I struggle through the endless summer.

Then, one day in late August, after Mark and I have returned from a trip to Vancouver, Gabe calls me at work.

"Alexandra, I need to see you. I'll pick you up after work." His tone is hard to read, but I am ecstatic to hear his voice.

"Umm..." I start to respond but, as is his style, he has hung up already. My heart beats wildly and a team of draft horses could not have held me back. I count each long minute until my shift ends, then I slick on some lipstick, smooth my hair into a loose knot at the nape of my neck, and run to the parking lot behind the clinic.

This time Gabe is waiting for me on his black and grey Harley. He looks incredible in his white T-shirt, his forearms tanned and muscular. A wide smile breaks across my face, my breath is thready, coming in random gulps. Gabe, who had been leaning against the black leather seat of the bike with jean clad legs crossed at the ankle, pushes away from the bike and opens his arms as I run the last few steps into his embrace.

He holds me tightly for a few precious moments, then lets me go as he hands me a skull-cap helmet.

"Come, Alexi. Let's get out of here."

"I'm afraid, Gabe." To be honest, I'm not sure if I mean of him, of myself, or of the bike. I have never felt so apprehensive in my life.

"Here, climb on behind me and hold on tight. I won't go fast." Despite my fears, I do as he asks and straddle the seat.

"Put your arms around me, Alexi," Gabe encourages as he slowly maneuvers the big bike out of the parking lot.

"Just lean with me. I think you'll enjoy the ride." I nod, but don't feel convinced. We proceed at a sedate pace across the bridge, then pick up speed as we follow the twisting and turning road along the edge of the lake.

The smells of late summer waft in the afternoon air; the sun warms my bare arms and legs. I tighten my hold around Gabe's torso, lean my cheek against his back and close my eyes. I am actually enjoying the ride. The roar of the engine coupled with the sound of the wind is hypnotic and I feel myself relaxing with each passing kilometre.

When we reach Kaslo, Gabe pulls over, puts the kick stand down, and turns off the engine. Stepping off the bike in one fluid motion, he removes his helmet and places it on the handlebars of the bike. He slants a questioning look in my direction.

"Well, did you enjoy that?" he asks.

"Oh, yes. That was really quite a lot of fun." I dismount with less skill and agility than Gabe, then hand him my helmet. I fluff my hair and smooth it back into place.

"You cut your hair," Gabe exclaims in surprise, as my hair tumbles to touch the tops of my shoulders.

"Yeah, more of a trim, really."

"You look as beautiful as always," he says, a warm smile in his eyes as he stretches out his hand to me.

We leave the bike and walk towards the lake to sit on a large, flat glacial boulder situated on the shoreline. From here, the lake view is impressive and unimpeded. The sun is setting behind the jagged mountain ridge and a nip freshens the air.

"Gabe, I've missed you. My life is bare without you in it. I feel so terrible; Mark assumes he's done something wrong. Apparently Dad called him at work and told him to get his butt back home to look after me. That's why he came home early." I squeeze Gabe's hand and nestle closer to him. "I am adrift in my own life, Gabe, and for the first time I cannot seem to get my bearings. Despite everything I've said in the past, I have fallen in love with you."

Turning sharply to me, Gabe pulls his brooding gaze from the view.

"No, Alexi. Don't say it." Gabe throws my own words, from a few months ago, back at me.

"But I do. I shouldn't, that is a fact, but I do anyway. I can't explain it or qualify it..." Gabe interrupts me, determined to stop my revelation.

"No. You must forget about me, Alexi. I am leaving for Australia tomorrow..."

I jump to my feet and whirl away from him, a shaking hand pressed against my racing heart.

"You can't leave me here. Take me with you." My throat is tight; the sentence barely squeezes out; a thin, reedy whisper. Even as the words leave my lips, I know how impossible they sound. Standing up, Gabe pulls me back into his arms, up against his chest, and tucks his chin on top of my head. The tears flow silently and I do not attempt to stop them as we gaze out over the still surface of the inky black water. Gabe strokes my hair, comforting me as he might Charlie.

"Stay here, Alexi. Stay here with Mark. This is your home, here amongst the wild woods of the Kootenays, beside the quiet lake." Turning me in his arms so that we stand atop the boulder hip to hip and chest to chest, he kisses me.

A long, slow kiss that is so exquisite in nature and achingly tender that even after he eventually pulls away from me, I am left entirely without conscious thought or ability to breathe. Slowly I open my eyes. I feel myself tremble inside. Finally, I draw a shallow breath.

"I don't know how I will bear being apart from you," I whisper, tracing his lips with my fingertip, storing their shape to memory.

"You will bear it, Alexi. The quality of your character, your loyalty, your honesty, determination, conviction, strength: all these things comprise who you are. The woman I fell in love with can bear this. A person with your integrity will learn to bear this because you must honour your wedding vows with Mark. Forget about me. *Forget* me." Gabe gently presses his hands into my hair, his voice, though strong, is velvety soft, his accent more pronounced than normal.

I rest my ear against his cotton-clad chest so that I can hear the steady beating of his heart as he cradles my head in his hands. The moment hangs there, suspended, with no beginning and no ending, until crystalizing, it becomes a memory, even though we were still standing in the present moment.

"Take me home, Gabe," I say quietly as I disentangle myself from him. There is a finality to my tone that seems to resonate between us.

"Yes, Alexi. It's time to take you home." Reaching for my hand, Gabe leads me back to the Harley and passes me a helmet.

The ride home is laced with poignancy as I gradually accept the fact that once Gabe returns to Australia, I will never see him again.

My mind races endlessly, frantic with thoughts of our impending separation and my deep reservations about my ability to cope with a completely shattered heart.

Dusk falls over us on our ride home and a chill fills the late August mountain air. I drink in deep gulps of oxygen trying to steady myself and I succeed. By the time we arrive back in town, I am prepared to say my final goodbye. I leave Gabe standing beside his bike, never once looking back.

And so I begin to learn the lesson of how to bear life without Gabe.

★ ★ ★

The cabin feels warm inside when I return from the mailbox. I toss the envelopes onto the kitchen counter and stoop to pat Charlie on the back.

"No news yet, my love." He looks up at me and blinks slowly, then sits down to ponder my words.

I decide to begin working on a commissioned painting I have been neglecting for several weeks. The city council had hired me to produce a large work to hang in the newly-renovated reception area of City Hall. Although the council has given me adequate time to create the piece, I feel an urgency to begin.

The canvases, three sections four feet wide by six feet tall, take up a substantial amount of space in my living room so it is with great care that I arrange my largest easel in the corner and begin the first panel. The commission has few limitations and I have been given free rein to indulge my artistic whims except for in the colour department: the work has to have a predominately pink theme.

Pink – pink is not my favourite colour to be sure, but thoughts of fully blossomed, gracefully arched cherry trees dance through my mind. The three canvases would work well for this and I sketch out a stylized concept on paper, pondering size and proportion before I proceed with the paints. The project progresses steadily and I pause after a few hours for a cup of tea and a snack.

I wait for the kettle to boil, resting my bony hips against the cabinetry, my fingers drumming aimlessly on the countertop. The clock on the sideboard strikes eight o'clock and I realize I should be having more than tea and a snack. I unplug the kettle and go to the fridge instead, surveying my options.

My appetite has been diminishing over the past several months and eating is mostly a chore, not a pleasure. I pull the bean and vegetable casserole Jillie dropped off earlier in the week, out of the fridge and place it on the hotplate to heat. Knowing it will take half an hour to fully warm, I return to the living room and begin to tidy my work space. Placing the brushes away, I gaze at my creation, happy with the results thus far.

The doorbell chimes just as I finish putting the still wet canvas into the storage area under the stairs. *Who could be calling at this time of night?* I think to myself. It is much too late for Jillie to be dropping in for an impromptu visit. Thinking it must be my neighbour, Lillian, looking to borrow something, I open the front door with a pleasant smile on my face.

My heart drums a wild tattoo and I am momentarily rendered speechless.

"Gabriel..." I say his name in breathless awe, wondering if my recent thoughts of him have conjured him up out of thin air.

Stepping across the threshold, he drops the small duffle bag from his grasp and pulls me into a sweet hug. He looks and feels and smells just like I remembered. Wonderful.

"I've missed you, beautiful," he says at last, releasing his hold on me and stepping back a pace. Gently he touches my face, concern swiftly lighting his dark eyes.

"You are not well." It is a statement, not a question. I shake my head. No, I am not well.

I take his hand in both of mine and pull him towards the living room. The faint smell of oils still lingers in the air.

"Come in, come in. Did you fly to Castlegar?" I ask. Castlegar is the closest airport to Kalsson and is about an hour's drive away.

"No, I flew to YVR in Vancouver, rented a car and drove for nine hours to get here." Looking more closely, I can see the odd grey hair showing in Gabe's thick, shiny locks and there is a fan of fine lines bracketing his eyes and mouth. Even in his state of exhaustion, he still is the best looking man I have ever seen.

"You must be weary and hungry. Let me get some food on the table for you, then we can catch up." I start to rise from the couch where we are seated but Gabe grabs my hand and pulls me back.

"Sit with me for a few minutes first, Alexi. I want to hear how you've been doing. Is Mark here?"

My left thumb instinctively crosses my palm and touches the heavy gold band on my ring finger. The right time to remove it had never presented itself. In my heart I still feel married; I could never tolerate the word *widow*. I shake my head. No, Mark is not here.

Gabe looks at my left hand and says, "I see." But he doesn't. He doesn't understand at all.

"It's a far cry from the Lake House," I comment as he surveys his surroundings, no doubt noticing how rustic the place seems.

"It's homey. Cozy. I like it, Alexi. It's very much *you*." He smiles at me and his dimple makes a brief appearance.

"Hey, look who's coming to see you," I exclaim. Slipping sedately down the stairs, Charlie ambles across the living room and proceeds to vault onto Gabe's lap with a demanding meow.

"Wow. This is our little runt? He's huge! I bet he weighs fifteen pounds." Gabe laughs as Charlie head butts him on the chest.

"Seventeen. Our runt weighs seventeen pounds." I have a silly grin on my face as warmth enters my soul and buoys it up higher and higher like a hot air balloon. I feel light, heady, delirious. Perhaps *I am* dreaming.

"He is delightful, Alexi. I think he remembers me." Gabe kisses the top of Charlie's head and gets a deep purr in response. Charlie turns three times then plops on Gabe's lap for a nap. Gabe turns his attention back on me.

"So tell me what's going on, Alexi. We don't exchange a single word in over ten years and then out of the blue I get an urgent letter from you asking for my help." Gabe's face is full of concern; his accent is more pronounced than I remembered.

"I didn't expect you to drop everything and rush to my rescue, Gabe. I should feel terrible that I dragged you all the way here, but if I'm honest, I'm absolutely astonished and thrilled that you came. It means everything to me that you are here." I can feel a rush of tears and nausea coming at the same time. Jumping to my feet, I excuse myself and stumble to the powder room where I experience a rash of dry heaves that last several minutes.

When the nausea subsides, I wash my face and smooth my grey hair into a long ponytail and pinch some colour into my cheeks. I return to the living room to find Gabe, head fallen back on the couch, fast asleep with Charlie cradled in his arms.

Watching the two of them peaceful in slumber again washes me with a tide of emotion. Tears well but do not spill. It is the first moment of profound happiness that I can recall since the hours before Mark's death. I tuck a cotton throw around Gabe's shoulders and, careful not to disturb either of them, I remove Gabe's Blundstone boots. It seems this time sleep trumps hunger.

I am resting on my side in a patch of sweet clover. My eyes are closed, dreamy. The sun warms my skin, kissing my exposed arms and legs with soft intimacy. All of my senses suddenly spring to alertness. I can hear a steady clop, clop, clop coming closer and closer. I smell an earthy, salty scent that sends my memory rushing for identification. I feel a soft blow of warm, grass-scented breath on my cheek; hair tickles my neck and bare shoulder. The taste of adrenalin shoots through my mouth as I sit up abruptly, opening my eyes.

There before me is the most exquisite horse I have ever seen. His soft brown eyes, laced with snowy white lashes, regard me with interest. He reaches forward again, blowing short, soft breaths into my tangled, twig-strewn hair. His dappled grey coat shines in the sun, his white tail swishing slowly from side to side.

Hesitantly, I reach out my hand and touch his silky forelock. Leaning forward, I blow into his nostrils. They flare, like soft, velvet bellows as he assesses my scent. He nickers and snakes his head from side to side in an invitation. Jumping to my feet, I leap effortlessly onto his strong back and, with a gentle nudge from my bare heels, he gallops through the field of clover.

Sitting in perfect harmony with the movement of the dapple, I raise my face and hands to the sky and feel the warm wind rushing through my hair. It is a moment of pure magic, a moment of delight. My body is alive. A symphony of sensation.

I awake from the dream with joy in my heart. And I am happy. I rest back on the pillow, a soft smile hovers at the edge of my lips and I think of Gabe who, at this very moment, is downstairs sleeping on my couch with Charlie cat. Tomorrow is going to be a red letter day. Reluctantly I fall back to sleep.

CHAPTER 6

...every moment is a gift...

Saturday dawns and I struggle from bed early unable to find a comfortable sleeping position. In my mind I leap out of bed ready to face the day. In reality, I creak and groan, slowly shuffling out from under the covers and heave myself upright as sharp pains stab my gut and lower back.

Peeking out the bedroom window I see that several centimetres of snow has descended from the dark November sky and thickly blanketed the landscape. Everything looks soft and beautiful, the evergreens bow down under the weight of their burden, swaying ever so gently from side to side. Flocks of Bohemian Waxwings gather in the tree tops to socialize, their sweet voices floating through the still air.

Going to the bathroom, I look in the mirror and I can't help but laugh at my scarecrow appearance; tufts of hair stick up, electric from the dry air in the cabin. My thin arms and legs lack all muscle definition and my breasts, once rounded and perky, have shrunken so that I am essentially flat-chested. Despite all this, today is bound to be one of the best days of my life. I can feel it in my soul.

I wash my face, then turn my attention to my unruly locks. I should have taken Jillie's advice and had the scraggly mess cut. With a flash of inspiration, I grab a pair of sharp scissors and, careful to keep the hair even, chop off a six inch ponytail. I run my fingers through my new do and decide it must be washed. Stepping into the shower, I shampoo and condition my shorn locks. It feels marvelous; short, clean, bouncy, fresh.

Half an hour later, I feel almost pretty for the first time in months. I dress in jeans and black turtle neck sweater that looks quiet nice with my salt and pepper hair. Downstairs, I can hear Gabe stirring and I quickly finish with my makeup, which of late, I have not been bothering to apply.

"Good morning, boys." On slippered feet, I walk over to the couch and manage to reach Gabe and Charlie before they notice me.

"Good morning, beautiful." Gabe smiles, his eyes soften, his face is relaxed after sleep. "It is lovely to be here with you, Alexi. I can't quite believe I'm actually here." He laughs then stretches and yawns loudly.

"I'm sorry I fell asleep last night before we even had a chance to catch up. I was absolutely exhausted." Gabe sits up, flings his feet over the side of the couch and stands. His garments and hair are disheveled but he looks wonderfully vital and alive.

"You look much brighter today. Did you sleep well, Alexi?" I sense a new level of perception coming from Gabe; an ability for thoughtful assessment that he did not have before. I reach for Gabe and he immediately opens his arms to me. I melt into him, reveling in his strength and warmth. Tilting my head back so that I can look at him, I smile.

"I had a wonderful sleep; I dreamed I was horseback riding in a field of clover. I have to admit that I was so excited to have you here that I could hardly fall asleep last night. I felt like a kid on Christmas

Eve." Reaching up, I smooth dark strands of grey and sun streaked hair back from Gabe's eyes.

"You have not changed a bit, Gabe. You're still a handsome devil."

"Thanks for your overly kind words, Alexi." Gabe sounds self-conscious, but he holds me tightly to his chest, his heartbeat is strong and steady.

"I didn't know you were a horseback rider," Gabe comments after a few moments silence.

"Oh, I'm not. It was just a dream." He does not comment but quirks an eyebrow skyward.

"Come, let me cook breakfast for you." Sliding reluctantly from the haven of his arms, I tug on his hand and he follows me readily to the kitchen.

"That sounds great. Speaking of horses, I'm hungry enough to eat one. But of course, now that I'm a vegetarian, that would not be appropriate."

"You're a *what?*" I squawk, astonishment raising my voice a few notes. "When did that happen? How did that happen?"

"I had an epiphany on my road trip to Alaska. One night, I was sleeping out under the stars, wondering, as I am wont to do, what I was going to do with the rest of my life. In the morning I woke up mentally refreshed; I had a sense of purpose and a clear vision for the first time in my life. I had a definitive plan and I knew exactly what I wanted to do." Gabe pauses, running a hand through his hair in a gesture so dear – so familiar to me – that I almost cried.

"I bought a journal that day and started writing down the future I envisioned for myself. I made a list of things I wanted to change; things I wanted to do. It was a very exciting time in my life. I quit cigarettes for good which was easy because I'd stopped smoking the day after you gave me what for in your studio. Do you remember that? You tore a strip off me!" Gabe is laughing at me again and it feels wonderful.

"I did not. Well, okay, maybe I did, but you deserved it." I can't help but smile at the memory. "I had a lot of kick back in those days," I recall.

"Anyway," Gabe picks up the thread of his story and carries on, "at the same time I became vegetarian, I stopped all excessive drinking, and made a plan to return home. Before heading home, I had to stop and say goodbye to the person who taught me more about life in one summer than I'd managed to learn in my entire life. I really owe you for that."

"You owe me nothing, Gabe. I'm pleased you found your path, even though it led you away from me."

"Part of my learning curve was that I realized that I'd be a real jerk to come back full of plans and try to use my *charm* to convince you to leave Mark and come to Australia with me. I did not want to be the sort of man that would use your vulnerability towards me to tear apart your marriage. That is the reason I had to say goodbye and leave without you. It was never because I didn't love you: it was because I loved you too much to ask that of you."

"It's so long ago, Gabe. We did what we needed to do to survive and go on. I have no regrets." Despite my words, I feel a tear slip down my cheek.

"Please do not cry, Alexi. I never wanted to hurt you." Gabe is at my side in an instant, holding me against his chest, comforting me.

"Don't worry about my tears, Gabe. They happen all the time these days. I don't even try to control them anymore; they are what they are. It scares the crap out of my sister Jillie. She gets very anxious and tries to get them to stop but you're not like that, Gabe. You can handle me being me, right?"

"Yes, Alexi. I can handle anything you need me to handle." He kisses my forehead, and with a gentle smile, pushes me towards the fridge. "Didn't I hear something about breakfast being made?"

"Right you are, smarty pants." I throw together the ingredients for a tofu scramble while the cast iron frying pan heats on the hot plate. I could have lit the wood burning stove, but it would have taken too long to get to temperature and Gabe might perish in the meantime.

"So why do you cry *all the time these days*?" Gabe asks as he helps me by mincing the onions and garlic. I pause, the water still running in the sink where I have been washing zucchini and red peppers. I silently debate how and when to tell Gabe about my illness. I turn the faucet off and slowly turn towards him. No point in delaying the inevitable. No point at all.

"I'm dying, Gabe. I wish I could soften or sugar coat it, but there you are. You are here because I don't have long to live and I need a home for Charlie. You are the only person I trust to take good care of him." I stop speaking and wait.

Slowly Gabe lays the knife down and places both hands on the counter; leaning, he drops his head forward. His long hair swings over his face so that I cannot see his eyes but it is easy enough to read his body. I reach for him and he automatically turns into the shelter of my arms. I can feel his body wracked with emotion as he comes to terms with my sobering disclosure. I wait, giving him time to absorb the information.

"It is cancer?" He finally asks, his face pressed against me. I nod. Yes, it is cancer.

"When did you find out?" His questions are coming fast. His breath is warm in my hair.

Pulling back slightly, I look into Gabe's sorrowful eyes. "Three years ago I was diagnosed with an inoperable tumour on the tail end of my pancreas and I was given no more than six months to live without treatment. Because of the proximity of the tumour to a major nerve bundle, I was not eligible for surgery. I was offered chemotherapy and radiation, which was estimated to extend my life by about three to six months." Gabe has remained quiet, listening intently as I share my story.

"Due to the terrible side-affects of these traditional therapies, I decided to seek alternative modalities instead and spent months traveling to both California and Mexico with my niece to receive a multitude of treatments. My oncologist told me that statistically, the chances of surviving this long after diagnosis is less than half a percent, so really, I'm one of the lucky ones." There. It was said. Now he knows the truth.

"You have not lost your optimistic attitude I see," Gabe notes quietly as he pulls himself gently from my arms and returns to the chopping board; he is understandably shaken but prepared to soldier on.

"And now? Have you been feeling worse lately?" His eyes are black with sorrow; his voice raw with emotion.

"Yes, I'm declining pretty fast these days and that is why I urgently needed to discuss Charlie with you. I think I may have used him as an excuse to communicate with you again. I noticed myself missing you lately, Gabe. Thank you for coming. It means the world to me." I tear up again. "See, here I go again. A constant waterfall."

"And where does Mark fit in to all of this? You are still together?" Gabe glances at me and I can see his eyes are guarded.

"No, but that's a story for another time. Let's get you fed first then we can catch up on everything that's happened in our lives over the last decade."

Later, after breakfast, we settle in the living room on the couch and, sitting next to each other, reminisce about the days at the Lake House.

"I see you still have the bronze hare. The hare with the stare you used to say." Gabe sounds amused as he eyes up the large, bronze Lepus statue sitting with long, floppy ears pinned back, a mutinous look in his eyes.

"Yes, the stare only a hare will dare." I laugh. And it feels good. "I couldn't possibly have left him behind. He was the first object d'art that Mark and I purchased after we bought the Lake House. I've always treasured that funky bunny."

"You brought the sideboard and the antique clock along as well, I see. I remember most of what you had collected in that lovely old house." Gabe sounds almost wistful. "I never though you'd sell that place, Alexi. I can't imagine why you did." He threads his fingers through mine and kisses the back of my hand.

"It was easy to sell it when the time was right. Maybe I'd better bring you up to date on how it happened that I'm living here now. It's a long tale; are you certain you're ready to hear it?" Gabe nods his consent.

"I want to know everything. Every detail."

So it is that I begin to gently unravel the story of how the I that Gabe used to know became the me that I am now.

"One year to the day after you left Kalsson for Australia, I walked to the middle of the bridge after work and made an important decision. I took the necklace that you had given me and I threw it out into the dark water." Gabe looks shocked but says nothing.

"For one solid year I had been stuck in the past unable and unwilling to move forward with my life. I had ended up in no man's land without a compass; the way forward was obscured by constant yearning for the past. I felt that my life was at the lowest point possible; that things could not possibly get any worse, but I was young and naïve back then."

"You did not seem naïve to me," Gabe interjects. I give him a cheerless smile at his comment and continue on.

"I shut Mark out emotionally and physically to the point where he had started to sleep in the guestroom and worked late almost every night. I gradually became aware that if I did not make a choice, I'd lose Mark through attrition. He had stopped trying to figure out what was wrong with me and right on the heels of that would come not caring about me. So, I finally made a choice and I threw away my only memento of you. I had to give my heart back to Mark and that meant I could not keep holding on to my love for you."

"I can't believe you tossed that remarkable necklace away. It was so beautiful." Gabe seems confused.

"I had to, Gabe. I had to let you go, so that night, after I walked home from the bridge, I opened myself up to Mark again and asked for his forgiveness. I told him about you. About how I had fallen in love without any intention of doing so and how it had taken me time to regain my equilibrium. I apologized for being unfair to him while I went through that difficult process and he accepted me back into his heart. I came incredibly close to losing him forever." I struggle for a moment, remembering the emotional turmoil we had lived through.

"It was difficult period of adjustment for both of us, but little by little we regained what we had lost in the marriage and after a time, it felt as if our bond had grown stronger because of what had happened."

"He must have loved you very much, Alexi. And he must have been very sure of your love for him. What happened then?" He asks after a brief pause.

"I decided to put aside my own desires and help Mark realize his dream of building an off the grid house. We drew up a five year plan that would see us design, build, and move into a self-sustaining, environmentally friendly green home on a small farm."

"That must have pleased Mark," Gabe comments.

"It did. You have no idea how excited he was about the project. It meant selling the Lake House, but with a five year plan in mind, it gave me time to get used to the idea and to become emotionally involved with the *green* home. We gathered ideas, decided where we wanted to build, designed the perfect house and purchased fifteen hectares of property twenty minutes outside of town. We were one year away from completing our project when Mark was..." My throat tightens, as it always does when I say the words "... killed in an accident."

I hear Gabe draw in a sharp breath and his eyes darken with emotion but he does not speak. His hand tightens on mine, support-ing me as I carry on.

"It happened on the evening of our twenty-third anniversary. He was struck by a car operated by an intoxicated driver. Mark died instantly. What followed was years of struggle. I struggled to stay alive...to find a *reason* to stay alive. I took time off work and with the help of my family and a good therapist, I concentrated on reviving my desire to remain. For the first few years it was unbearably difficult and I was not sure I could make it..." Gabe pulls me close and presses a kiss to my temple as my voice clogs with emotion and fades away.

"We can stop here if you want, Alexi. I know this cannot be easy." I shake my head.

"No, I'm okay. Slowly, day by day, I got stronger," I continue, finding my voice again. "Light started filtering into my life here and there and I could see potential in being earthbound for a while longer. I started painting again and found that grief had added a deep layer of meaning and maturity to my work that was strangely obvious on canvas."

"That completely makes sense to me," Gabe says as he continues to hold me in his arms, stroking my hair.

"My paintings had already become quite popular in the year or two after you went back home, but when I started to paint again after Mark's death, I could hardly keep up with the demand. It felt good. It gave me a focus and the business aspect drew me back to society, back to social interactions. I was making very good money from my painting and decide to reduce my hours at the clinic to part-time so I could focus more on painting."

"That was brave of you, especially since you so enjoyed your job at the clinic."

"Not so much brave as necessary. I needed to paint to cope. It's as simple as that. Anyway, it was during these years that the lawsuit I laid against the driver that had killed Mark raged on and on in court. Jillie and my parents were staunch and stoic in their efforts to bring the driver to accountability. It took over three years, but we finally won the battle."

"You must have had very good legal advice," he observes. "Those types of cases can be tricky to win."

"I did and it was tricky, but we won, nonetheless," I pause before taking a deep breath and continuing.

"My life had, after years of difficulty, settled into a calm and even enjoyable pattern of painting in the studio at the Lake House, attending gallery openings and unveilings, publishing a coffee table book of my most acclaimed works, and in general finding some purpose in my life when once again, my life took an unbelievable turn." I reflect for a few moments, then carry on.

"My pancreatic cancer diagnosis was shocking. I did not fit a single risk factor for this disease: older, male, African-American, obese, diabetic. I was so far removed from this group that it took some time to diagnose my vague symptoms of mild stomach cramps and weight loss. By the time I was diagnosed, the tumour was large and impossibly placed for surgery. This cancer has a mortality rate of ninety-six percent in twelve months. I was deemed terminal."

"My God, Alexi. I wish I had known. You should have told me; I would have come in an instant." Tears shimmer in his eyes.

"No, Gabe. This was my battle to fight. I couldn't ask you to fight it for me." I rub my icy fingers across the back of his hands and marvel at how strong and warm they feel.

"I packed my bags and with Jillie's daughter Amanda in tow, I did a circuit of alternative treatment clinics in California and Mexico. Amanda, a naturopathic doctor with a fledgling practice in Montreal, assured me that these clinics were world leaders in alternative care."

I pull my legs up under me on the couch and place a cushion against the small of my back trying to relieve the pain that constantly riddles my bones.

"I had detox treatments, I.V. vitamin C, vitamin D17 injections, stress and nausea reduction through visualization, yoga, meditation, and a mountain of herbal and Ayurvedic concoctions. When I returned home, I felt good. Better than I expected actually. So I decided to resume the plans that Mark and I had almost made a reality."

"You felt you owed that to Mark?" Gabe queries.

"Yes and no. I didn't *owe* it to him, but I *wanted* to do it for us. I sold the almost completed *green* house and acreage we had bought years before and purchased this place instead. It is smaller and closer to town, which suited me better."

"You did not worry about living out here all alone?" Gabe wonders.

"Yes, at first I did, then I got used to it. Once I took ownership, I hired a contractor to take this place, this one hundred year old Doukhobor log cabin, and make it energy efficient. The renovation crew re-insulated the house, installed solar hot water, photovoltaics, battery banks, instant hot water, rain catchment and cistern systems, and high efficiency appliances. The cabin already had a wood burning cook stove and fireplaces so all I had to do was remember how to cook on one. By the time it was done, this little cabin was running on solar power and had enough kilowatts left over to sell back to the grid."

"What a big project, Alexi. It was gutsy to take it on all alone." There is respect and awe in Gabe's voice

"I felt Mark with me every step of the way. He would have been so pleased with how it all turned out. And I love it. It may have been his dream initially, but it has been an exceptional experience for me from beginning to end."

"You must have been so proud of yourself to manage all that and at the same time take good care of your health." I smile at Gabe.

"Yes, it was an exciting time of my life, as strange as that might sound. That first spring on the farm, I hired an arborist who showed me how to prune the old, scraggly fruit trees to encourage production again and I spent a fortune bringing in loads of high quality soil for my vegetable garden. By my second year on the farm, I had such a bountiful harvest that I could share it with friends and family. I attribute my statistically improbable extra years of life to the fact that I have been nourishing not just my body but my soul as well."

"Nourishing your soul...I know what that means now, Alexi." Gabe's words are spoken slowly, quietly.

"I've learned to live in the moment, for the moment. Living without a future makes you redefine every single aspect of your life, Gabe. And there at the forefront of it all, shining bright like the sun, is gratitude. Gratitude for each hour, each day, each season. Every moment is a gift and I am grateful."

Gabe, who has been quietly listening to me while still holding my hand, now draws me into his chest, my head tucked under his chin as he rubs his hands up and down my arms.

"You never cease to amaze me," he whispers, his heart pounding against my ear. I tilt my head back and kiss the prickly edge of the angle of his jaw. "I am profoundly saddened by your loss, Alexi. Although I never met him, I know Mark was a good man and that he loved you very much indeed. He would have been proud of all that you've accomplished since his death."

We sit quietly, both reeling, me from the telling and Gabe from the hearing of the events that lead to my current situation. After a few moments I say, "Now that you've heard every detail of my past decade, it's your turn to tell me all about yours."

Gabe groans. "I knew you'd want to hear the nitty-gritty details." Prevaricating, he suggests, "Shall we go stretch our legs and have a look around the property first?"

"Sure. I'd love to show you the place. I must say, however, that Sunnymede is not at her most picturesque in late November. Come, you can judge for yourself."

We gather our coats, boots, and essential outdoor gear and stroll around the property as I point out the areas of interest, like the photovoltaic panels on the roof. Gabe is particularly interested in the well that supplies the water to the house. A small solar array stores energy in a battery which runs a DC pump that then pumps water from the well into a five thousand gallon underground holding tank. The tank, placed up the hill from the house, uses gravity to feed the house with sufficient water pressure to meet my requirements. The system, once installed, is low maintenance and entirely free.

"But what about those long winter months when you don't get any sun?" Gabe inquires.

"Then I use the water stored in the tank. Once the sky is clear again, the pump starts again and refills the tank. The new photovoltaic technology has increased light sensitivity and does not require direct sun to work well. Their efficiency has vastly improved over the last few years, so the battery pack is almost constantly being charged."

I show Gabe the charge light on the battery pack to demonstrate how, even on a high cloud day like today, the system is still working.

"That's great. I'm thinking how such a system might work for me in Australia. My farm is flat, but I get constant sun, so perhaps with a larger solar array and a larger pump, I could create the pressure that I need to feed the house." Gabe is deep in thought as he carefully scrutinizes the control panel in the well-house.

"You have a farm?" I ask, my teeth chattering together as the cold sneaks its way through the dense layers of clothing and nestles in my bones.

"My God, Alexi. You're lips are blue," Gabe exclaims as he glances in my direction. Peeling off his coat he drapes it around my drooping shoulders.

"You'll get cold..." I begin to protest.

"Don't you say a single word," Gabe snaps, dragging me by the hand towards the house. "You should have told me that you were freezing." I smile weakly because, even though his gaze is dark and foreboding, it is pure *Gabe*. And it is heavenly to have him here to care for me.

"I'm sorry," I say, the silly smile still on my frigid lips. My legs, not used to Gabe's quick pace, give way and I sink to my knees in the powdery snow. My breath wheezes in and out of my lungs in painful gasps and I place the back of my gloved hand against my mouth as bile rises in my throat. Squeezing my eyes shut, I use a visualization method I learned to help overcome my nausea.

I think of an army of tiny workers closing a solid metal gate at the base of my throat forcefully blocking the path from my stomach. I concentrate on the details; the feeling of the workers helping me, the strength of the gate, the solidness of the blockade.Slowly, the nausea subsides.

I lower my hand from my face and notice that Gabe has crouched beside me in the snow and has quietly waited while I battled within. His self-directed anger has disappeared, his eyes softening as he takes my hand.

"Come, beautiful. Let's get you back inside. I'll make you a nice cup of tea." Leaning heavily on Gabe, I hold his arm as we move slowly to the house while every part of my body protests.

Once inside, I go to the medicine cabinet in the powder room and take a painkiller. I generally do not resort to painkillers preferring instead to use acupuncture but my acupuncturist is away this week on holiday and I do not have another session booked for a few days. When I return to the kitchen, Gabe is making a pot of tea.

"I'm going to lie down for a few minutes, Gabe."

"That sounds like a good idea. I'll bring you a cup of tea when it's brewed."

Stretching out on the couch, I pull the cotton throw around my shoulders and tuck a pillow against the small of my back hoping to warm up my chilly body. I feel better as my eyelids drop over my dry, weary eyes and that is my last coherent thought as I drift off to sleep.

The smell of burning pitch and the sound of a crackling fire wakes me up and I am aware of being cozy and warm. Stretching my arms and legs, I struggle to an upright position. Gabe, sitting in the armchair beside the fireplace with Charlie on his lap, is looking at my book: *The Essential Hollingberry Collection*. They look good; the two of them together, quietly reading. I glance at the clock; it chimes six times. I have been asleep for hours.

Gabe lowers the book and smiles at me.

"You looked all done in, Alexi. I thought you'd feel better after a good rest. Are you warm now?"

"Oh, yes. That fire warmed me right up." I notice another blanket has been added on top of the throw while I slept. "Thank you for looking after me, Gabe."

"My pleasure." Putting the book aside, Gabe places a pissed off pussy on the floor and bending down, he stokes the fire, adding several split logs to the glowing embers.

"I've heated up a casserole I found in the freezer. Would you like some?" He asks as he straightens away from the fireplace.

"Amazingly enough, I do feel hungry," I respond. "Jillie will be coming by in about half an hour; why don't we wait and invite her to join us for dinner?"

"Sure, I'd love to finally meet her. I'll set the table and have everything ready for when she get here." Gabe picks Charlie up and drops him on my lap.

"Here, Charlie. Keep your mom company," he says, then strolls to the kitchen singing a Robbie Robertson tune in a deep baritone. Some things never change.

Putting Charlie down, I wander over to the window and pressing my nose against the cold pane, peer out into the darkening night. The morning's snow looks crisp in the clear of the night sky, the moon illuminates the trees just enough for me to see that the eagle has landed again on a low branch of the spruce tree at the edge of the woods, beyond the garden. He looks majestic against the snow-ladened conifers and despite the distance and the darkness, I can feel the piercing gaze of his yellow eyes.

"I can't believe he is here," I whisper to myself excitedly.

"Who's here?" Gabe asks from beside me. I shriek.

"Shit, Gabe! You scared me."

Who's here?" Gabe asks again, looking into the night with me.

"You see that bald eagle over there? He's been flying by or landing on that branch almost every day for about a week now." I explain.

"How do you know he's a he?" Gabe asks.

"I know here," I say, placing a loose fist on my abdomen.

"He certainly is magnificent." Gabe acknowledges.

As if he is aware that he has an audience, the eagle spreads his wings and with might and grace, pushes off the limb into the November night sky.

"Wow, that was a treat," I exclaim as I pull the heavy drapes over the cold windowpane.

"You must be eager for a shower, Gabe," I say as I realize he must feel grubby from his long trip. "Go upstairs and use my bathroom, if you want. There are clean towels in the drawer beside the sink."

"I won't be more than ten minutes," he calls over his shoulder, already halfway up the stairs.

When he returns, all freshly shaven and showered, I go myself to wash up before dinner.

By the time the doorbell rings, I have managed to subdue my hair, which had gone flat on one side as a result of my nap and I have reapplied blusher and lip colour so I won't scare the crap out of Jillie. Downstairs, I can hear Gabe opening the door and introducing himself to Jillie.

I make my way down and greet Jillie with a hug.

"Hi, honey," she says, then whispers in my ear, "Who is this gorgeous guy?" I smile and pull away from her embrace.

"Have you two introduced yourselves? Gabe, this is my younger sister, Jillie. Jillie, this is Gabe, a dear friend of mine visiting from Australia." I can tell from Jillie's face that she is gobsmacked as Mark used to say.

"I don't recall hearing you talk about a friend coming from Australia," she states, looking at me with an arched and inquiring brow inherited from our mother.

"It was a last minute sort of trip," Gabe answers for me, trying to quell Jillie's curiosity.

"Well, that all seems rather odd to me." Jillie removes her coat and gloves and I place them in the hall closet.

"Come in and have a seat. We held dinner for you; I hope you haven't eaten yet."

"I'm starving. We didn't have time for lunch today so a hot meal sounds wonderful."

"Gabe's heated up one of the casseroles you left for me, Jillie. Have a seat and we'll get it on the table right away." I help Gabe get the meal ready by tossing the salad with oil and vinegar dressing while he serves the casserole.

Once seated, we begin the meal and conversation is halting and somewhat stilted.

"Are you staying for long, Gabe?" Jillie asks as she pauses to sip the white wine Gabe has poured for her.

"I'm not sure yet. I'll stay as long as Alexi needs me."

Jillie darts a glance in my direction and despite myself, I feel annoyed with her for peppering Gabe with questions. Okay, maybe *peppering* is too strong a word; but why can't she just mind her own business?

Trying to sidetrack her, I ask about my niece, Amanda.

"She'll be here on Monday for your fiftieth birthday party. I told you that last week, Alexi. Don't you remember?" Jillie's tone is lightly scolding, as if I was a naughty or dim-witted child.

"Um...yes, now that you mention it, I do recall." Gabe glances at me with a questioning look but makes no comment. He is no doubt unaware that my birthday is in a few days.

"I hope you're not still trying to get out of the party I've planned for you," Jillie says, helping herself to more casserole and another dinner roll.

"Jillie, you know how I feel about that," I rebut, trying not to let an edge sharpen my reply.

"How *do* you feel about it?" Gabe queries, his voice deep and concerned.

"I love that Jillie has worked so hard to get the family and my friends together for my birthday, but honestly, I don't know if I'll have the stamina to participate," I turn pleading eyes to Jillie, willing her to understand my concern.

"You know how it goes with me, Jillie. Some days it's all I can do to get out of bed. Some days my back aches or I have nausea. I just don't want to disappoint everybody by turning up green around the gills."

"You'll only disappoint us if you refuse to come," she replies smartly finishing her glass of wine in a gulp.

"You should listen to your sister, Jillie. She's trying very hard to tell you politely that she can't cope with a party. You should respect her wishes." Gabe's voice sounds respectful but firm.

"*Really?*" Jillie gives Gabe her *I'm-not-impressed* stare. "And how do you know what Alexi can cope with? I have never seen you around before yet suddenly you're an expert on what she needs?" Jillie is pissed off and pushes back from the table abruptly. "I've got to get home. I have to work very early tomorrow."

"Jillie," I call, trying to catch her before she reaches the door. "Don't be angry, Jillie. I'll do my best to be ready to party on Monday." She pauses long enough to kiss me on the cheek and mumble a goodbye before she rushes from the house.

"Well, I though that went really well," I say, laughing facetiously. I shake my head in disbelief as I gather up the dinner plates.

"What the hell is wrong with her? Does she not realize that you are dying?" Gabe asks incredulously.

"She knows. It's very difficult for her. She tries hard to help me; does so much for me. Deep down she is angry...afraid...and terribly sad. Until she contends with these emotions, my illness is like a red cape to a charging bull. She runs at it full tilt because she can't accept that it's going to win and that I'm going to die."

"Some support that is," Gabe snorts with derision.

"Don't, Gabe. She's doing the best she can and I am thankful that she comes every day to try and ease my suffering, despite the fact that she truly believes that I should be in palliative care now." I circle the table and, taking Gabe by the hand, I pull him in for a hug.

"Besides, everything is going to be just fine now that you're here." Gabe tightens his hold on me and kisses my temple.

"I can't stand to see you hurting, Alexi. You're so fragile; so precious. All I want to do is protect you from any more pain."

"I wish I could say not to worry and that I'm tough as old nails, but this ancient body of mine is tired out. It's been a hell of a ride, Gabe, a helluva ride..."

God damn it. Tears are rising, clogging my throat, my eyes. Big breath in. Big breath out. In...out. The tears recede. I clear my throat and step out of Gabe's arms, needing to compose myself.

Refreshing my smile, I take Gabe's hand in mine.

"Let's see what we can find for dessert." In the kitchen I look through the cupboards until I find my prized applesauce. "Would you like some of this on soy yogurt?" I brandish the jar of golden sauce.

"Absolutely." I serve the creamy white yogurt with an ample portion of sauce and Gabe accepts the bowl from me eagerly.

"Did you grow the apples for this yourself, Alexi?" Gabe asks.

"I sure did. They're an heirloom variety called Northern Spy and they hail from New York. It is a versatile apple that is good fresh, cooked, dried, and canned."

"Very tasty."

"I know it's late, but tell me about you're farm, Gabe. Are you growing crops? How many hectares do you have?"

"It's thirty-five hectares and there is a vegetable garden, but no other crops. It's actually an animal rescue sanctuary."

"Oh, Gabe! That's fabulous. I'm so proud of you. Just imagine all those times you told me you didn't know what to do with your life." I reach across the table and touch his hand. "I'm just so pleased for you. How did you go from a nomadic gypsy on a motorbike to an animal rescuer? That's gotta be a good story."

Gabe launches into the details as he finishes the bowl of applesauce.

"When I got back to Sydney, I went straight to my townhouse and listed it on the market. Then I went home for a few weeks to stay with my parents."

"They must have been thrilled to see you after three years abroad," I exclaim.

"Oh, yes. They both cried when I arrived at their front door unannounced. You forget how worried parents get about their fully grown offspring."

"And who can blame them?" I question.

"Anyway, I told them about this beautiful and wise woman I had met in the West Kootenays. I told them that knowing her had changed me and that I was ready to start doing something useful with my life."

"No doubt they were very excited to see you interested in life again," I murmur, leaning back in the dinning room chair as as I sip the green tea Gabe made after dinner.

"Well, first I had to explain why they would not be meeting this wonderful person. I told them that she was married and had given her heart to someone else a long time ago. They were sad for me because I could not be with you, but they understood that I had come away with valuable life lessons that I was ready to implement."

We clear the table and wash the few dishes from the tea and dessert before moving to the couch where, in front of a roaring fire, Gabe continues.

"After my stay with my parents, I began to look for an acreage that would suit my needs. I also enrolled in a one-year, full-time veterinary technician course. During that year, lots happened.

First, I found and purchased an old, dilapidated farm not far from my parents' vineyard. Then, from the local teens at risk program, I hired and trained six kids to fence, paint, mow, plumb, and repair. I hired a local handyman to oversee the kids while I attended school during the day. The class was small, with only twelve students and the pace was fast. I learned a lot about animals and animal care in a very short period of time. My grey matter was smarting from all that studying."

I laugh, imagining him trying to keep up with a class full of young, eager students.

"I met Lauren in class and we became study partners. She was also a mature student trying to gain skills to make her employable."

"Lauren?" I query with quiet interest.

"Lauren had just left an abusive marriage of ten years. She was a single mother and needed to be able to support herself and her three year old daughter Jasmine."

"You like her?" I can tell that he does so my question is rhetorical. He nods anyway.

"She's smart, funny, a good mother, and the hardest worker I've ever seen." His eyes are bright with emotion as he describes her. I, despite myself, feel a stab of envy. "She started to help me on weekends on the farm, doing everything from the bookkeeping, to ordering supplies, to unloading feed shipments. Lauren would bring Jasmine along, who happened to be one of the sweetest little kids I'd ever seen."

I snort. "I didn't have you pegged as a guy who'd go bananas over a kid," I say feeling the uncomfortable and jagged edge of jealousy slide into my heart.

"Jasmine made me go bananas over her. She was a bundle of crazy energy and pure joy." He is smiling as he recollects the days when Jasmine was a toddler.

I can feel a burn in my chest and for once it's not from the pancreatic cancer. No, this burn is even more deadly than that. It is the burn of hatred and jealousy. Hating that, while my life got burdened with one blow after another, Gabe's life bloomed like a beautiful rose.

"I guess they were your first rescue case," I snap, the words tasting poisonous as they leave my mouth. Gabe pulls sharply away from me, putting distance between us on the couch. A slash of colour forms on his cheeks.

"That's rude and uncalled for. Never once has Lauren asked for my help. She was the top student in our class and I offered her a job immediately upon graduation. I was lucky she accepted the offer. She works hard for every penny she makes and Lauren never fails Jasmine in any way; she deserves kudos for all she's accomplished in life." Gabe's voice has a hard edge to it that I have never heard before.

"Of course she accepted the job: rich, handsome, single boss. What did she have to lose?" My tone is sarcastic despite myself.

I squeeze my eyes shut, blocking out the image of Gabe's angry face. I'm being a total shit and I can't seem to stop myself. Clearing my throat, I get to my feet and walk gingerly to the stairs.

"I'm not feeling well; I'm going to go up to bed." Slowly, with the use of the railing, I mount the stairs one tread at a time. I flop face down on the bed and let the tears flow in a silent torrent. Some time later, I fall into an exhausted sleep, the salty tracks of my tears dried upon my pale, smooth skin.

I feel arms wrap around me; a warm body presses up behind me, immediately banishing the chill from my bones. I think of Mark, how he used to spoon me during the long, cold nights of winter. But Mark is dead. It is Gabe who is offering comfort now. Too embarrassed to face him, I mumble an apology for my terrible behavior into my pillow.

"Shh..." He tucks strands of loose hair behind my ear and leans over my shoulder to kiss my salty cheek. "We all say things we regret, Alexi. If you knew Lauren, you would not say such things about her."

Turning in the circle of his arms, I press my face into his neck.

"I am truly sorry, Gabe. Sometimes this life of mine makes me struggle to stay centered. You know? To not be pulled off track by despair. Sorrow. Jealousy. Anger. Grief. All those emotions that don't really help me but that visit me from time to time just the same. I try to remain my optimistic self as life deals me one big blow after another, and honestly, most days I am very positive...but every now and again I am bamboozled by my own circumstances. I had no right to lash out with an intent to hurt someone you care about and for that I am extremely sorry. So much for being a woman of beauty and wisdom." I pause, then say with a half-hearted smile, "More like a woman of sour grapes and lemons."

Gabe's lips quirk upward in a faint smile at my dismal attempt at humour. Not a substantial enough smile to reveal the dimple, but a smile just the same. He strokes my hair gently and kisses my cheek.

"Let's not speak of it again, Alexi. I understand and accept your apology. Thank you for that."

We fall silent in each other arms for a few minutes, cuddling close to each other in body and spirit.

"I'd like to hear more about your farm, Gabe. I promise not to be snotty."

"Shush. Enough about that. What do you want to know?" He pulls back a little from me so that he can spread a comforter up over our legs, then, leaning on his elbow, a pillow under his head, he gives me an assessing glance.

"Everything."

"It's not getting too late? I don't want to wear you out."

"No, I'm wide awake now. I want to hear it all."

"Okay, then." Rolling onto his back, he nestles clasped hands behind his head and begins talking.

"Once Lauren and I graduated from the vet tech program, we started working on the farm, preparing to receive our first animals. The boys did a wonderful job whipping the barn, corrals, and fences into shape. The three-bedroom house had been fully renovated by a contracting company while I was at school and was finally ready for occupancy. A small cottage beside the barn had been updated as well and Lauren and Jasmine moved in so that they might avoid paying high rent in the city and eliminate commuting expenses at the same time. Since Lauren's ex-husband had left her virtually bankrupt, this arrangement worked well for both of us."

"How long until you got your first rescue?"

"One week after settling into our new homes, we received word that a pig had fallen off a slaughterhouse transportation truck and had been spotted wandering, wounded and bleeding, along the streets of suburban Sydney. We hitched the trailer to the truck and set out, the three musketeers, ready for an adventure. It was a hot, dusty day and that pig was not keen to be loaded on the trailer. It took hours of dogged work to finally get her up the ramp and safely in the trailer.

Once we got back to the sanctuary, Pinky, as Jasmine named her, refused to disembark. So she spent her first night at the farm in the trailer on a pile of straw, apparently deciding she liked the trailer after all. We treated her road burns as best we could, gave her food and water, and left her to decide on her own when she wanted to come down the ramp and into her new pen."

I chuckle at his story, imaging how proud they must have been to have gotten Pinky successfully home after such a struggle.

"And then? Did the calls start coming fast after that?"

"We were getting two to three calls a week and soon we had dogs, cats, chickens, another pig, goats, and a pony. It was completely daunting those first few months. I'd asked two of the teens at risk to stay and work for me full-time and they agreed. A government program paid part of their wages and we had been granted..." I cut in sharply.

"You said *we* not *I*," I exclaim in startled wonder.

"So I did." He smiles at me and kisses the end of my nose. "We not I." He rolls the words on his tongue like he is tasting honey.

"Sorry, I interrupted."

Gabe carries on from where I had butted in.

"*We* were granted charity status which gave us a number of marvelous opportunities financially and in gaining the trust of the community. I spent many days taking local vets for lunch and explaining our vision. We toured schools and set up booths at the markets making the public aware of our services. We also started a fund-raising campaign because I could see that my finances would be in shambles after just a few years if I didn't stop the gush of cash flowing into the sanctuary. Lauren has a great head for business, as it turns out, and she masterminded several fundraisers that landed us some substantial donors."

"She sounds very talented." This time I can comment without the green haze of jealousy clouding my words.

"She is. I could never have made it this far with the sanctuary without her at my side."

"It seems to me like it's about time you march her down the aisle and put a ring on her finger." I smile, but I am saddened by the idea; sad that our chapter is coming to an ending. I am happy for Gabe however, despite my own sense of loss. He deserves a person like

Lauren; someone to share his dreams, his excitement, his sense of accomplishment, his love.

"It's been almost ten years now that we've worked side by side and I care for her deeply, but I have never been able to get over my love for the blue-eyed lady of the Lake House." His tone is velvet-soft – a whisper, really. "I have never stopped loving you, Alexi. My body and mind moved on but my heart was left behind with you. I didn't want to *move on* in that regard. One fierce love in a lifetime seems like enough to me." Gabe rubs his fingertips over the back of my frail, faintly purple hand where it lies on the coverlet between us.

"Don't give up on an opportunity for love because of me, Gabe. You deserve more than a brief summer of unfulfilled love. If you open your heart to Lauren, you might find a love so amazing that you would wonder why you had never noticed it before. Does she love you?" I can't imagine why she wouldn't.

"I think so, but I never encouraged romance. She knows I'm still in love with you..."

"It must be breaking her heart to know you've come to see me," I say, tears welling up as I imagine her pain. "You must call her and tell her that I'm dying and that this is the only reason why you came to see me."

"Is it? Is it the only reason, Alexi? You don't have feelings for me anymore?" Gabe's questions are filled with anguish.

"Of course I still have feelings for you, Gabe, but I'm dying. There is no time left for us. You have a full life still ahead of you. Fill it with love; real, immediate, physical love. Don't you want that in your life?" I touch his face, wanting more than anything for him to be happy.

"I do, but I always dreamed that it would be with you." Gabe closes his eyes, a weary expression slips across his face. "When your letter arrived at my parents' address, they called me right away. I couldn't believe it when you asked me for help. I hoped that...I don't know exactly what, but that somehow we'd be together at last." He sounds drained; defeated.

"We are together, but not like that and not for long. I am sorry, Gabe." I run my hand down the plane of his face, my thumb coming to rest on his full lower lip. Leaning forward, I kiss the edge of his mouth.

"I don't regret us for a single second, Gabe." I whisper. "You taught me that it is possible to love deeply and fully. Twice. Before you, I never would have believed that such a notion was possible."

"I have no regrets either, Alexi. How could I regret the best moments of my life?" Of their own accord, our bodies come together; clinging, pressing, moulding.

We kiss, lips and legs entwine, our arms holding tight to one another. The flame of passion is still there between us raging, like it always had, but I know it is time to bank that fire; time to let it dwindle down to nothing more than embers. Pulling back a fraction, I ease away from Gabe emotionally while remaining in his embrace.

Steering for less treacherous ground, I ask, "What are your plans for the farm now, Gabriel?"

Loosening his arms from around my body, Gabe rolls onto his back and rubs his fingertips slowly across his eyelids. He does not speak for a few moments, his eyes are black, bleak in the dim light of the bedroom. I can see him struggling to accept the withdrawal of my physical love; his gradual coming to terms with the ending of a long held dream.

Clearing his throat, he says gruffly, "About a year ago I was given five emaciated horses that had been left beaten and neglected in a farmer's field. It took some doing, but we got them to trust humans again, fattened them up and started training them for pleasure riding.

It turns out I'm rather good with horses." He smiles, his mood brightening just slightly as he speaks of the horses.

"It wasn't more than a year before they were mentally and physically ready for adoption, which incidentally, was not my original plan. However, it dawned on me that if I could train these wild, beaten or abandoned horses, and I could find good homes for them, then I could take in more horses to be rehabilitated. I keep the calm and quiet horses and use them for working with handicapped kids. We have a gal, Janice, who has special training in therapeutic riding and together we organize sessions at the sanctuary." Gabe seems happy to distract himself by talking about the ranch and I am excited to hear every detail. I snuggle up against his side as he continues.

"The kids love it. Jasmine helps teach all the basics of grooming, I teach tack care and tacking up, and Janice actually teaches the riding lessons. My dream now is to build a covered riding arena and offer a range of riding opportunities for kids with handicaps. The government has helped some with funding, but it's a huge capital outlay, so we've been focusing on fundraising." I am awed by Gabe's passion yet I can't help but remember that he'd always had fire in his soul.

"I think I can help you with the arena, Gabe." I slip out of his arms, slowly get off the bed and open the top drawer of my antique dresser. I pull an envelope from the drawer, mindlessly running my fingertips over the thick watermarked paper.

"How so?" Gabe asks, his interest piqued.

"Here. Look at this." I slide a single, heavy sheet of paper from the envelope and pass it to Gabe.

"It looks like money in a bank account. Lots of money. What does this have to do with me? With the arena?" Gabriel hands the paper back to me.

I sit on the edge of the bed and take his hand in mine. "I'm going to gift it to you. I'll sign it over to you tomorrow. I'll get Al to drop by early in the morning so I can sign the necessary documents and transfer the funds to your charity." I am so thrilled with the idea that my words jump and tumble over each other in an effort to leave my mouth.

"You can't give away your life's savings just like that, Alexi. What will your family say?" I laugh at his look of astonishment.

"First, it's not my life's saving. My lawyer sued the intoxicated driver who killed Mark and we won. This is that settlement. I want you to have it for your project. You are doing valuable work, Gabe. I've waited a long time to find a suitable use for that money and I know Mark would approve. Secondly, my family is well looked after in my will, so don't you worry about them."

"I can't..." I cut Gabe off abruptly.

"Yes, you can. Imagine how much it will help all those kids in need. Can you really afford to say no to them?" My argument is persuasive and I can see Gabe rethinking his refusal. He looks over-whelmed with emotion; his Adam's apple bobs as he struggles to find a response.

"Thank you," he finally whispers.

"There's something else I'd like you to have, Gabe. I'll go get it." I slip off the bed again and shove my feet into woolly slippers.

"I can't accept any more gifts, Alexandra," he growls in a firm tone.

"You won't be able to refuse this one," I call over my shoulder gaily as I go downstairs and pull a painting out from under the stairs. It is the picture of the charred stump; in my mind, this painting has belonged to Gabe ever since the moment he laid eyes on it over ten years ago. I wipe a cobweb off the bottom edge of the frame and carry it slowly up to the bedroom.

"I want you to take this picture with you when you leave. I've always wanted to give this to you and now I can."

"It would be worth a small fortune, considering the selling price of your work these days." Gabe can't help but be drawn back into the brooding depths of the scene.

"Do not worry about the cash value. I want you to have it because you always understood it. Every now and again, when you look at it, think of me." Gabe takes the painting and leans it carefully against the edge of the bed before beckoning me into his arms.

"Thank you. I will cherish it."

"Gabe, it's well past midnight and I am barely keeping my eyes open. I'm going to call it a day. Are you okay to make up the bed on your own downstairs?"

"Poor darling. You've had a long day. Don't worry. I can get the bed ready, no probs." He kisses me on the forehead and squeezes me in a long hug before he clambers off the bed, and taking the picture with him, goes downstairs.

"Good night, Gabriel."

"See you in the morning," he responds.

CHAPTER 7

...all is as it should be...

T he last day of my forty-ninth year and the first day of December dawns to a brilliant blue sky. The sun busily melts yesterday's snow while the tree boughs jump up in relief as globs of softened snow plop to the ground in noisy, messy piles. Birds of all colours and sizes zip from tree to tree energized by the reprieve from the blustery weather of the past few days.

Charlie had graced me with his presence and we had slept companionably together all night. I slept well; a deep, exhausted sleep that was tinged with relief. Relief that, at last, many of my loose ends are being sewn up. All that is left to do is to mentally prepare Charlie for the trip to Australia.

I already had him checked by the vet to make certain he is in good condition for long distance traveling. I purchased a large cat carrier that is regulation size for air travel and an old cotton towel lies inside the cage to help him stay warm and cozy during the flight. Several cans of his favourite food plus a small bag of kibble are already slipped into the back of the carrier, along with a bottle of Bach Flower Rescue Remedy. Charlie is accustomed to taking

Rescue Remedy for his trips to the veterinary clinic so I do not anticipate any problems with him accepting it. I have even written up a long list of feline foibles that will make the transition easier for both Gabe and Charlie. In short, Charlie is ready to depart at a moment's notice.

Stroking Charlie's dense fur, I began to talk to him about living with Gabe. And Lauren. I tell him to expect a big change in weather, but that the quality of care and love he will experience will not change at all. He stares at me with wide, wise eyes, seeming to catch my drift. A friend of mine once told me that animals fare better with big changes if we talk to them about it prior to the event. On the off chance that she was right, I continue to chat with Charlie, hoping the move will not rock his world.

Later, after my morning ablutions, I find a note downstairs on the kitchen counter:

> *Good morning, beautiful!*
> *I've gone to town on an errand. Will be back by lunch.*
> *Love you, G.*
>
> *P.S. I called Lauren and told*
> *her about your donation.*
>
> *She is very pleased and excited.*

I smile to myself as I think how such a large cash infusion will help them progress with their charity work. Now they can concentrate their energy on the facility, the animals, and the kids instead of fundraising endeavors.

Finding myself at loose ends, I decide to work on my nearly finished commission. The pink cherry blossoms on the three canvases are cheerful in the morning sun and I find myself happily painting as the morning moves towards noon.

At lunch time, like clockwork Jillie turns up on my doorstep with a basket of fresh fruits, vegetables, and homemade bread.

"Hi, Jillie." Thanking her, I take the basket and put it on the counter. "Do you have time for a coffee?" I ask.

"I'd rather have tea, Alexi. I'm all keyed up as it is." Jillie leans against the counter and rubs a weary hand across her brow. She looks tired with dark smudges under her eyes. My dying is taking its toll on her.

"Sure. I'll make a pot. Tough day at work?" I guess.

"Yeah. It's been hellishly busy, plus the new girl quit just when I had her fully trained."

"Come on, let's sit in the living room." I lead the way even though Jillie's been in my cabin a thousand times before.

"Oh, wow. I love that," Jillie admires my cherry blossom painting, commenting on the delicate use of several hues of pink.

"It's a commission for the City Hall reception area. I need to get it done before I..." I stop myself in time, "...before the grand opening next month." Jillie doesn't notice as I fumble my words.

"It's good, Alexi. I swear, you've been painting better then ever lately." Turning back to look at me, she changes the subject: "Are you ready for the party tomorrow? Amanda is very excited to see you."

"And I can't wait to see her," I return. Amanda and I correspond regularly by e-mail so she is well aware of my rapidly declining health. Because of Jillie's resistance to alternative therapy, Amanda and I decided it was best not to advertise our close association particularly as it includes regular counsel from Amanda on the latest therapies. Amanda had been my only supporter when I decided to buck the chemo-radiation system; even my parents had voiced concerns about my decision. So be it.

"Where is Gabriel? Has he swanned off to Australia already? Maybe the snow scared him away," Jillie snorts.

I pour the freshly brewed tea and serve Jillie. "Do you want a sandwich?" I ask her, not responding to her snarly comment about Gabe.

"No, but I'd kill for a cookie." I grab a few from the cookie jar and serve them on a small, hand-painted, porcelain Foley plate, a relic from the days when Mark and I would go antiquing together.

"I have it on good authority that these are the best cookies in town," I say with a smile.

"Hey, I made these." She returns my smile as she recognizes her own baking and acknowledges the compliment.

"Yep, that's how I know they're good."

"You didn't answer my question about Gabriel, by the way." She looks at me over the rim of her tea cup, one eyebrow arched. Shit. She noticed.

"He's in town running errands," I respond casually.

"I guess you'll be bringing him to the party?" Jillie asks, sounding anything but thrilled.

"I could leave him here at home, but that would seem rude after he travelled so far to see me." I remain calm, trying to control my irritation. "He won't disrupt any of your plans, Jillie. I promise." I lay my hands over hers in an effort to allay her concerns.

"Oh, God, Alexi. You're hands are freezing cold. And look how purple they are." Jillie pulls her hands abruptly away and I try not to feel affronted.

"Yes, they've been rather cold since it snowed." I tuck the offending appendages in the large patch pockets of my knitted sweater.

"Harrumph. I still say you should be in a care facility, not suck out here in the middle of nowhere. At least then you'd have a good, reliable heat source."

"Jillie, my fireplace heats the cabin perfectly well. I don't need to move to town to stay warm." I can feel my energy draining away like cold water after a bath. I was going to need to ask Jillie to leave if she didn't depart soon of her own accord.

Perhaps sensing the nature of my thoughts, Jillie grabs another cookie and takes her leave. At the door, she pauses, turns back and, with the cookie in one hand and her purse in the other, she hugs me awkwardly but a fraction longer than normal. She averts her misty eyes and rushes out the door.

"Goodbye, beloved sister." My voice is but a faint whisper that she cannot hear. Fatigued, I lean back against the door, sliding to the mat as my knees buckle. I rest my head back, my eyes hot and burning as unshed tears blur my vision.

I can feel nausea roiling in my stomach and I scramble to my knees in an effort to get to the toilet before it's too late. Slowed by exhaustion, I do not reach my destination and I vomit the tea I just drank onto the hardwood floors. It pools in an ugly, dark puddle in front of me. I am thankful that I have not eaten yet today. The retching drains me completely and I slowly collapse to the floor in an untidy heap.

Minutes later, Gabe returns home to find me on the doormat unable to gather the strength to get up.

"Let me help you, Alexi," he says tenderly scooping me into his arms and carrying me upstairs to the bathroom. "Rinse your face and mouth, then I'll help you into bed." I mutely obey him with scarcely enough reserves to do his bidding.

True to his word, Gabe tucks me in as he might Jasmine and kisses my cool forehead.

"Have a good nap, beautiful," he whispers, a sweet, sad smile on his face, his hands lingering on mine.

Waking some time later, I feel remarkably better and I ease out of bed to run a deep, hot bath. Adding a healthy dose of my favourite bubbles, I undress and step into the hot water as the Peter Gabriel song *Solsbury Hill* runs through my head. I piece together some of the lyrics from a spotty memory and begin to sing, at first with little volume, but then with gusto as I gain confidence.

"What's all the racket?" Gabe asks, tapping on the half open bathroom door before entering the room.

"Good afternoon to you, too," I retort smartly. "It's not a racket, it's a lovely song. By the way, did I invite you up here?" I ask, feeling heat rise in my cheeks. I make sure my naked body is fully covered with bubbles.

"Yes. You sent a letter inviting me to come. I have the original downstairs..." He's teasing me.

I laugh, feeling the hot water restoring my spirits.

"Sing for me," Gabe coaxes. "I never knew you liked to sing."

"I'm a terrible singer. I only sing when nobody can hear me. Besides, I don't know the words..." I trail off, running out of excuses.

"Come on, sing it for me. Pretty please?" Gabe sits on the edge of the tub and I feel sure my face must be beet-red by now. I can't refuse his sad, puppy dog eyes.

"Fine. It goes something like this," I acquiesce then bravely start to sing. Gabe joins in, our voices twinning together, the deep and the soft. The lyrics come easier as we sing and together we sound beautiful.

"I like that song. And you sing it very well." A gentle smile plays on his lips. "Very well, indeed."

"Well, thanks. You sounded pretty good yourself. Now you had better vacate the bathroom so that I can get out of this water before I turn into a prune."

"A very lovely prune, however," Gabe jokes as he takes his leave.

Popping his head back around the edge of the door he says, "By the way, this evening you'll want to dress up in something special because I have a real treat planned for you. You'll need to stay up here for about an hour just before dinner time." He has a cheeky grin and a light dances in his eyes. "In the meantime, would you like a cup of soup?"

"Screw the soup. I want to know what surprise you have planned. Whatever could it be?" I'm full of curiosity now. I can't begin to imagine what he's been planning.

"You'll have to wait and find out later," he calls cheerily over his shoulder as he goes back down the stairs.

Before I have a chance to get dressed, Gabe calls to me from the living room, "Alexi, Al's here to see you." I put on my robe and go downstairs to sign the papers that Al, the family lawyer, has drawn up in preparation for the transfer of the funds to Gabe's charity. When I had called him just before Jillie's visit, he'd been more than happy to stop by today with the documents. In addition to being our family's solicitor for years, he is also my father's best friend.

"Al, it's great to see you. Thank you for coming on such short notice. I just got out of the tub so I apologize for my attire." I tighten the robe's belt around my waist.

"Think nothing of it, my dear. It's a pleasure for me to help you in any way that I can." Al, well past retirement age, has enough appetite for life to still enjoying working three days a week. At six foot three, he is an imposing man both in size and personality, and my family loves him not only for his frank conversation but for his infectious laugh as well.

"Do you have time for tea?" I ask, knowing full well that Al *always* has time to sit and shoot the breeze with a Wainwright over a cuppa.

"That'd be lovely, my dear girl." I hang his jacket in the closet and gesture down the hall.

"Please take a seat in the living room, Al. I'll get the kettle on, then we can sign those forms."

Gabe is in the kitchen warming the soup on the wood stove which he has successfully started from a box of newspapers and dry kindling stored beside the stack of chopped wood.

"I'm going to make tea for Al. Do you want to join us, Gabe?"

"Sure. We can eat this later." Gabe pushes the pan to the cooler back edge of the cast iron stovetop where it can stay warm without overheating.

"Let me make the tea, Alexi. You go socialize with Al." I go up on my tiptoes so that I can kiss Gabe's smooth cheek.

"Thank you, Gabe."

An hour later, Al leaves, having regaled us with stories of past legal anomalies that always seem to intrigue him. A copy of the signed document lies on the coffee table and I give it to Gabe.

"You should keep these for your records," I say, pressing the sheets of paper into his hands.

"That's a good idea," he responds, placing them in his travel bag that has found a temporary home beside the couch.

"Now, are you ready for a bit of very late lunch?" Gabe asks as his stomach growls in hunger.

"Absolutely. Let's eat."

When we have finished lunch, I set up my easel and resume working on the third and final cherry tree panel. It feels good to be finishing it at last and I am pleased with the overall result.

"Charlie and I are going to pick a book from your library," Gabe says, a sweeping hand gesture indicates the loaded bookshelves nearby, "and have a little cozy up on the couch."

"Do you want to put some music on, Gabe?" I ask. "I've got a bunch of CD's in the sideboard."

"Let's have a look at what you've got." Humming, he opens the doors to the Edwardian mahogany-inlaid sideboard to reveal a wide selection of CD's.

"I've not heard this one in years," he says, slipping a disc into the player. The room fills with the cheerful sound of Claude Bolling's Suite for Flute and Jazz Piano.

"Good choice, Gabe. I love this CD."

The clock strikes five times and Gabe, closing his book, shuffles the sleeping cat onto the couch.

"I've got to kick you out soon, Alexi. Are you almost finished?" Gabe comes over and stands behind me, his hands resting quietly on my shoulders as I add minute detail to the finished painting.

"Actually, I'm done." With a flourish, I sign my name on the bottom right hand corner of the third canvas in vivid pink paint.

"Very nice," Gabe encourages. "I'm sure they will be well pleased with these."

I clean my brushes and put them away, then place the canvas with its counterparts in the corner of the room. The overall effect of the three canvases together is enchanting.

"I wasn't sure about painting with predominantly pink, but I think it all worked out in the end. Once the paint dries, I'll have to get these over to City Hall."

The doorbell rings and Gabe urges me towards the stairs.

"Time to clear out," he says with a laugh. "Go put on your best dress and in about an hour, I'll come to get you." I slowly mount the stairs, wondering again what on earth he's dreamed up.

Since it won't take me an hour to get ready, I decide to take a nap first and stretch out on the quilt covered bed. I can hear Gabe's baritone voice as he laughs and talks to whomever it is that has arrived at the cabin. Gradually I drift off into a light, dreamless sleep only to awake forty-five minutes later feeling much refreshed.

I decide on a plain black, knit dress with long sleeves that button from the wrist half way to the elbow. Its elegance is understated and flows down from my slender waist in a straight fall to my shins. I put on black hosiery and a pair of low-heeled, sling-back pumps. With an application of makeup and a few minutes with the curling iron, I feel ready for anything. I dab perfume on my wrist and neck, then wait impatiently for Gabe's summons. I can feel butterflies in my stomach but for a pleasant change, it's due to excitement, not nausea.

Moments later Gabe comes up to the loft to get me.

"Wow, you look amazing," he exclaims. "That dress sure suits you." He has changed into black slacks and a dark green cotton dress shirt. He looks impossibly handsome and extremely pleased with himself.

"Let's go down, Alexi." He takes my hand and together we descend the stairs slowly, one step at a time.

The dining room table is set with a white tablecloth, candles, and a beautiful bouquet of white roses graces the sideboard. The table, set for two, has a glorious array of delicious looking dishes on display.

Pulling a chair out for me, Gabe helps me get settled, then seats himself.

"Happy Birthday, Alexi." He lifts his glass and salutes me. "I know it's a day early, but you'll be so busy tomorrow with Jillie's party...I wanted to do something special for you...with just the two of us."

"I'm at a loss for words..." Tears well up and I dab at them with a white linen napkin. "This is a real treat. I've never had a meal catered in my home before. How ever did you manage to arrange it?"

"Pure magic and a lot of help from the Kitchen Cowards Catering Company," he responds, his rambunctious laugher playing havoc with my heart.

"Well, thank you. Everything looks mouth-watering."

"All the items are Thai inspired but made with mild spices and are, of course, vegan. Here, let me serve you." Taking my plate, Gabe loads it with spring rolls, Som Tum papaya salad, sweet and sour tofu on a bed of vegetables, tofu Ma Muang, Pra Rak and a helping of jasmine rice.

"I won't be hungry for a week after this feast," I exclaim, placing the linen napkin on my lap.

"There is no alcohol in the beverage; it's sparkling water with lime infusion. I thought spirits might not be advisable with your supplement regime."

"You have thought of everything, Gabe. Thank you." I raise my crystal glass and we clink the edges before sipping the refreshing drink.

The food is marvelous, each mouthful an explosion of tastes, some new, some familiar. Chewing slowly, I sample each dish finding that the Pra Rak broccoli and peanut dish is my favourite. Gabe favours the sweet and sour dish.

"We must remember to call the Kitchen Cowards tomorrow and tell them what a superb job they did with this meal." I lean back in

216

my chair and silently thank the universe that the mildly spiced foods had not unleashed a bout of nausea.

"I'm going to clear the table now, but I want you to sit by the fire and relax, okay?" I don't argue. What's the point of turning fifty if you can't take time to enjoy it?

When the table is cleared, Gabe brings a tray full of hot drinks and places it on the coffee table.

"Umm...there's four mugs on that tray, Gabe. Are we expecting company?" Right on cue, the doorbell rings.

"Yes, actually we are. I'll go answer it." I can hear the voices of a man and woman as Gabe greets the mystery guests at the front door.

"Alexi, let me introduce you to Juliette Bell and Maurice Coultard. Juliette, Maurice, this is Alexandra, the special lady I was telling you about."

"You're the famous Canadian soprano," I exclaim excitedly, recognizing the striking woman before me. Juliette laughs, the sound light and musical, just as one might expect from an acclaimed singer.

"I have several of your recordings. I particularly enjoy the Italian Renaissance compilation." Eagerly, I shake her hand and welcome them both.

"Maurice plays the lute and has accompanied Juliette on several of her recordings. He also has a flourishing solo career and teaches early Baroque music at the University in Ontario," Gabe explains.

"Please, come in and sit down." Gabe ushers the guests into the living room. "I've prepared chamomile tea just as you requested, Juliette. And there's honey here, too if you want it." Gabe pours the tea and adds honey to Juliette's, who nods when he lifts an inquiring eyebrow.

Maurice, who until this point has been all smiles but no words, speaks for the first time: "We are pleased to be here tonight to celebrate your fiftieth birthday. Gabriel's request was so touching, Juliette and I felt we could not refuse." He smiles, the edges of his neatly trimmed mustache lifting slightly to reveal small, even teeth.

"It's true. After talking to Gabriel on the phone, there was no way we could say no." Juliette chimes in enthusiastically.

She is a remarkably attractive women in her early fifties. Her blonde hair is pulled into a neat chignon, a double stand of pearls circles the long column of her throat. Juliette's sleeveless dress is midnight blue, fitted, and long. She is simply stunning.

"We'd better explain how this all came about," Gabe states, relaxing on the couch with a cup of tea in his hands.

"We met at the luggage carousel at YVR airport," Juliette informs me, jumping in before Gabe can continue. "We started chatting as we waited for our bags to arrive and realized that by coincidence, we were all driving to Kalsson. Gabriel was interested in the concert we are giving tomorrow night at the Imperial Theatre, so we gave him our phone number in case he had difficulty obtaining tickets."

"So this morning, quiet early, I might point out, we received a call from Gabriel." Maurice has joined Juliette in hijacking Gabe's story. "He asked if we would be willing to do a performance for a very special lady who is celebrating her birthday."

"Umm...I don't know if you're aware of this but my birthday isn't until tomorrow..."

"Don't concern yourself about that. What's a day this way or that amongst friends?" Maurice smiles again, his soft voice is warm and friendly.

"We threw together a few pieces from the concert we'll be performing tomorrow plus a few from our last engagement," Juliette explains, pulling a folded sheet of paper from her clutch. "I've written down tonight's program for you; you might recognize some of the Italian songs from the Renaissance recordings."

I take the paper from her and glance at the list.

"Yes, I am familiar with some of these. What's this last one?" I point to a song noted as TBA at the bottom of the sheet.

"That's a special request from Gabriel," Juliette responds, smiling. "He said it's one of your favourites, so I quickly brushed up on it in the hotel room and on the way over here in the car. You'll have to forgive any mistakes I make on that one." She smiles warmly, a tinkling laugh falling from her lips as she smooths a tendril of hair behind her ear with a manicured hand.

"I feel privileged to have you in my home giving a private performance. I thank all three of you for giving me the gift of a lifetime." My eyes well up and a single fat tear drops with a plop on the back of my hand. My very thin, faintly purple hand.

Gabe moves across the couch quickly to sit next to me and takes my cold hands between his large, warm ones, then kisses me gently on the lips.

"Are you ready to begin?" He asks, turning his attention to Juliette and Maurice. They nod. Maurice retrieves his lute from the hallway, then seats himself beside the fireplace while Juliette stands on the opposite side, her hands neatly folded together.

"Before you start, I should let you know that sometimes I need to leave a room...abruptly..." Maurice gently cuts in, "Don't be concerned that you'll inconvenience us. We will simply continue on once you feel better again." He has such kind eyes, I think to myself. I let out a sigh and relax. Gabe must have explained my condition to them already.

"Thank you for your understanding," I say, settling against the cushions.

Maurice removes the lute from the case and spends a few minutes tuning it. Charlie, who had been sleeping on the couch beside me, jumps down and makes hasty tracks for the bedroom at the first sound from the strings. Apparently the lute is not his favourite instrument.

Beginning with a Claudio Monteverdi song, Juliette fills the cabin to the rafters with her huge, soaring voice. Goosebumps spread up my arms and legs as her voice, nimble and crystal clear, trills its way through the fast and demanding Italian lyrics.

Juliette sings a series of short songs, then takes a break while Maurice plucks out two solos by Franciscus Bossinensis and Pietro Paolo Borrono. Once rested, Juliette continues the program with several well known arias which have been arranged for lute accompaniment.

"I've come to the end of the program," Juliette eventually announces as the last note of a Mozart aria fades from her lips. "The final song this evening is by Edvard Grieg. Alexandra, I understand, from what Gabriel has told me, that Solveig's Song is a favourite of yours. I have not sung it for many years, and never with lute. However, when Maurice and I practiced it earlier in the hotel, we thought it sounded quite acceptable. We hope you enjoy it."

I glance at Gabe. Our eyes meet; I smile, a soft, wistful turning up of my lips. For a brief moment I feel young and carefree again. I recall how incredibly handsome Gabe had looked ten years ago behind the wheel of the blue Mustang; how we had spent the day together learning about each other. That was the day Gabe was introduced to classical music for the first time.

That was the day I had fallen in love with him.

The single, sombre notes of the song are plucked out on the lute as Maurice plays the introductory bars. Looking at Juliette, Maurice pauses for a fraction of a second as Juliette picks up the first deep, resonating notes. She sings in Norwegian, her voice breathtakingly beautiful and filled with anguished emotion.

Gabe has given me a precious gift; I squeeze his hand as tears glint in my eyes, then slip slowly and steadily down my cheeks.

When we have said our final goodbyes to Juliette and Maurice, Gabe and I return to the living room and sit in front of the fire, recounting our favourite moments from the evening. Both musicians had been gracious and generous with their time and their talent.

"You must have pulled out all the stops to get them to agree to come tonight, Gabe. Lucky for me, you've got buckets of charm, otherwise that special little concert would never have happened." I glance at Gabe. His eyes are closed, but he is smiling. Happy.

"I need to get some sleep, Gabe. Tomorrow will be a taxing day. I have to go to Jillie's place at about five in the evening. She won't tell me what all she has planned, but I'm sure it will go on well into the night. Would you like to come?" My voice is hopeful.

"If you want me to come, I will come," he replies, turning his head to look at me.

"Yes, please. I'll need all the support I can get."

"Are you sure you want to go, Alexi? You could make an excuse..."

"No. I should go. Jillie has put a lot of effort into this party. I don't want to spoil it for her."

"If that's what you really want, then I'll come and support you."

Standing up, I walk over to Gabe and kiss him on the cheek.

"Thank you for everything, Gabe. It was a remarkably special evening. Good night."

"Before you to up to bed, I have a little gift for you." Gabe reaches into his travel bag and fishes out a pretty silver box tied with a red ribbon.

"Gabe, you cannot possibly give me anything else for my bir..."

"Please, just take it and don't argue." Gabe presses the box into my palm. I turn it over and over in my hands, hesitant.

"I can't..."

"Please..." Gabe unties the ribbon and lifts the lid then passes the box back to me. "Please take it."

"Oh, it's beautiful." I gently pull the vintage locket out of the box and hold it by the delicate silver chain.

"Open the locket, but be careful," Gabe cautions. I pop the intricately carved locket open to reveal a tuft of orange and white fur and a lock of Gabe's dark hair.

"Did you snip some of Charlie's fur?" I ask in amazement.

"I most certainly did," he responds firmly. "He won't miss that little bit." I click the locket closed; a surge of love wings through my heart.

"Here, help me put it on, please." Lifting my hair, Gabe closes the clasp at the nape of my neck and the locket drops to my decolletage, shimmering against the black fabric of my dress.

"There. Now, wherever you go, we will not be far from your heart." Gabe's eyes are dark with emotion.

"It's lovely. Where did you get it?" I turn the locket over and notice that the back has been engraved with the words: *For my beautiful friend. GH.* The font is heavily scrolled and matches the essence of the vintage piece.

"I got it about four years ago at an antique market in Sydney. I thought it would suit you, which it does. I don't want you throwing this one off the bridge, you hear?" His tone is gently, playfully scolding.

"Never. I promise to keep it forever. Thank you, Gabe. Now, I really must go up to bed," I say with conviction. I kiss his cheek again, then wearily climb the stairs

"Oh, Gabe, I keep meaning to ask you – do you still have your Harley?"

"No. I sold it before I returned to Australia. Those things are *terribly* dangerous, you know." I snort in an undignified manner but say nothing as a faint smile curls my lips. I can't believe he's still taking the mickey after all these years.

"Sleep well, beautiful."

"And you."

In the darkness, I lay awake unable to fall asleep despite my best intentions and exhausted body. My mind is busy with thoughts of the evening and I feel restless. Getting up, I put on my thick robe, socks, and slippers, then slip quietly downstairs without turning on the lights. I inch my way through the darkness, broken only by the flames of the fire. I can see the outline of Gabe slumbering, out-stretched on the hide-a-bed. Charlie is curled up on his chest like a little fox.

I pull the drapes back and look out into the still, bright night.

"Couldn't sleep?" Gabe calls softly from the bed.

"Oh, I'm sorry I woke you. I'm tired but too restless to fall asleep." I settle on the window seat and stare out at the wintry scene.

"Is he here?" Gabe asks, coming to stand beside me in his T-shirt and boxer shorts; Charlie is cradled in his arms, half asleep.

"No." I know Gabe is referring to the eagle who has been tugging at the edges of my attention for the last several days.

"Scooch over," Gabe says, putting Charlie on the floor. He sits behind me, leaning up against the wall of the window seat and pulls me back into his arms so that we both can look out over the yard.

"I happened to see your dad in town today," Gabe remarks. "I passed him on the street and only just recognized him. He's aged quite a bit."

"Yes, he's had few health issues these past two years. How did your meeting go?" I ask, imagining my dad could have been unpleasant to Gabe.

"Very well, actually. At first he was guarded with me, then I explained that you had written to me and that I had come directly to see you. I told him despite what he might think, you have always been faithful to Mark and that nothing had ever happened between us for which he should feel ashamed. He was overwhelmed and had needed to take a seat for a few minutes. He thanked me for being a good friend to you and then left without further comment."

"I'm glad you talked to him about us, Gabe. He never treated me the same after he met you at the Lake House. It was as if I was guilty until proven innocent. Now that he knows the truth, he can put it out of his head."

"And your mom, does she mistrust you also?" Gabe asks.

"No. She believes me. She knows how much I love Mark. Even now, with him dead all these years, I still love him. I still feel *connected* to him. Some days I miss him so badly, Gabe, it's like a gut wrenching pain inside of me from which there is no escape." My throat tightens, the words clog and come out high pitched, cracking.

"I know, my love, I know." Gabe soothes me with his soft tone and warm hands.

We settle into silence, the only sound is that of sappy wood popping in the fireplace.

"You know, Gabe, I'm eternally grateful to you for coming to see me. And for agreeing to look after Charlie. I feel utterly relieved knowing he's going to be well loved by you." I lean farther back into the comfort of his arms and pull an afghan blanket over our socked feet.

"It is the least I can do, Alexi, and I am honoured that you asked me."

"Are you chilly?" I ask. I can feel him shake his head. The drapes are open so that despite the cold, we can watch the silvery shadows, cast by the full moon, playing on the snow. The reflections of the moonlight make the eerie landscape a bright yet monochromatic image.

I feel Gabe's body heat sinking into my pain-riddled back and a sigh of unbidden pleasure escapes my lips as the ache slowly subsides. I rub my cheek on the soft cotton of his shirt and inhale Gabriel's clean masculine scent. My eyelids drift drowsily down, almost closing and I feel Gabe press a feather-light kiss to my temple.

We sit like this for some time, watching, with languid eyes, the snow-dusted trees. Now and again Gabe tightens his arms around me and I press deeper into the security of his safe haven, lulled by the steady and reassuring beat of his heart.

Charlie wanders quietly to the window and with a soft meow, jumps with the strength and agility of a much younger cat, onto my lap. Purring and kneading, he stares at us as if transfixed.

Gabe and I take turns stroking his soft coat and chucking him under the chin. Occasionally our fingers touch in silent conversation. Finally, after several attempts, Charlie curls into a tight ball on my lap, whips his tail over his nose, and falls asleep with a deep, languorous sigh. I smile into the darkness; all is as it should be.

The clock strikes midnight. I have reached my fiftieth birthday. Statistically impossible, I have beaten all the odds. But my body is tired now. The need to let go has grown stronger with every passing day, yet I remain. Diminished. Dwindling. Ebbing away like the fading notes of Philip Glass' violin concerto. Slowly, slowly to nought.

Unaware that I had fallen asleep, I am suddenly awakened. Outside I can see the eagle swooping, low over the forest, towards the cabin. I watch, alert and breathless. The eagle has never come this close before, always preferring to keep some distance from the house. He is circling just feet away from the window now; he turns and looks directly at me, his piercing yellow eyes vivid against the silver moonlight

I am mesmerized. Bewitched. I lean forward towards the window-pane, pulling gently out of Gabe's arms. He is asleep; I can tell by the steady rhythm of his breathing, the looseness of his limbs.

"Gabe," I whisper urgently, "the eagle is here. He is so close I can almost touch him." I get no response. I feel myself being pulled farther forward; I am almost floating as I gaze back at the majestic bird, his feathers gleaming in the moonlight.

Suddenly, he circles and wings powerfully towards the evergreens; he looks back at me over his outspread wings. The moon shines as bright as a spotlight on the pure white feathers of his head. Magical. A messenger from the Creator.

As he surges away from me with powerful strokes, I cry, "No, don't leave me!" Turning from the window, I look at Gabe, peaceful in his rest. And Charlie, curled happily in a ball on my lap, is content. The eagle is waiting – almost impatiently – for me at the edge of the woods, soaring then circling and soaring again.

"I must leave you now," I whisper to my beloved slumbering companions. My throat closes, tight with emotion, and I speak no more.

I feel light – truly buoyant – my heart is wide open as I look back towards the dark forest. The eagle beckons me, urging me to follow him as he glides seamlessly into the trees, guided by the light of the moon. Without regret, my soul extricates itself from my weary, worn out shell of a body. My moment is finally here.

There is no reason to stay.

EPILOGUE

Lauren glances at her watch. The time crawls by as she waits anxiously for the arrival of the flight from Vancouver, British Columbia. Her stomach tightens nervously as she anticipates Gabe's return. She missed him terribly, even though he was only gone for three weeks. She had been on edge ever since Gabe, out of the blue, packed a bag and announced he was going to Canada to help a friend in need. He didn't have to tell her that the friend was Alexandra; she could tell by the way he acted. By the way he withdrew from her the moment he received her letter.

Although it is mid-December, the temperature has risen to an unseasonable high of twenty-nine degrees Celsius. Lauren wipes a bead of perspiration from her forehead with a shaky hand, then carries on pacing like a caged lion. Her petite, slender body, held taut with nerves, moves methodically from window to window. Watching. Waiting.

She is wearing a short white skirt with a deep red sleeveless blouse that accents the black sheen of her shoulder-length bob. Her white, high heeled sandals tap a quick staccato on the ceramic floor tiles as she moves restlessly around the arrivals lounge. She is as beautiful and delicate as a wild orchid, with huge, expressive black eyes and a smile, that when in attendance, spreads like the morning sun across her face.

Nearby, Jasmine slumps in a beige, vinyl clad chair, the heel of one worn out runner rests on the edge of the seat as she reads the current edition of Equine Today. Her jean shorts are frayed at the edges; her hair, long and glossy, is held back in a ponytail. Like her mother, she is breathtaking, but as of yet, she is unaware of her beauty.

"Come sit down, Mum," Jasmine calls, patting the empty seat beside her. "Pacing won't make him get here any sooner."

"I'm not pacing," Lauren replies, trying unsuccessfully to calm herself.

A group of elderly people and mothers with young children move slowly down the corridor towards the arrivals lounge. It won't be long now, Lauren thinks to herself, her heart beating like a tom-tom.

She sees him at last, striding briskly towards her, a cat carrier in one hand and his travel bag in the other. He lowers both to the floor as he reaches her, wrapping his arms around her tiny frame.

"Lauren," he whispers, emotions limiting his ability to speak. "I missed you." He takes her lips in a passion filled kiss and she presses against his body, feeling herself melt into his strength. Tears seep from beneath her closed eyelids and she cannot find her voice.

"Why are you kissing my Mum?" Jasmine asks, having quietly joined Gabe and Lauren.

"Jasmine, my darling," Gabe releases Lauren from his embrace and pulls Jasmine into a hug, kissing her rosy cheeks. Looking over the top of Jasmine's head, he gazes at Lauren who has taken a tissue from her purse and is dabbing at her tear-stained face.

"I was kissing your mother because I love her and I hope that she will agree to marry me. That is, if you're okay with that, Jasmine?"

Pulling Lauren into the hug, the three of them stand in a circle, laughing and crying all at once.

"Yes, Gabriel, I will marry you. You sure took your time in asking." Tenderly, Lauren reaches up and smooths the lines from his travel-worn face. They kiss again until Jasmine clears her throat.

"It's fine by me if you two want to get married, but can't *that* wait until you get home? Come on, let's get out of here."

A loud demanding meow emanates from the cat carrier. Squatting down in front of the carrier, Jasmine sticks her finger through the gaps in the metal gate and rubs the soft coat of the cranky feline.

"Who do we have here?" Jasmine asks, swiveling on her heels to glance up at Gabe.

Reluctantly Gabe lets Lauren go and comes to stand beside Jasmine.

"This is Charlie. He was Alexi's cat and it was her dying wish that we give him a happy, loving home for the rest of his days. Do you think we can provide that? He's a fussy old bugger, but I promised Alexi that we'd look after him." Lauren looks up sharply when she hears a catch in Gabe's voice. Instinctively she wants to comfort him, but she holds back not wanting to intrude on his moment of sorrow.

"Of course we can give the old boy a good home," Jasmine states excitedly. "That's what we do; we look after animals that need a place to call home." She opens the carrier door and pulls Charlie into her arms.

"Gosh, he's huge and ever so soft." Her eyes are sparkling as she kisses and pets the cat, who settles contentedly into the arms of his new friend. Another one falls under the magic spell of Charlie, Gabe thinks to himself. That cat could charm a mouse from its hole.

Beside him, Lauren quickly takes Gabe's arm in hers and rests her smooth cheek against his deltoid. "I'm sorry, Gabe," she says quietly so that only Gabe can hear. "I know how much you love her." A pulse ticks in Gabe's cheek and sadness shadows his dark, smarting eyes.

"Yes, I loved her." All about them there is a buzz of activity, but for Gabe and Lauren, they are cocooned from the hubbub as their eyes meet; communication, rich in complexity and history passes between them without a word being spoken. He takes a long slow breath in and releases it just as slowly, closing his eyes for a moment before opening them again. Then he smiles. A warm, open-hearted, loving smile that shifts the moment from the past to the present. From melancholy to joy. From loved to love.

"Come, ladies." Gabe picks up his bag and, taking Lauren's hand in his, leads the way towards the exit doors. Jasmine pops Charlie back into the carrier, closes the door, and dashes to catch up, hauling the awkward cage with youthful enthusiasm.

Outside, the brilliant sun of December beats down on the tarmac. Gabe stops for a moment and raises his face to its rays, relishing the feeling of rejuvenation that the sun brings. Beside him, Lauren feels love leap wildly in her heart and a smile, gentle as a summer rain, caresses her lips. Taking Jasmine's free hand in hers, the three of them leave the terminal together. It is time to go home.

ACKNOWLEDGEMENTS

It is with a grateful heart that I thank the following people for their insight and support in bringing this book to fruition: Mariam Ordubadi and the team at FriesenPress, Ruth Foley, Georgina Eden, Roberta, Dreena, Lori, and all of you who took the time to read and comment on the manuscript.

My life has been touched by several extraordinary people, each leaving an indelible mark on my heart and soul. You have been instrumental, in your own unique way, in inspiring me to express myself. In chronological order, I would like to thank Tom Foxcroft for occasionally marking my creative writing with *well done*. Alice Rich, whose talents are boundless and who walks through life with beauty. The role model, the leader, the trusted friend – Larry Goldstein. John Snively – a mentor, a healer, a poet. And Muni Fluss, filled with quiet grace, the extoller of the wisdom of the heart.

To my darling husband, I thank you for your faith in me and for offering your strong and steady love.

FURTHER READING AND
LINKS OF INTEREST

B.C. SPCA
www.spca.bc.ca

International Fund for Animal Welfare (IFAW)
www.ifaw.org

Creston Wetlands
www.crestonwildlife.ca

West Kootenay Tourism
www.gokootenays.com

Becoming Vegan: The Complete Guide to Adopting A Healthy Plant-Based Diet by Brenda Davis, R.D. & Vesanto Melina, M.S., R.D.

Diet For A New America by John Robbins

CPSIA information can be obtained
at www.ICGtesting.com
Printed in the USA
LVOW10s2235081116

512195LV00002B/63/P